A FEAST OF EPIPHANIES

A FEAST OF EPIPHANIES

And Other Stories

Dale Harris

ISBN: 978-1-7777228-1-4

In memory of Lloyd Harris,
who helped me understand
why Jesus was a storyteller

ACKNOWLEDGMENTS

This book would not have been possible without the gracious help and warm encouragement of many wonderful people. I especially want to thank Rachael Harris, whose imaginative writing prompts inspired so many of the epiphanies in this humble feast. Thank you, Rachael, for taking up that storytelling challenge with me during the Covid spring of 2020. Your enthusiasm for creative writing was contagious (no pun intended) and helped bring some much-needed light to those first dark days of the pandemic.

I am thankful to Leland Harris and Ramy Owiar, who both shared their artistic talents to give these pages a touch of visual class. Their elegant illustrations have added the equivalent of a thousand evocative words to many of the stories in this book. (Leland on "Christopher," "The Tattoo" and "The Patchwork Quilt"; Ramy on "New Clothes," "The Words of Zumisura," "The Day's Last Dance," "The Paper Crane," "All is Bright," "Kangaroo Care," "The Binding" and "A Feast of Epiphanies.")

I want to thank my friends at the Corner Church, especially Pam Verhagen, Wendy MacLean and Rhoda Gomes, who shared their honest reactions to many of these stories back when they were still in their earliest form. Their enthusiastic response helped me believe that they might be worth sharing more broadly.

Dani Harris spent many hours reading, editing and responding to these stories, one by one as they came into being and then all at once after they had been collected into one place. Her honest feedback, critical eye and attention to detail have made them far better than they otherwise could have been (just as I am a far better man than I could have been without her). Thank you, Dani, for getting behind me in my passion for writing and believing in me even when I found it hard to do so myself.

Above all, I am grateful to the Lord Jesus Christ, who is for me an endless source of reasons to write. We have it on good authority that the whole world would not have room enough for all the books that would have to be written, were we to record every wonderful thing he has done. I am not so bold as to suppose that I have added much to that vast library of his deeds with this modest volume, but inasmuch as he is the ultimate inspiration for every story in it, I offer it to him here as one small record of his on-going work in me.

Soli Deo Gloria, 2023

CONTENTS

Preface

Fred Craddock once said that all preachers should make a regular habit of reading fiction, short stories especially. Craddock was an ordained minister, a New Testament scholar, and one of the twentieth century's most well-respected preachers. He taught homiletics—the art and craft of preaching—at Johnson University in Tennessee, and his reasoning for this particular homiletical advice was twofold. On the one hand, the Bible was given to us primarily in narrative form, so preachers need to understand the unique way stories communicate if they are going to handle the Word of Truth rightly. On the other hand, all the best sermons have a strong narrative structure, even the most didactic of them. Preachers who want to hone their craft, then, need to hone their storytelling skills, and one of the best ways to do this, Craddock claimed, was by reading the work of gifted storytellers.

I was an English teacher before I became a preacher, so it did not take much to convince me of Craddock's argument on this point. I would only want to expand it beyond the pulpit and apply it to all aspects of the spiritual life. Human beings are, I think, wired for story. This should come as no surprise to anyone who takes the book of Genesis seriously, when it says that we are made in the image of God. If it's true that in some way human beings reflect the divine likeness, then it stands to reason that we would resonate on a deeply spiritual level when it comes to telling stories, given the fact that God chose the sacred story of the Bible as a means of revelation.

It would certainly explain why storytelling played such a central role in the ministry of Jesus. One of the most firmly established facts about the historical Jesus, a fact that even the most skeptical of historians are convinced of when it comes to the life of this first-century Nazarene rabbi, is that he employed storytelling to powerful and lasting effect in his teaching. The many parables of Jesus should come rushing to mind the moment we acknowledge this. The one about the passionate shepherd who left ninety-nine sheep in the pen to go looking for the one that was lost, the one about the reviled Samaritan who took care of the bludgeoned man at the side of the road when all the respectable religious types refused to help, the one about the shrewd steward who used his master's wealth to make friends with the world, the one about the widow who pestered the judge incessantly for justice: the list is long and diverse. And to this day, the narratives he used to convey what life with God is like still pique curiosity and spark imagination. Yeast gets worked into dough. Treasure is hidden in fields. Sowers sow seed. Wedding parties are thrown for the poor and the dejected.

It wasn't limited simply to the stories he told, either. In an even wider sense, the mission of Jesus—what he came to do and how he set about accomplishing it—was all bound up with the narrative life of ancient Israel, fulfilling the story of God's people by writing it a beautiful, if unexpected concluding chapter. He chose twelve apostles to parallel the twelve legendary heads of the tribes of Israel. He gathered up the symbolism of the Passover feast and offered it to us in the sacred meal of Holy Communion. He retold the creation story, the Exodus story, the story of Israel's exile and return, all of it through his passionate death and world-changing resurrection. If he was the Son of the Storytelling God, it should not surprise us for a moment to discover how his very life retold the narrative of redemption that this God had been speaking over his people for millennia.

Francis Schaeffer, one of the more prominent voices in twentieth century evangelicalism, used to wax philosophical about the fact that in the Christian faith we have been given "propositional revelation." This was the term he liked to use, and especially in his book *He is There and He is Not Silent*, he makes much theological hay out of the idea that God did not leave us guessing about who he is, rather he gave us revelation in the form of propositions—clear statements that express concrete facts. He was referring to the biblical witness when he said this, and early on in my life as a follower of Jesus, this idea was hugely influential. I was convinced that God had given us the Bible especially so that we could make propositional statements about him.

Maybe. But as I've grown in my faith, I've come to realize that the Bible is not predominantly a book of propositions, so much as it is a messy, rapturous, divine/human narrative of exhilarating and oftentimes heart-aching proportions. It is possible to wring propositional truths out of the story, of course, but such bullet points about the character of God no more capture the divine reality than a glass of orange juice does a gloriously bright and freshly picked orange, after the fruit has been wrung lifeless and the rind tossed aside. If you really want propositions about God, read Thomas Aquinas. If you want to encounter the God and Father of our Lord Jesus Christ, open your heart to hear the story he has told in the pages of his good book.

Because we are wired for story.

As a preacher, I have firsthand experience of how deep the wiring goes, because I have the joyful burden of preparing a talk each week on the ways and things of God, which I get to share with a gathered community of listeners. Inasmuch as I was a high school teacher before I became a pastor, my preaching can sometimes be overly didactic, even pedantic if I'm not careful. But I was, more specifically, an English teacher, so I do carry with me into the pulpit a great appreciation for the power of story. And here is a mystery I have observed: something indescribable seems to come over a congregation when the preacher, in the middle of all their homiletical propounding and exegetical point-making, begins to tell a story. You can almost feel the whole group sit forward collectively, as one body, as though the temperature of the room had changed slightly, or a refreshing breeze had just passed over us all. Heads incline. Bodies engage. Eyes squint slightly with the happy labor of visualizing the events as they're being narrated. And then comes the release, of tears or laughter or both, when the problem is resolved, the mystery unveiled, the villain vanquished, or whatever conclusion the particular story was pointing us to. And as it happens—and those who've experienced this will know it's true—a space for divine revelation opens up.

The collection of short stories you are holding began in the spring of 2020, as a writing project my teenage daughter and I took on, trying to stay sane through the early days and worst moments of the Covid-19 pandemic. We would take turns coming up with a writing prompt, give ourselves a week to finish it, and compare the stories we each wrote in response. Write a story set at a high school dance was one such prompt. Write a ghost story. Write a story based on a historical figure, or one involving a sea voyage, or one where the last line is exactly the same as the first. As the pandemic stretched from weeks into months, I started to have a growing number of stories that felt like they might say something cohesive if they were all gathered together in one place. I added to the pile a handful of stories I had written previously, in the nooks and crannies of my spare time as a pastor over the years, and soon I had enough to fill a book.

I did not intend for any of them to be specifically pastoral, or even necessarily Christian. I was just trying to tell some stories that personally piqued my curiosity. Nevertheless, some of the earliest writing advice I ever received—I think it was Earnest Hemmingway who first said it—was "write what you know." And after fifteen years of pastoral ministry, one thing I am beginning to know well is how mysterious it can be when the supernatural presence of God starts to make itself known in the ordinary stuff of everyday life. Not that all the stories in this volume deal with the ordinary and the everyday. Some of them are decidedly out of the ordinary in the telling. What they share in common, though, is an attempt to describe what it is like to brush up against the real presence of the divine, and an attempt to imagine how things can be different once we have.

As you explore this collection, you will encounter mystical origami masters, visionary mothers, clairvoyant guitarists, unlikely wisemen and much more. Some of the stories are so fanciful as to be fantastical, others are starkly real, perhaps at times too real. It will be up to you to determine which is which. But real or fantasy, please receive each as one man's attempt to clear out some imaginative space for an epiphany or two to happen. If any of them accomplish, in the reading, even a few of the things they did for me in the writing—inviting new perspectives on the divine and new ways of imagining life with him—take that as further evidence that we truly are made in the likeness of a wondrously wise Storytelling God.

1.

Christopher

Looking back, I think at some point one of us should have said that we were just too old for such things anymore. Traipsing through the forest with wooden swords and homemade cloaks was fine when we were kids, but we were going to be eighth graders that fall, and most guys our age had long since given up hunting imaginary dragons in exchange for more grown-up pursuits, like girls and sports and dreaming about their first car.

But old habits die hard, I guess.

They certainly did for me and Christopher, anyway; we had been adventuring in the river valley on the edge of town for so long that we knew every grove and gulley of it by heart. We had even mapped them out. All our favorite fantasy novels included elaborate maps of the imaginary kingdoms their adventures were set in, and we took our cue from them. I had stolen a roll of newsprint from the closet where my mom stored the stationery and spread out a good six-foot length of it on my bedroom floor. Christopher and I then set to work with a couple of black Sharpies, tracing out the whole river valley as best we could from memory. Every site of every adventure we'd ever had found its place on the map: the Cave of Bludgeon the Troll, the Golden Meadow of the Star Elves, the Shrine of Alonwyn the Unicorn, and of course, at the furthest end of the map, the castle of Logrim the Wizard, who ruled the whole federation of the eastern kingdoms with wisdom and war. We did our best to achieve the look of the calligraphy on the maps in the Lord of the Rings books, but neither of us really had the patience for it. The ink soaked through the paper, of course, and stained the carpet in my room terribly.

In preparation before setting out on this, our greatest and (as we would come to understand in retrospect) our final adventure, I had opened the map to a spot in the upper left corner, a region we had tentatively labelled as the Western Wastelands. There I had drawn the shape of a single smoldering mountain.

"This is the lair of Diabolus the Dragon," I explained in a hushed voice when Christopher finally arrived, and we were pouring over the map. "According to the Lore Master of Elandor, Diabolus guards the Demon-bane, a magical staff that has the power to banish evil once and for all from the Seven Lands."

"The Demon-bane?" Christopher repeated. We had done this often enough that he knew how to play his part without any prompting.

"Yes," I said. "It's an ancient staff carved from a branch of the Mystic Willow, the sacred tree of the Star Elves."

"And polished," Christopher suggested (though he said it in the tone of one well-schooled in this ancient lore, regardless the fact that he was actually inventing it there on the spot), "and polished with the tears of a dying Phoenix."

"Yes," I agreed, as if I had studied the same ancient lore as he had. "Yes, and the blood of a wyvern."

"How will we get there?" he asked.

I pointed to a line on the map marked out as the Wall of Emperor Tyranius. We both knew well enough that this was the old railroad track west of town, and if we followed it to where it bent away to the south, we would find a trail that led through an overgrown cow pasture and down into the most densely-forested stretch of the river valley, a place we had labelled as the Forest of Shadows on the map.

"We follow the Wall of Tyranius," I said, as though we hadn't wandered up and down that railroad track a hundred times already that summer. "When we find the ancient Elf Road of Taris, it will take us down into the Forest of Shadows."

"Will we have to cross at the Ford of Brynnwyn?" Christopher reached to point at a spot on the map as he said this, and even though the spell of our role playing was almost complete, still I noticed four ugly, brownish bruises just above the wrist as he did.

"It happened again?" I asked, a thirteen-year-old boy once more, so quickly that the shock almost startled me.

Christopher wouldn't look at me but kept his eyes fixed on the map. "It's nothing," he said softly. But I didn't speak for a long time, so finally he said, "Look. He came home drunk last night, and he and mom were having it out. I don't really want to talk about it. I got caught between them is all. It's nothing."

I still didn't speak, so he looked at me angrily. "Forget it, Peter," he said. "It's nothing."

A final quiet moment passed, and I gave in at last. "No," I said quietly. "No, we'll need to go further on past the Fords, till we get to the Goblin Bridge." The Goblin Bridge was an abandoned beaver's dam that we took to cross to the far side of the river. It was perilous crossing at the best of times, but especially when the water was high, and we seldom used it without soaking one or two of our sneakers.

I was rolling up the map and getting ready to go, when Christopher reached for an old duffel bag he'd brought with him.

"I made these," he said, "for the journey." He pulled out a longish shape, bundled in an old blanket. He unwrapped it and set between us two of the most beautifully crafted weapons I had ever seen.

"I carved them out of some wood I found in my dad's shop."

"But Christopher—" I'd heard the story of the time his dad caught Christopher's older brother taking lumber from the shop without permission, so I knew profoundly the risk he had taken.

But that wasn't my only cause for awe. The two swords were exquisitely wrought. That's how they would have said it in one of our favorite fantasy novels, anyway, and certainly, for all their being the craftmanship of a thirteen-year-old boy, they were. He had carved the blades with his pocketknife till they were flat and smooth and rounded. He must have found a can of metallic spray-paint in his father's garage—another great risk—because they gleamed as though they were made of some magical steel. He had even glued chips of colored glass (broken beer bottles, perhaps) and translucent plastic to the hilt, to serve as gemstones.

The grips of each were wound with strips of real leather.

"Where did you get—"

"I cut up one of my dad's old coats," he said with a grin. My incredulity must have been writ large on my face, because he added: "Well, he'll never miss it. I found it in an old trunk in the basement."

He had made loops out of two pieces of rope, to fasten them to our belts. "I've named mine," he said, tying it in place. "It's called Star-edge."

I looked hard at mine, still hesitating to take it. It wasn't that I didn't want it, but I thought of the bruises on Christopher's forearm, and the broken beer bottles that he'd turned into gems for the hilt. I imagined his mother or father, finding an old leather coat all cut up in his bedroom, and suddenly that homemade sword seemed almost a sacred talisman to me, forged in dragon fire and quenched in the blood of a thousand foes.

"What should I name mine?" I asked at last. I took it tentatively in hand and swung it once or twice. It whooped sharply as it slit the air. Christopher was watching me closely, and I could tell from the light in his face how pleased he was for me to take the sword, how worth the risk it had been.

"Dawn-blade?" he suggested. "Shadow-cleaver?" He had read far more than I had and was quite good at naming things. Most of the names on our map, in fact, had been his invention. "Light-wielder?"

This last one rang especially true for me. "Yeah," I said, gripping it tightly, testing its weight the way I imagined a knight ought to do. "Light-wielder's good."

I strapped Light-wielder to my side. I had lifted two oversized beach towels from my mom's linen closet to serve as traveler's cloaks, and when they were tied in place we set out.

The journey to the Wall of Emperor Tyranius was uneventful. My house was close to a field at the edge of town. On the far side of the field, past the old ball diamonds and a run-down cluster of playground equipment, across a ditch overgrown with tall grass and at the end of an indistinct trail, there grew a long stretch of pine trees, a bit of a windbreak planted there time-out-of-mind. These were so closely grown that it usually took some work to push through them, but that was part of the appeal, for once we were on the other side of those pines, closed off completely from the rest of our sleepy little town, we really felt as if we had entered an alternate world.

The Wall of Emperor Tyranius ran along this length of pine trees for a good three miles. We scrambled up the gravel embankment and picked our way from railroad tie to railroad tie. With Light-wielder strapped to my side and my adventurer's cloak fluttering around my shoulders, it took next to no work to make believe we were in fact walking the battlements of an ancient imperial wall, built some time (according to Christopher's lore) in the fourth age, to keep out goblin marauders.

"What will we do when we reach Diabolus?" Christopher asked. He drew Star-edge from its scabbard and cut the air with a sweeping arc. "Do you know what his weakness is? Every dragon has one."

"The Lore Master of Elandor tells of an ancient prophesy: that only the light of two stars combined can pierce the dragon's side." I was making it up as we went, but given the names with which we had christened our swords, it came to me almost effortlessly.

"Good," he said, nodding in approval. We talked over possible interpretations, though we each knew what two "stars" the prophesy must have been referring to.

Suddenly Christopher stopped and pointed with his sword. "Look!" he said ominously. "The Elf Road of Taris!"

"Yes. And a whole band of ogres guarding the way to the Forest of Shadow!"

The ogres looked suspiciously like a handful of cows, standing stupidly out to pasture and entirely indifferent to our arrival, but Christopher and I both knew without saying that the ogres of the Forest of Shadow were notorious shapeshifters.

"There are too many of them to take in open combat," Christopher was saying. "Best we go by stealth."

We crouched and crept along the fence, through the tall grass and cautiously toward the forest. We must have had a true rogue's skill in stealth, because the ogres took no notice of us whatsoever. We were almost at the forest, when suddenly Christopher leapt into the open.

"We've been spotted!" he bellowed. The ogre nearest us was perhaps a bit startled. It skittered away a few yards while Christopher hollered at it, swinging his sword in the air as though laying all his hero's mettle on the anvil, there to be tried and tempered. I drew Light-wielder and swung it too, though I was not nearly so bold around farm animals as he was and couldn't actually bring myself to holler.

When the ogres had been duly chased off and the Elf Road of Taris was well cleared, we proceeded toward the Forest of Shadows, now travelling again in the open. The air was heavy and resin-scented when we entered, and in the dim light it was a simple thing to imagine a goblin lurking behind every trunk and fallen log. Christopher signaled me to move cautiously.

In the pines overhead, two crows began screaming at us viciously, one of them leaping into the air with a flurry of black feathers.

"Spies of Diabolous," I whispered, as though every adventurer knew without being told that the crows in these parts, however ordinary they may look, really served the Demon Dragon of the Western Wastelands. "He'll know we're coming now."

The journey to the bottom of the river valley proceeded slowly. Every now and then some gnome or sprite would skitter by, and one of us would classify it according to our mythical bestiary. These creatures bore a strange resemblance to ordinary squirrels and chipmunks, but Christopher and I both knew that the Forest of Shadows was crawling with fairies, so we were not to be deceived.

We came at last to the Goblin Bridge and our first real adventure. It had stormed the day before, so the water was high for midsummer and the going treacherous. We had traversed it often enough to be confident, though, and were able to cross this time without even wetting our shoes. This was good luck, I thought, because one time Christopher had actually lost a shoe in the mud, and for the next many days he bore across his shoulders the mark of the beating he'd received for it. We always crossed as carefully as we could after that.

There was a dense thicket of trees growing along the bank on the far side of the Goblin Bridge, and the only way forward was along the water's edge. Christopher went first, so it was probably he who stepped in it, but it was all so quick that neither of us really knew what was happening until it was upon us. All I know is that suddenly, my lower calf, near the ankle, was burning with fire.

I heard Christopher scream out even as my own pain registered, and when I looked, something fat and bright had come to rest on my upper thigh, and then the fire shot up through my leg. I screamed, too, and as I did, I realized that the air was swarming with those fat, bright shapes.

Christopher was swinging violently with his sword and screaming indistinctly. I had forgotten mine and was batting the air with both hands. The fire stabbed into my arm and then my chest, and at some point, abject terror must have set in, because I bolted, splashing out into the river to get away and flinging my arms madly about my head, wet sneakers be damned.

I splashed four or five frantic yards into the water, until the river was eddying around my upper thighs and the towel around my shoulders was heavy with it. The spots on my legs and chest still burned angrily, but I was no longer being swarmed. Looking back, I saw Christopher splashing his way into the river, too, still swinging his sword gallantly and throwing out a heroic wake of water as he came.

I was crying, breathlessly. His voice still had the pitch of a scream in it, and I could see a horrible welt swelling on his arm. Neither of us dared to make-believe we'd stumbled on anything other than what it was.

"Wasps," he said, when he could speak with his normal timbre again. "Must have been a nest."

"Are you—" I said between gasps. "Are you okay?"

"They got me on the legs a couple of times. And here." He lifted his arm to inspect the welt.

We fell silent. The water curled around our legs and between us disinterestedly. I dared a backward glance and could see the furious wasps still swarming frenetically about the riverbank, but they seemed to have lost interest in us.

Another long moment passed, and then, unexpectedly, Christopher started laughing.

"That was amazing!" he said.

"But Christopher—" I was badly shaken and took more time to see the humor of it, standing with my mother's beach towel over my shoulders and my wooden sword in my hand, chased away in terror by a mere swarm of angry wasps.

"Your shoes…"

"Who cares about shoes?" Whatever joke Christopher saw in the situation, his laughter was catching. I tried to grin weakly. "Who cares?" he said again. "That was amazing!"

I took a step forward. My ankle was beginning to hurt alarmingly now, though the cool water was soothing. The sting on my chest ached intensely. "Well, we did come for adventure," I said feebly. But I was still pretty shaken, and I couldn't help it: I started crying.

"Hey," Christopher said, seeing my tears. And I couldn't tell if he was still role-playing or not, but it was the most genuine "hey" I had ever heard, as if he had comforted someone who had been violently hurt before and knew exactly how to do it.

He stepped toward me and said it again. "Hey, Peter. It's alright. We're alright." And then, for the only time he had ever done so in all our long friendship, he put his arms around me and pulled me in to that "hey," firmly against his chest. He had younger brothers, of course, and I guess he had learned from them how to hold a man close in his distress.

"Would it be okay?" I asked, when the tears were gone but I hadn't quite started to feel embarrassed. "Would it be okay if we turn back now?"

Christopher laughed. "Yeah," he said. "If Diabolus is anywhere near as bad as those wasps, we may want to come back and fight him another day." He splashed toward the far bank, and I followed. When we were at last on dry ground, we both still had our shoes, though they were sopping wet and caked with mud.

"Do you still wanna—you know—adventure on the way back?" he asked, wringing out the edge of his beach towel cloak. Mine was too heavy with water to wear well anymore, so I took it off and draped it over my arm.

But I nodded. We were far enough from the wasps now that my sense of the heroic was returning. "Let's call that the Hive of the Fire Wraiths," I suggested.

Christopher drew his sword. "Come," he said, the note of a warrior ringing again in his voice. "Let's return to Logrim to warn him that the Fire Wraiths are advancing on the western edge of his kingdom."

So we set out once more, back through the Forest of Shadows and up along the Elf-road of Taris. When we came out into the open again, we saw that the ogres were still there, standing dumbly in their bovine forms. But we'd already had enough adventure that day and had no interest in chasing them this time. Instead, we scrambled back up the gravel embankment of the Wall of Tyranius and started making our way home.

It was when we had pushed through the stand of pine trees and had started crossing the field that we encountered our greatest trial, my greatest ordeal, and to this day, my heaviest shame. Because as we were passing the ball diamonds, I noticed up ahead a cluster of kids from school. I didn't say anything, but instinctively I untied the wooden sword at my belt, with a single silent motion, and dropped it, along with the soaking wet beach towel, into the tall grass along the ditch. It was full of stormwater from the day before, and the sword and cloak both were irretrievably lost.

But I said nothing, and Christopher had yet to notice them standing there. He was still swinging his own sword playfully in the air at nothing in particular.

"Peter!"

I knew the voice that called me. It was Julian. He was one of the more popular kids in my class and had even been expelled once for drinking a stolen bottle of his dad's vodka behind the school gym. He was leaning indolently against the chain link fence of the backstop with two or three other kids our age. One of them held a smoldering cigarette, though none of them, to my knowledge, really smoked. There was a girl with them whom I had admired from my desk in the far corner of our classroom all that spring, though I hadn't seen her since school had let out for the summer.

"Well, look who it is!" Julian said again, and there was an edge to his voice that was almost threatening.

"Peter and Christopher," said one of the boys with him. "What you guys up to?" It was more a challenge than a question.

Christopher was further ahead of me and pulled up mid-swing with his sword. I hung back.

Julian straightened up from leaning against the fence. "Nice fairy cape, Chris. And what's with the sword?"

The other boy laughed. "Probably for beating back the other fairies." Everyone was laughing but Christopher now. He looked back at me, and I couldn't meet his eyes.

"Leave him be," said the girl, and I couldn't tell if the note of mercy I heard in her voice was sincere or make-believe. But Julian stepped forward. "Is that what it's for?" he asked. "Let's have a look."

He reached, and Christopher gave no resistance when he pulled the sword from his hand. "Julian, please," was all he said.

Julian was holding it by its wooden blade, like an inverted baseball bat. A diabolical grin crept over his face then, and even though I had slunk back a few paces more from them, I could see his knuckles whiten around the wood. "Nah," he said over his shoulder. "I don't think this would make a good fairy beater. It's not strong enough."

And then he turned slightly and swung it suddenly with great force against the steel post of the backstop. The crack of it resounded across the field, and I winced. The sword shattered in two, and the hilt end went spinning off. Julian dropped the blade end gingerly at Christopher's feet, splintered and broken. The whole while Christopher was staring with unseeing eyes, retreating into himself and unwilling to look Julian in the face.

"Come on Julian," said the girl, and this time her tone was clear. "Leave him alone."

Julian turned. The boy with the cigarette flicked the smoldering butt toward Christopher and turned too. I had hoped they'd forgotten me, but just before they wandered off, Julian looked over his shoulder. "See y'round, Peter."

I nodded faintly.

Something somewhere startled a cow in a field on the far side of the trees, and I could hear it mooing, distantly. Whatever it was must have startled the other farm animals, too, because following the moo came the bark of a dog, and then, unmistakably, the single crow of a lonely rooster.

When they were gone, Christopher turned to me with trembling eyes, but I couldn't lift mine to meet his. He said nothing but stooped to pick up his broken sword. He looked at me again, and I could see that he saw how mine was missing.

"Just—" I said softly, pushing past him and starting across the field. "Just forget it, Chris. Julian's a jerk."

I didn't look back, but after a moment I could hear the shuffle of slow footsteps in the grass beside me. We walked home in total silence. My welts from the fire wraiths no longer hurt me, but with every step, still, I could feel a searing pain burning in my chest.

2.

The Tattoo

The waiting room was surprisingly pristine, given the part of town I was in. I don't know what I was expecting—ashtrays smoldering on stained countertops, perhaps, dirty magazines piled haphazardly on the coffee table, maybe—but it wasn't this. The place was almost fastidiously tidy. An elaborate Turkish rug covered the floor, the tassels arranged so neatly on either edge that I wondered absently if they had been combed out. The couch I was sitting on was threadbare, it's true, but only charmingly so. In the corner, a floor lamp with multiple branching arms cast a soft orange glow over everything, and on the counter, a single incense burner smoked faintly, making the air sweet, but hardly pungent.

I had arrived early. There was a heavy curtain separating this waiting area from his studio, and through the thick cloth I could hear him working with a client. He was speaking softly, his voice mingling indistinctly with the faint clicking sound of some machinery or other.

The wood-paneled walls were hung with framed drawings—examples of his work, I assumed—and I passed the time by pouring over them. There were the usual skulls and arrow-pierced hearts, some of these so grim as to be almost ugly, but there were also more transcendent images: warrior angels with wings of fire, elaborate floral patterns, mysterious inscriptions in stylized script.

The clicking sound stopped, the voices grew slightly louder, and almost with a flourish the curtain parted. He was done with his client and was bringing her into the waiting room.

"You will see," he was saying, "that there's still a faint shadow left, where it was. Another two or three sessions and that will be gone too. But even now, I'm sure, you'll be pleased with the change."

"I don't know how to thank you," she replied. He had produced a handheld mirror from behind the counter, and she was using it to inspect the side of her throat, up and around, as far as she could see, to the back of her neck.

I tried to respect her privacy, but since I myself would be undergoing the same procedure shortly, I couldn't help but glance out the corner of my eye.

Whatever tattoo had been there—on her throat and around her neck—it was certainly gone. He was right, there was still a faint shadow left behind, but so faint that I never could have told you what the image was that had once been in its place.

"I don't know how I can possibly repay you," she was saying. Tears were forming in her eyes, and they gleamed with all the light of the multistemmed lamp in the corner. "He forced me to do it, you know. And the tattoos were all so awful. He said it was so that no one would want me if I ever left him."

I tried hard not to overhear so personal a confession, but I couldn't help it.

"The others weren't so bad, but on my neck like that? There was no way I could keep it hidden."

The tears were glistening brightly on her cheek now.

"It's my pleasure," he said quietly. He didn't look in her face but seemed rather to be inspecting the spot on her neck where he had been working. "Like I say: two or three more sessions and it will be a thing of the past. There are, of course, some scars that even I can't remove, but those, too, will heal with time."

When she was gone, the tattooist—or perhaps more accurately I ought to call him the untattooist—addressed himself to me.

"You must be Mr. Wilson," he said. He stepped behind the counter and consulted his agenda book. "My three o'clock?"

"Thank you for seeing me. They told me that you remove tattoos—the best in the city, is what they said—and that you are willing to—how would you say it? Take on pro bono work?"

He looked up from his book. "If the story warrants it," he said, "I do it for free."

He nodded toward the door. "Take her, for instance. I can't tell you her whole story, but it's enough for you to know that when she was young, a man she had given her heart to marked her as his own with tattoos all over her body. Well: she's left him behind now, but of course, something like that doesn't fade so easily, does it?"

"And so you—"

"When she came to me, his mark was everywhere. Arms, back, upper thigh, throat. A case so tragic as that, of course I did it pro bono. What price could anybody reasonably charge? The throat tattoo was the hardest. It's a very vulnerable place, you know."

I wondered vaguely what part of her story he had left out as *too* personal, if he was willing already to share this much. But there was a profound note of compassion in his voice, and it prompted me to share my story too.

"Years ago, I had a lot of demons I was fighting. I mean that metaphorically, of course." I added that quickly, because at the first mention of my demons he looked at me hard—harder than I would have expected. "The drink, you know. And worse. And one night—I don't remember much of it—but the next day, I had this."

I couldn't look him in the eye, for shame, but I pulled up my sleeve to reveal a poorly rendered Celtic cross, upside-down and bleeding great gouts of blood, glaring up defiantly from my forearm. The image itself was hideous enough, but it had been a shoddy job all around, and the artistry made it look almost comical in certain lights, a laughable attempt at looking fearsome.

I could tell nothing from his face, but he looked at the image for a long, pensive moment.

"Does it qualify?" I asked at last.

He looked at me again with that hard, piercing light in his eye. "You will have to tell me," he said strangely. "It is entirely up to you." He rubbed his chin and looked at the image again. "And are you still fighting your demons?" he asked indistinctly.

I held my breath for what felt a long time, and then exhaled heavily at last. "I do want it gone," I said. "Everywhere I go it's always long sleeves and heavy coats. Even in summer. And it's not just the image—though that's bad enough—but what it reminds me of, who I was."

He looked at me a third time, piercingly. "I've seen worse," he said. "But if you want me to, I will do it."

I nodded, and the next thing I knew he had pulled aside the curtain again and ushered me into his studio. A chair not unlike a dentist's chair stood in the centre, though it looked far more comfortable than I had anticipated—and again this surprised me so much that I wondered once more what I had expected. A machine festooned with cables and wires stood in one corner, gleaming so spotlessly that I assumed it must be what he used for the procedure.

He gestured toward the chair and asked me to have a seat. I watched him closely while he busied himself in a cupboard, producing bottles of disinfectant, swabs, gauze and other items I couldn't identify.

For the first time I noticed how strangely he was dressed. He wore gloves that covered his hands well past the wrist, though I expect this was for the sake of hygiene. But they were, remarkably, dark black. So were his pants and his high-necked sweater. Everything on him was black, in fact, except for a bright red scarf which he wore, not stylishly, but wrapped tightly to the chin. He wore a beret, too, pulled low over his brow. This, together with the soul patch on his chin, made him look almost like the caricature of a beatnik, or one trying too hard to affect that appearance.

The whole time he worked, he spoke. "I had one client," he said, "Who had been a—what do they call it these days? A skinhead? You know the type. He had the worst hate you could imagine printed on his knuckles. Said he did it so that when he punched someone, they would see the reason why, even as the fist flew at them."

He had turned his attention to the machinery now, preparing it carefully and moving it toward my chair.

"If you can believe it, he even had—well, I can't repeat it, the slur itself—but he had it emblazoned on his forehead, right there, so that anyone looking him in the eye would know exactly how much he hated. And who."

He had turned on the machine now, and it began to hum faintly, like a fan whirring on a hot summer night, or rain falling steadily on a lazy afternoon. "But would you believe it? He left that life behind. All of it. The gangs, the hatred, the violence. Almost a supernatural change, if you will. But sometimes, you know, changes on the inside don't show up on the outside so easily, do they?"

I couldn't tell if he was laughing now, but his voice certainly shifted, if subtly. "And then, when he came to me, he had fallen in love. Can you believe it? And mark this: to the last woman he ever could have loved in his skinhead days, and the last woman who ever would have taken him, back then."

He pulled a wheeled stool over and sat down next to my inclined chair, leaning over me. "But, as they say, love covereth over a multitude of sins." He picked up the laser-needle, attached to the whirring machine by a thick black cord. "Please," he said. "Pull back your sleeve and lay out your arm."

I did.

"So these two wanted to be married. Can you imagine? And he told me that he couldn't bear the thought of standing up to say, 'I do,' with that old hatred written all over his face."

"Sounds like the perfect candidate for pro bono work."

"Perhaps," he said absently. "Perhaps they all are. Anyway, he was able to marry his lovely bride, without any of the old ugliness standing between them. He even sent me a wedding photo."

He gestured to a framed picture on the wall. A beautiful bride, dark-skinned and radiant, stood next to a young man in an inexpensive-looking suit. His face shone brightly with one of the sincerest smiles I had ever seen, no shadow in sight.

"They look happy," I said.

"They are. And so am I to have helped. Now—" There was a lamp on a retractable arm over the chair—again not unlike a dentist's chair—and he pulled it over me, flooding my whole body with a blinding white light. "Let's see what we can do about this."

"Will it hurt?" I asked. It only now occurred to me to ask.

"Yes. I'm sorry to say, but it will hurt very much."

"They say that even the best tattoo removal techniques leave a mark behind—" I was talking now only to steel myself against the first stab of the needle—"that you can never really get it all. But that man in the photo, if he really did have a hateful slur on his forehead, you certainly can't see any sign of it."

"Most techniques do leave something behind," he said. "But I have developed a device that—well—it hurts, like I say, but it gets it all. Now please, Mr. Wilson, if you will hold still."

It did hurt, though not as much as I had expected. There started up a steady clicking sound, and a stabbing fire shot through my skin. I winced and turned my head to see what was happening on my arm. I was somewhat startled to see how intently the untattooist was bent over his work, furrowing his brow with such intense concentration that he might have been wincing himself.

"It's not possible except there be some pain," he said, and there was something in his voice I hadn't heard before.

To distract me, he began talking in an ambling way about some of his other clients. Each story, he explained, was entirely unique. The first—and this was the case that had started him out doing this kind of thing for charity—up until then he had simply been a tattoo artist—but the first was an old man who had been in Auschwitz. He had survived, but not without the dehumanizing number of that awful death factory engraved on his arm.

I commented on the irony, that he would have done a tattoo removal for a survivor of Auschwitz, only to go on and remove those neo-Nazi slurs from the skinhead fiancé in the photograph.

"Every story has a story," he said enigmatically. "And anyway, the two cases aren't so different as they might seem."

At any rate, word started to spread like only good news can, after that first client. An ex-con came next. He had taken a tattoo during his time in prison, mostly to protect himself by identifying with one of the gangs on the inside.

"He was completely reformed, of course, and on parole. But the mark of the past was still haunting him. Couldn't get work. Couldn't find love. That one was an easy removal, though. It hurt very little."

But there were grimmer stories to come. One client had received her tattoo as part of an elaborate initiation into a mysterious cult that she had since escaped. Another had been tattooed as a child by the worst kind of abusive parent. There were some stories that even he would not tell, but only alluded to vaguely. And all the while he spoke, he worked with his furrowed brow and his steadily clicking needle over the upside-down cross on my forearm.

And I felt a profound wave of appreciation welling up in me, despite the pain, to consider all the lives the untattooist had changed. I thought of my own ridiculous tattoo, slowly vanishing beneath the piercing laser-needle of his device, and I felt new channels of gratitude opening in me as it did.

I can't say how long it took, and before he was done my arm was aching fully to the shoulder, throbbing with a slow, dull pain. But then, almost without warning, the droning of the machine stopped. He wiped my arm with an alcohol swab, set down the needle, and pushed his stool back.

"I think, Mr. Wilson, that will do for today."

I only noticed the shadow left behind because I knew there would be one. If you did not know the story, you never would have imagined that my forearm had not always been so soft and clean as it was in that moment.

I was at a loss for words. Bubbling over with gratitude, I reached instinctively for my wallet. "How can I—"

The untattooist blinked weakly and his voice sounded strangely far away. "Please, put it out of your mind. There's no need to repay. You may wish to return, though, to see if more of that shadow can't be removed."

He pulled back the curtain and ushered me into the waiting room.

"And of course, if you ever come across a story that might warrant my services, perhaps you'd be so kind as to send them my way?"

I reached for his hand. Surprisingly, however, he didn't take mine. He stood there almost as if he were favoring his arm, and I wondered if it wasn't trembling slightly. "Yes," I said, lowering my hand awkwardly. "Yes, of course I will."

He showed me to the door, and with a warm farewell, I stepped out into the greasy street. Somewhere far away a siren was screaming.

I was only five minutes down the road when I realized I had left my wallet behind. I'd set it down when he had refused my payment, and I'd inadvertently left it on the counter. I turned back.

The parlor had a closed sign hung in the window now—it was well past five o'clock—but I tried the door and gratefully discovered he hadn't locked up.

"Hello?" I called out, but the parlor was unnervingly silent. It made me think vaguely of a tomb. The curtain was drawn, but there was light behind it, and beneath the cloth I could see shadows moving, suggesting to me that he was still there. I stepped up and looked through.

His back was to me, and he was looking into a mirror by the bright overhead lamp he had used during my procedure. I could see that he had removed his gloves and his sweater. The red scarf was draped over the chair and the beret was set aside on the counter.

I spoke again, and he turned at the sound. "I forgot my—" I began to explain, then stopped with a startled inhale. There were tears in his eyes, but that is not what caught my breath. Rather, as he turned toward me, I saw that his forehead—that part of it that had been covered by the beret—was inscribed with a hideous racial slur, an ugly skinhead tattoo.

He nodded at me and raised his hand. As he did, I could see, in the hard light of that overhead lamp, that the knuckles were tattooed with hateful letters. I followed the hand as it lifted to his throat, and there, where the scarf had been, I saw the most tragic tattoo I could imagine, up the neck and around the back of his head. He nodded again.

"As I said," he said softly. "It's not possible except there be some pain."

And he lowered his hand again, but now I wept at what I saw. For there on his exposed forearm, distorted and so shoddily-done as to be cartoonish, I saw a grotesque cross, upside down and bleeding great gouts of hideous blood—my own tattoo—throbbing freshly on his bare skin.

3.

The Patchwork Quilt

And then one night Ashlyn's insomnia finally became unbearable. Mark was sleeping luxuriously on the pillow next to her, his rhythmic breathing almost infuriatingly serene. She had always known him to be a sound sleeper, but that night he seemed especially oblivious to her tosses and turns—or, indeed, to what had caused them—and when she could take it no longer, she flung herself from the covers and found her way into the cold living room.

Her mother's antique hope chest sat next to the couch, a simple cedar box that had been crafted by her great-great-grandfather Kirk for her great-grandmother's wedding day, and handed down from one generation of matrons to the next on her mother's side. She seldom looked in it anymore, but she knew there was an old patchwork quilt among the keepsakes it contained. It was folded neatly near the top, so she found it easily enough in the dark, saving herself the trouble of having to turn on a light and rummage for a blanket in the linen closet.

It was difficult to settle into the faux leather cushions of the couch. She had never found this couch to be terribly comfortable, but Mark had insisted on it because it matched the modern décor he wanted for the living room. Cold moonlight washed over her through the half-closed blinds, and it might have been this that made her shiver the way she did. She burrowed, almost cowered under the quilt, pulling it to her chin and folding her body into a tight ball beneath it.

It took a long time for the spinning coin of her harried thoughts to rattle finally still, but in the end it did.

She woke poorly rested the next morning. Pale sunlight had replaced cold moonlight at the window, and outside in the yard, loud enough that it reached her even through the glass, a handful of starlings were bickering furiously with each other. She had slept very deeply, but even so she'd had a dream so unsettling that she felt as though she hadn't slept at all.

In her dream, she was sitting in a crowded church, somehow aware that she was not properly dressed for the occasion and greatly distressed that this might be noticed. There was a groom with his party at the front, and though she never saw his face, he looked vaguely familiar to her. A priest rose, or perhaps it was a minister—she could never really tell the difference—and then an organ started up.

It was not the typical bridal march that played. It was both more compelling and more terrifying, like some celestial orison coming from somewhere far away. Ashlyn did not see the bride process down the aisle, but when she looked, there she was, standing at the front with the groom. She wore a simple linen dress, the style very old-fashioned, and the fabric—this stood out to her especially—seemed particularly rough for a wedding dress, but brilliantly white. Her head was bowed with a reverence so intense as to be almost agonizing.

The priest lifted his arms and began to pray, though the words sounded as though they were coming from the organ itself; certainly they did not seem to be coming from him. "O Eternal God," said the voice, "Creator and preserver of all mankind, send Your blessing upon this man and this woman whom we bless in Your name, that they, living faithfully together, may surely perform and keep the vow and covenant between them made this day."

And in one gathered voice the whole church said an amen, then fell still, though in her dream Ashlyn could not find the word in time. When her amen finally came, it was so late that it sounded out singly through the silent church, echoing so conspicuously that the bride at the front looked at her suddenly, and Ashlyn was startled to see that her eyes were streaming with tears.

And then she woke.

It was not the content of the dream that troubled her, she thought, as she pulled herself to sitting on the couch and began folding the quilt to put it away. The weeping bride notwithstanding, it was not especially disturbing, and even somewhat commonplace in its details. It was simply far more vivid, more solid and more textured, than any normal dream should have been—so real as to be somehow oppressive. That, and the piercing sound of the music in the church, is what had left her so unsettled.

She smoothed the folded quilt in her lap, ready to return it to the hope chest. It might have been the touch of the fabric, or perhaps the brilliant white, but something suddenly caught her breath. The patch of the quilt that happened to be facing up at her, now that the quilt was folded, was a square of unusually rough linen. She was quite weary from her restless night and perhaps not thinking clearly, but even so it seemed to her that it was made of the same cloth—the very same texture and color—as the wedding dress in her dream.

A moment passed and she became aware that she had been holding her breath, staring at the quilt.

"But really," she said at last in a dismissive voice, "it could have been from anything. And what would you expect a wedding dress to look like?" She heard Mark stirring in the bedroom down the hall and rose quickly, putting the quilt away with a furtive glance over her shoulder.

They spoke very little over breakfast. Mark indicated that he would be home late from work that night, and Ashlyn said something allusively about not much being new. He attempted a tentative peck on the cheek on his way out, but she shied away, and in the end he left without so much as a warm goodbye.

The difficulty with insomnia, of course, is that after four or five nights of it, you begin to worry throughout the day that the coming night is going to be no better than the ones before, and this worry puts your nerves in such a knot that, insomnia or not, there's no way you'll ever fall asleep.

That's how it seemed to Ashlyn, anyway, as she lay there late that evening, staring into the dark with unseeing eyes. Mark had indeed been home late, so late that he simply assumed she was asleep when he came into the room, settling in beside her without a word. She wondered if he would have said anything even if he had known she was awake, and this train of thought made her all the more restless.

At last, she rose and made her way to the couch. She found the quilt and curled up beneath it, hoping against hope that it might work the same magic it had the night before and coax her into sleep.

When she finally did drift off, she began dreaming immediately. What surprised her was that she knew very clearly it was a dream this time, but that knowledge was not at all reassuring. Instead, it only intensified her feelings of helplessness as she watched the events unfold.

A slim man was standing alone in a barren field beneath a slate-grey sky. He was wearing a plaid shirt, crisscrossed with bright red and stark black. He wore old-fashioned suspenders and held a brown felt hat in his hands, which he wrung nervously between his fingers. Looking closely, she saw that the field was not just barren; it had been ruined. The crop that was once growing there had been pummeled flat, and the hailstones that had done it—some of them as large as a man's fist—had not yet melted away.

The man said nothing, but his shoulders were stooped, and they sank even lower as he surveyed the damage. Ashlyn felt compelled to say something, but, as sometimes happens in dreams, she could find no voice. The man's shoulders began to tremble slightly, and then he collapsed to his knees.

What happened next is what caused Ashlyn to wake, though, because instead of burying his face in his hands as she expected him to do, the man lifted them, raising his palms in a gesture that she could only describe as abject submission.

"Please," he whispered. "Bring my family through this."

It broke Ashlyn's heart to hear it, and his posture was so beautiful but also so awful that she looked away, almost willing herself awake as she did.

It was not quite morning when she opened her eyes, and the light in the living room was dim. She sat up and pulled the quilt into a heap on her lap. She was certain she had seen the fabric of the man's shirt before—the colours were so vivid—and she rooted among the patches, terrified to discover that she had.

She found it in one of the four corners. It was only a single square of plaid, and because it was crisscrossed with such dark black, she could tell even in the grey light that the red was an intensely bright hue. She stared at it for a moment, and then, because the weight of her dream was still upon her, she buried her face in the quilt, stifling her tears with a choked cry.

She was still thinking about it at dinner. She and Mark were eating together these days only by force of habit, though they had started preparing their own meals. Weeks ago, they had given up on even the most superficial efforts at conversation. Looking back, she wondered if she said what she did only because she was trying to avoid the unsettling conclusion she was coming to about her dreams and that quilt. At any rate, she looked at him across the table and finally asked, "Do I know her?"

It was all she needed to have said. Mark had just taken a bite, and he lowered his fork slowly. His eyes were fixed on hers, but she could not read them well. And anyway, in that moment she felt for the first time in a long time that she did not much care what his looks meant anymore.

He didn't reply, so eventually she said, "Well?"

The pause that followed was excruciating, but at last he spoke. "Stephanie," he said, and then, after another agonizing pause. "It was Stephanie from work." He looked down into his plate.

Ashlyn stared at him for a piercing moment, and then quietly pushed her chair from the table and left the room.

That night she abandoned even the pretense of sleeping in their bed but took the quilt and spread it on the couch. Mark passed her on his way into the bedroom. She was sunk deeply into the cushions, the quilt pulled tightly to her chin, refusing to look at him.

"I—" He faltered. "I am so sorry, Ash."

When no reply came, he shuffled grimly off to bed.

Sleep still took a long time to come, though less than it had on previous nights. Her dream this time was just as vivid as the others, but she was expecting it tonight, so it was somehow less unsettling.

She saw two small boys standing near a table in a kitchen, while a woman worked away on an antique-looking sewing machine. The boys were close enough in size and appearance that she took them to be twins. They were making a martyr's effort to stand still, while the woman fitted them for the clothes she was sewing. Because they were twins, the outfits matched, two identical sets of overalls. They were made of a bright blue material speckled with white dots, though looking closer, Ashlyn saw that the dots were really tiny anchors printed onto the fabric.

What surprised her this time was that she recognized the sewing machine so easily. It was the very sewing machine her grandmother had used with her, when Ashlyn would visit as a little girl, and they would work on projects together.

Time is often hard to piece together in dreams, but it seemed that the very moment this dawned on her, one of the two boys looked directly at her. And she gasped, because she suddenly realized that it was her uncle standing there, her mother's younger brother. She knew it was him only in the way one knows things in dreams. She could not have recognized him otherwise because she had only met him a few times as a grown-up, and in all those memories he was drunk. There was some dark story attached to him that her mother would never share, though she did say once that she had chosen Ashlyn's father especially because he was the complete opposite of her brother.

It occurred to Ashlyn—and this was the thought that lingered with her inescapably the next morning—that she'd never known her uncle had a twin. But she didn't have time to absorb that strange detail in the dream, because the two had given up holding still and had begun to tussle. She couldn't tell if it was playful or in earnest, but either way, it struck her as very violent, and they tumbled out of the kitchen, locked in each other's arms.

The woman said something to call them back, but the struggle carried on, and then Ashlyn watched as she sighed and buried her face in her hands. Ashlyn supposed it was in exasperation, but at just that moment the sound of the boy's quarrel died away and the room became perfectly still. She could hear the woman whispering into the silence. Ashlyn thought at first that she was speaking to herself, but as the voice whispered on, she realized she must be speaking to someone, though they were definitely alone in the room.

"O God," she said. "Please make this worth it." She said much more than this, but those were the only words Ashlyn could make out.

She was not surprised when she woke that morning to find a patch in the quilt, toward the centre, made of bright blue fabric printed with white anchors.

After that, Ashlyn started to look forward to nights on the couch with the quilt. She still often struggled with insomnia, sometimes terribly, but she always drifted off eventually, and when she did, she always had the most vivid dreams.

In one, she stood in a shadowy bedroom in a house which she thought she had been in before. An old man in striped pajamas lay on the bed, so warm with fever that the bedclothes were pulled back. A girl knelt at the bedside, squeezing his hand and praying earnestly. When the girl looked up, Ashlyn recognized the face of her great-grandmother, looking much the same as she looked in the only photo Ashlyn had ever seen of her as a child.

In another dream she saw a girl that she knew almost instantly to be her grandmother, standing in a throng of people on a street in Toronto, one hand holding tightly to her father, the other waving a triangular-shaped pennant. The crowd cheered uproariously while a parade of men in sailor's uniforms marched past, and Ashlyn knew that this was the day of Toronto's V.E. celebrations after the war. She watched as one of the parading men came close. He stooped and picked up the little girl in an embrace so tight that Ashlyn knew they must be related, and when she looked at the girl's father, there were the kind of tears on his cheeks that a man can only weep when his prayers have been answered.

Each morning Ashlyn would wake from dreams like these and scour the quilt. It was not always easy, but invariably she would find the patch she was looking for. Here was a bit of striped cloth that she knew must have been a man's pajama top at one time. There was a bright patch the same color as the pennant she had seen in the parade. Every dream, it seemed, had a corresponding patch in the quilt, or perhaps it was that the dreams were coming from the patches themselves. The thought almost embarrassed her to put it that way around.

During this time, something of a thaw—perhaps even a spring— in her interactions with Mark had begun, as well. She still refused to sleep in their bedroom, but one night, after another tense and perfunctory dinner, she asked him if it really was over between him and this Stephanie. Mark assured her earnestly that it was, and for the first time since everything had come to light, she found she believed him.

Another time, late in the afternoon, he came home early from work and asked if he might take her out. She agreed only with great reluctance, but they went to a spot they used to frequent when they were dating, long before the betrayal. There, over two untouched cups of coffee he offered her a sincere, if faltering apology, more heartfelt than anything she had ever heard him say before. And when she came home, she felt, if not exactly close to him, at least not so far as she once had been.

And then one night, deep in sleep on the couch and buried almost completely under the quilt, she dreamed the hardest dream of all.

She was standing in the dimly lit parlor of someone's house. A sombre-sounding clock was ticking insistently in the corner, and solemn men and women were drifting infrequently in and out of the room. In the centre stood a coffin, far too small to have been there for anything but the saddest of tragedies. It was open, and the flowers arranged around it seemed to beckon Ashlyn forward, though she could not have moved even if she had wanted to.

A man and a woman dressed in black came in, stepping up to the tiny casket. They peered into it pathetically, the woman pressing a handkerchief against her mouth, and the man looking almost defiantly resolute.

"So lovely," the woman whispered. "Doesn't she look just too lovely?"

The man nodded. "Did they name her?" he asked softly.

"Hope," came the reply. There was a long silence, filled only with the sonorous tick of the clock. "And they say," the woman said at last, "that she sewed the little dress herself. So lovely…" She trailed off, and the two wandered away.

Ashlyn pushed through the fear that paralyzed her and forced herself to the centre of the room. The sight of the little one lying in the casket brought her heart into her throat and held it there. The child was clothed in a beautiful dress made of some satiny pink material. Ashlyn had no time to weep, though, because at just that moment another woman came into the parlour, and she recognized her, through the black lace veil that shrouded her face, as her own great-grandmother.

She was young, of course, as she had been in previous dreams, but old enough now to be a brand-new mother. And from the way she trembled to look into the casket, Ashlyn knew at a glance whose child it must have been in that tragic pink dress. The mourning woman sobbed openly, and then to Ashlyn's surprise—though it was less surprising now, since she had seen it happen so often in her dreams—she knelt, still weeping freely.

"Please," she whispered. "Please, may something good still come of my little Hope's life. May this not be for nothing."

It was such a strange thing to have said in that moment, but it seemed to Ashlyn that the words were not really coming from her at all, but that a voice more simple and more beautiful than any she had ever heard before was speaking, a celestial orison sounding from somewhere very far away, but closer to her than the beat of her own heart.

"Please may this not be for nothing."

And then Ashlyn woke. She could hardly bear searching among the patches of the quilt, but it did not take her long to find one made of the softest, pinkest satin she could imagine. When she saw it, she pressed her face against it and repeated to herself the words of the prayer she had dreamed, over and over again in a breaking voice.

Though she resisted it tenaciously, the echo of those words guided her thoughts back to her own loss. It had been more than a year now since she'd thought of it, the little girl she could never bring herself to name. She and Mark had given up trying for a child after saying goodbye to her, and at some point—she knew it was true, though she could not say exactly when—they had given up on each other, too.

She stared intensely at the pink square of cloth in her lap. She knew at last what she would name the little child she'd never got to hold, and she felt it urgently that she must.

She moved beneath the shadow of that dream all morning, but before the day was through it had begun to feel more like a shade than a gloom. That evening at dinner Ashlyn let her eyes meet Mark's in a way she had not done for many weeks. She held his gaze so long that he even dared a tentative smile, a testing of the waters.

"I've been thinking," she said at last. "I would like it if we could…" The words were difficult for her to find. "I mean, if you would be willing to—if we could see someone. To talk, you know? About what happened between us. And to see if we might find a way forward."

He was still very tentative. "Together?" he asked.

She nodded faintly. "Yes," she said. "Together."

He was nodding too. "I'd like that very much."

Ashlyn still slept on the couch that night, but for the first time in months she dared to believe that it would not be like this much longer. And that night she slept deeply, and dreamlessly, such a sleep as she'd not had in a very long time.

4.

The New Parson of Petit-Wasmes

The day the superintendent arrived in the village of Petit-Wasmes, two parishioners were waiting at the inn to welcome his carriage. They were modest men, their hats doffed meekly and their shoulders stooped with the weariness of poverty. Hans Visser was a foreman in the coal mines, and down there in the sooty darkness he spoke with the bark of a man used to being obeyed. Standing on the porch of the village inn, however, to welcome a prestigious doctor of theology from the University of Amsterdam, his voice barely lifted above a whisper. Jozef was the village baker. He had been billeting their parson since he'd arrived that summer, and it was he who had written the superintendent to come see about him. He was lean, for a baker, and his hands were veined and knobbed, hardened from years of pounding dough.

"Welcome, Heer Opzitcher," he said hesitantly, clutching his hat as though it were one of the soiled dishcloths he used to mop up spills in his bakery. "I am Jozef Vos, who wrote you. We are glad to welcome you to our humble village and so grateful you have come. We trust the journey was pleasant."

The superintendent did not exactly look at Meneer Vos, at least not face to face. He wore a pair of soft leather gloves, which he was carefully removing, one painstaking finger at a time, and this absorbed the better part of his attention.

"It is a serious matter," he said at last, still not looking at the baker. His gloves were now off, and even though the evening was dim and there were no streetlamps to see by, he seemed to be inspecting his fingernails closely, as though he were worried they might not be clean. "A most serious matter to make the kind of accusation you have made against a minister of the gospel."

Hans the coal miner wrung his hat so tightly that it would probably never be worn properly again. "Quite so," he said timidly. "But Heer Opzitcher, you must understand. The situation is in fact as serious as we said."

The superintendent tucked his gloves beneath his arm, removed his black high hat carefully and addressed himself to the door of the inn.

"Does he know you've written me?" he asked vaguely.

Hans and Jozef exchanged glances. "No," said the baker. "Outside of his duties as our parson—his preaching and the sacraments and such—other than that, I mean, we speak very little."

"And when we do," added Hans, "it's often very hard to make sense of what we're speaking about. Visions and ramblings, mostly. We were hoping, Heer Opzitcher, that with your experience in these matters you would be able to help him see reason. We are, after all, just simple men." The look on his face suggested that, though he was painfully aware of his obsequious tone, he could not suppress it for trying.

The superintendent had reached the door of the inn. He stopped with his hand on the knob and looked in the direction of the two villagers. It was a very damp night, and they were in that purgatory of seasons between late winter and early spring. A cold fog was settling over the village, and the night air was smeared grimy with it. Even so, a brilliant moon must have been gleaming somewhere overhead, because despite the fog it was not impenetrably dark, though it might have been better if it were. In all that mist, everything looked only ugly and shapeless and sullen.

"Is there a café or taverne here at the inn? Shall we have a koffie and talk?"

He gestured gregariously, opening the door as though he were the host and they the guests of the village, and so the three of them found their way into a back room of the inn. It was a dimly lit café, almost empty at that hour of the evening.

"No doubt, Heer Opzitcher, our modest little café must seem a laughable thing next to the bustling cafés of Amsterdam," said the baker.

The superintendent glanced around the room. The greasy lamp light gave the whole place a sickly yellow hue, made worse by the choice of décor. The peeling wallpaper was a hideous scarlet and the soiled table linen a faded green, a putrid color that reminded one vaguely of mold or bile. "Indeed, it is," he said, setting his high hat gingerly on the table. "But if the koffie is good I suppose that is all that matters."

The koffie was not particularly good. Even so, Hans and Jozef could not have afforded it, and they exchanged an embarrassed look as the superintendent placed his order. The host knew Hans and Jozef well, of course, and knew equally well why they were meeting with this sharply dressed visitor from Amsterdam. He was one of the laymen, in fact, who had urged the baker to write the superintendent, so he discreetly brought them each a half pint of beer with the superintendent's koffie, offering it all as compliments of the house.

"Most kind," said the superintendent. "Most kind. And now, about our parson here at Petit-Wasmes—"

"As I said in the letter," the baker broke in, "we mean him no ill will, and certainly no disrespect—"

"But his preaching," said Hans. "It is incomprehensible. He talks of Jesus as the beauty that lies within the petals of every sunflower, the Morning Star that gives every starry sky its light—gibberish like that, Heer Opzitcher—in the pulpit of a Sunday morning!" Perhaps now that they were indoors, Hans felt more like a coal miner than he had out on the street, but whatever the reason his voice seemed to have more bark in it than before.

"We have seen him at times almost as if in a trance, staring at the sunrise, or watching the night sky, sometimes for hours even."

"And instead of attending to the—er—the needs of the flock, he spends his time sketching in his notebooks. They are quite filled with idle drawings from what I understand. He's drawn portraits of us, sometimes without us knowing—and—" The coal miner leaned in here, his voice dropping, though the room was empty enough that no one would have heard anyway. "These are not always flattering, except for a few drawings of some of the village girls."

The superintendent said nothing, but a grave look clouded his face. He took a slow, thoughtful sip of his koffie. "Your letter said something about his manner in presiding over of the Lord's Supper?" he said, setting the cup down.

Hans blushed and looked toward Jozef.

"Well," said the baker, clearing his throat. He leaned in, too, and spoke in a furtive tone. "Last month at the Lord's Supper, he directed us to admire…" He seemed to have trouble finding the words and looked to Hans for corroboration.

Hans nodded. "Admire is one way to say it, yes."

Jozef tried again. "Well: he asked us to admire the sparkle of the wine in the cup. It was most unexpected."

"'See how it sets off the sheen of the chalice,' is how he said it, and then something about the beauty of the Lord's body, the richness of his blood." Hans was clearly agitated as he spoke, though the superintendent stared impassively at the tabletop, his arms folded tightly across his chest, listening. If he shared the coal miner's consternation over this aesthetic indulgence at the Lord's table, it was impossible to tell.

"It was almost indecent," said Jozef, as if the superintendent needed some prompting. "Heer Opzitcher," he said, "we are simple folk, not used to such flights of fancy, and certainly not in our worship."

"These are most unusual carryings-on," said the superintendent slowly. "I can understand it causing you concern, but I see nothing

33

especially unorthodox in them, however out of the ordinary. You would not be surprised to learn, I suppose, that your parson did not do especially well in his training for the ministry. He failed his examinations for theological school in Amsterdam, and he struggled at missionary school in Brussels. We had hoped that an appointment in a place like Petit-Wasmes would suit him well. Among a flock more—" and here he spoke with the greatest of delicacy—"more earthy, shall we say, with more immediate needs. We had hoped he would find his footing in a place like this."

Hans and Jozef exchanged another look. Jozef took a deep breath, and Hans a long pull at his tankard of beer. "There is also the question," Jozef said at last, "of his hygiene, and his health."

"Has that been a problem? He is a young man, and hale. I would not expect there to be concerns in that regard."

"Life in Petit-Wasmes is hard for all of us, to be sure," said Jozef. "But even among the coal miners—and they are the least likely to notice—but even among them it gets mentioned. He is often unkempt. Was taken with fever for two weeks last month. Even if his ministry were sound, which as we say we're not sure it is, but even if it were, the parish worries that he is not well."

"Not well?"

"Sallow cheeks, sunken eyes. He eats very little and seldom takes meat. I suppose it would be better for him if he didn't sleep in the straw like that, but as it is, he's often…" Jozef trailed off discreetly.

"There are women in the parish who simply cannot bear the stench of it sometimes, he gets so strong," said Hans bluntly.

For the first time in this interview, a look of real alarm crossed the superintendent's face. "Meneer Vos, I beg your pardon, but what could you possibly mean? Sleeping in the straw? Surely the church at Petit-Wasmes has provided better lodging for their parson than that?"

Jozef blushed slightly. Hans drained the rest of his half-pint at a gulp.

"Oh yes, Heer Opzitcher, to be sure we did," said the baker tentatively. "Why, I myself put him up in my own bakery. It's a modest room, to be sure, but comfortable. I dare say luxurious by village standards."

"Then why would he be sleeping in the straw?"

"He gave it up!" said Hans, bringing his empty mug down with a clap.

"Gave it up?"

"There was a vagabond come through town some months ago," said Jozef, turning bright red. "He came to the church seeking alms, and what little we could spare, he received. Over the span of a week or so, he and the parson became better known to one another, and come Sunday—and from the pulpit no less—Parson Vincent announced that he had offered up his lodgings at my bakery to this homeless derelict, and that he would be sleeping in the shed behind the inn here, in obedience to the teaching of our Lord."

"To be fair," added Hans. "The Gospel lesson that Sunday was Luke 9:58."

"The Son of Man has nowhere to lay his head," muttered the superintendent reflexively to himself.

"Be that as it may," continued Jozef, "he gave up his rooms in my bakery to a homeless vagabond, without the least consultation with me on the matter. And since then, I've been billeting a derelict, and our parson has been sleeping in the straw, in a hut behind the inn like some filthy zwerver."

"And he goes about his duties here looking exactly as though he *were* a zwerver."

"This is most alarming," said the superintendent. "Has no one put it to him, how unbecoming it is for the town parson to carry on like this?"

"Has no one put it to him? Have you not been listening?" The exasperation in Hans's voice was undisguised, and he might have said something regrettable, but Jozef placed a hand on his forearm and interjected.

"With all due respect, Heer Opzitcher, this is what we have been trying to say. All such efforts to speak reason to Heer Parson fall on deaf ears. He rattles on about the rich young ruler who had to sell all to follow the Lord, or how the Son of Man came not to be served but to serve."

"And offer up his life as a ransom for many," said the superintendent reflexively again.

"Yes, offer up his life, he says, and then he becomes distracted by a flower in a vase at the window, perhaps, or the angle of the sunlight as it sets over the corn fields—"

"A flock of crows springing up into the sky," added Hans.

"The silhouette of the cypress trees edging the road—"

"The shape of a haystack—"

"And it's all we can do to get a coherent word out of him after that."

The superintendent had finished his koffie and was staring into the dregs at the bottom of the cup, swirling them thoughtfully.

"No," he said at last. "You were right to contact us. This will never do. Sleeping in the hay like a vagabond, no less. It's the kind of thing that undermines the dignity of the priesthood. Most unbecoming for a minister of the gospel."

"Then you will attend to it?"

He looked up from his cup and met their eyes fully for the first time that night. He nodded grimly. "I will. He will either come to see reason, or the parish at Petit-Wasmes will soon have a new parson."

The cups were all drained now. The two villagers rose. "Thank you, Heer Opzitcher. Thank you."

"If you will excuse me now, Meneer Vos, Meneer Visser. It has been a long journey for me, and it is quite late. I shall retire for the night. But please, be assured. I will call on your parson first thing tomorrow morning. One way or another he and I shall come to an understanding, and your concerns shall all be addressed."

The baker and the coal miner shook the superintendent's hand warmly and found their way into the street.

They had not been more than an hour with Heer Opzitcher, but it was long enough that the fog had rolled through, and the sky had cleared. It had turned out, in fact, to be a brilliant night. The moon above was a dazzling crescent of pure white light, and the sky was ablaze—one might almost say aswirl—with the starry host.

Jozef Vos looked up, and despite the weight he felt from his interview with the superintendent, he couldn't help but comment on it. "There may be frost tonight," he said.

Hans said nothing, but he nodded in the direction of the street. A man was standing there in a threadbare coat and a woolen scarf. His hands were thrust into his pockets, and he was gazing up motionless into the night.

Hans gave Jozef a knowing look, and they both nodded sadly.

"Good evening, Heer Parson," said Jozef at last, affecting as neighborly a tone as he could. "A beautifully brisk night, isn't it?"

But the parson said nothing and continued staring at the sky.

Hans cleared his throat and raised his voice slightly. "I say, Heer Van Gogh—Parson Vincent—good evening to you!"

At the sound of his name, the parson seemed to start, as if returning suddenly from somewhere far away. He looked at the two men, and even in the moonlight they were sure of the piercing look in his blue eyes; they had seen it often enough. His red beard was quite overgrown, and his copper-colored hair was disheveled, giving him the air of a mystic, perhaps, or a prophet of old.

"Good evening, Meneer Vos, Meneer Visser," he said at last. "Do you see the stars tonight? Doesn't it put you in mind of the Psalm, how the heavens declare the glory of the Lord and the skies proclaim his handiwork?"

"Indeed, it does," said Jozef awkwardly, and then after a pause: "Heer Parson, will you be sleeping in your room at the bakery tonight?"

Van Gogh tilted his head slightly, lost in thought. "My room?" he said to himself. "Tonight? No, I think not. As our good Lord said, foxes have holes and birds have nests, but the Son of Man has nowhere to lay his head."

"As we've heard," said Hans softly.

It wasn't clear if Van Gogh heard him or not, but at that very moment a beatific smile dawned slowly across his sunken face, so clearly that even in the dim light Hans and Jozef could make it out. He laughed softly, somewhat sadly, and then nodded up in the direction of the night sky.

"But didn't he also say," he whispered, and it was not at all clear who he was speaking to, "that he who has eyes to see, let him see? Oh yes, and if we had his eyes, we would see indeed."

5.

Ghosted

I got my results

                    Your results?

From the test

                    Oh. Did you pass?

Haha very funny

                    No, seriously

Seriously? It was positive

                    So you passed?

No I didn't pass. What's the matter
with you?
I'm pregnant!

                    Pregnant?
                    How could you be pregnant?!?

As if you didn't know
Well?
Are you still there?

                    I don't know what to say. I
                    thought you were taking your
                    MCAT today and now you tell
                    me you're pregnant?

WTF!? MCAT?

                    I guess there goes med school.

What are you talking about MCAT?

                    Have you told mom and dad?

Med School?!

                    Do you know who the father
                    is?

Again, very funny. It's you, idiot

                    How could it be me?

As if you didn't know.
Don't be an a-hole

Is this Julie?

Julie? Who the hell is Julie?
Look if you've been screwing around
on me again, I swear to god

Julie? My sister Julie?
Who is this?

It's Peg. Who is this?

I think you might have texted
the wrong number.
I'm John

My name's John

I thought you were my sister
Julie. She has a new cell. The
number's not in my contacts

She was taking her MCAT
today
Was gonna text me the results
when she got them. I just
assumed.
Ummm, sorry?
It sounds like things aren't
great for you.

Hello?

Are you still there?

Hello?

O my god
I can't believe it
Look I'm sorry. My bf told me to text
him at this number when I got my
results.
Oh god
I gotta go
Please erase this whole convo from
your memory. Though I'm sorry I
called you an a-hole and all that.
Please just forget it

Hello?

You there?

                    Yes?

So did Julie pass?

                    Ummmm, yeah.
                    Flying colors as always.

Sorry to text you so late
Did I wake you?

                    Nah, it's ok

I told my bf

                    About your MCAT results? :)

Right. My MCAT. lol

lol? Who uses lol anymore?
Haven't heard that since I was a
kid.
Anyway, how did it go?

Have you ever been dumped by text
before?

No

It sucks. But its even worse when
you're pregnant and you're couch
surfing cause your parents kicked you
out and you thought maybe this guy
was gonna take care of you and he
doesn't even have the guts to call you
in person let alone meet with you face
to face

I bet

And you know what he said? I don't
have time for this. WTF? Don't have
time? As if having a child is something
you just pencil into your agenda book
or something? Like I'm just sitting
around with nothing to do but have
his stupid kid all on my own

Oof

Oof is an understatement. Cause then
he put it out on Facebook that I was
cheating on him. That way he can
deny it's his baby, I guess. Even
though he's been sleeping around ever

since we started dating and I know
this for a fact. But it doesn't matter
cause everyone believes him and now
I'm like a social leper or something.
No one will talk to me or answer my
texts

I don't know why I'm telling all this to
a perfect stranger. It's just, I literally
have no one else to talk to

Hello? You still there, or did I blow it
with you too?

                      No. I'm still here. It's just, I
                      don't know what to say

Maybe you don't have to say anything.
Maybe there's nothing to say

                      Maybe

You're up late, anyways. I hope you
don't mind me dumping like this

                      Well, I couldn't sleep anyways

Join the club

                      I guess
                      I was thinking about Julie
                      actually

Your sister?

Yeah. She passed the MCAT,
like I say.
It's hard for me because I
haven't told my mom and dad
but I didn't make it in school
this year

No?

Nah. Things kinda got away
from me.
I don't know
I dropped out mid-semester
and I've been faking it, you
know? Pretending I'm going to
classes and all, but really I've
just been blowing my time.
Hiding out in the library.
Playing video games in my
dorm.

I was going to tell them this
week. The day you texted me
actually. Only now with Julie
going to med school, it makes
me twice the loser I guess

I don't know if I would say loser.
You're not homeless with some idiot's
baby inside you

Nah, I guess not

Sorry. I don't know if that came
across the way I meant

Nah, it's okay. But I was thinking about Julie because she's always doing that kinda thing

What kind of thing?

Passing her MCAT and going to Med School and like that. Making me look bad

You ever wonder?

Wonder?

Nvm

Wonder what?

Nah. I just thought its strange our text threads would cross like this when we're both, you know

Falling apart?

Yeah. Anyway, I should sleep

Okay

Okay

Peg?

Yeah?

Nothing

What is it?

Nvm. dwai

Dwai? I've never heard that one
before

Dwai? Don't worry about it?
Where you been? It's been
around for years

Guess I missed that one. What's up?

I'm just lying here staring into
the dark. No one to talk to.
Roommate's out with his gf.
They're partying down the
hall. Friday night stuff. But I
can't go join them

I could use a party right now

Not me. It's not really my
thing. When I started here in
Sept I tried. Got really sick the
first night
I can barely show my face now
So now I just lie here when
Friday night comes, and
wonder

Wonder what?

Just why?

Why?

Like why it's always got to be
so hard. You try, you know,
and even your best efforts
don't seem to make any
difference
I went to the Grand Canyon
when I was a kid. You ever
been?

I wish

Well I have. My mom always
wanted to take us kids. Not
sure why. But I remember I
hucked a rock over the edge to
hear what it would sound like
when it hit the bottom. Only
the wind and the distance and
whatever was so bad that I
never heard it land. It's like that
you know? You do what you
do as best you can and you
hope it makes a difference.
Only it's like listening for a
rock you dropped in the Grand
Canyon to hit bottom. You can
bust your eardrums straining to
hear it and just silence. That's
what it's like for me

Peg?
You there?

John?

Yeah
It's been a while
Were you ghosting me?

Sorry. My plan ran out on my phone
and I was broke so I couldn't renew.
Anyway, I got it sorted now. You're
my first text on the new plan :)

You got some money?

A job

Oh yeah?

Lousy waitress at a lousy restaurant
but at least it's something

Maybe I'll come by sometime

Haha very funny. You don't even
know where I live

How's it been?

Well I got news
Twins

Wow

Yeah

No really. Wow

Totally cut ties with their dad though.
I moved to the city. Trying to start
new

Me and Julie are twins

No kidding?
Coincidence

Yeah

How's staring into the darkness been going?

Not great
lol

You tell your mom and dad about it?

Nah. They still think I'm
pulling down a 4.0

You still listening for the rock to hit
the bottom?

Sorta
Listen when your twins come
don't give them corny matching
names like Julie and John. Take
it from someone who knows. It
sucks

Haha. But I always thought that was
nice!

Take it from me

Peg?
You there?
Peg?

Sorry. I missed this. Working

No problem

What's up?

I'm gonna tell them tonight.
Mom and dad about school.
Just needed some moral
support. Mom will probably get
it. She gets stuff. But Frank's
likely to blow his top. He's big
on responsibility and hated
putting up the money in the
first place

You call your dad Frank?

Only at times like these. He's
not my real dad

No?

Nah
Mom was a teen mom. I never
really met my dad. Which
totally sucked. Probably made
me the flop I am

Oh

I'm sorry

I forgot

No. It's okay. I get it

I'm sure it won't be like that for
you though

I hope not. Listen, if it goes south
with Frank and your mom, you can
text me any time

Thanks. You're the nicest
perfect stranger I ever met

Well I feel I owe you

Owe me?

It was pretty grim for me that night I
texted you, after I told Rick about the
babies and he dumped me. I don't
know if I would have made it. I was
about to do something
I won't say what but it wasn't pretty
And then I thought of you getting that
text and I thought what the hell, why
not give it a try? And you answered. I
don't know what I would have done if
you weren't there
And then your last text, before they
cancelled my phone plan. It sounded
so dark for you that I had to get back
in touch.
That's why I decided to get the job,
which of course led me to move to
the city

Clean break and all
And that's how I got back on my feet.
I mean if it wasn't for you I'd
probably still be couch surfing in St.
Paul

John?

You there?

Who's Rick?

I guess I never told you. My bf's name
was Rick

Hey. My roommate and his gf
just got here. I gotta go

___

John?
Been a long time. Hope you're good
Wondering how it went with Frank
and mom?

___

John? You there?

___

I don't know if maybe I screwed up
something without knowing it, or if
maybe you're not doing so good and
can't take texts now. I don't even know
why I care, only, our threads crossed,
and I sorta feel like that musta been for
a reason

Please don't be like Rick to me

                      Peg?

He lives!
I was gonna put out an Amber Alert for you

                      Very funny
                      Sorry I was ghosting you. I had
                      some things to sort out

You talk to mom and dad?

                      To Frank?
                      Yeah

And?
How did it go?

                      Not so great. Frank wanted to
                      enlist me

Nice

                      I mean it. He was seriously
                      going to drag me down to the
                      recruitment office

I hate the army. I'm a pacifist at heart

                      That's what my mom said. She
                      pushed back and said that if I
                      couldn't make it in University,
                      how was I supposed to make it
                      in the army?

That's what I would have said

They really went at it for a bit

I would have backed you up if I had
been there

Yeah

So now what?

Maybe I'll become a lousy
waiter in a lousy restaurant
somewhere.

Then you could take after me!

Yeah. And my mom,
apparently. It's how she put
herself through night school

Hey?

Yeah?

Which St. Paul?

Which St. Paul?

You said you were couch
surfing in St. Paul. But there's
St. Paul Minnesota, and St. Paul
Alberta

You know about St Paul Alberta?

Is that where you grew up?

Yeah, why?

Nvm

You okay John?

I haven't asked for a long time. How has the pregnancy been going? You must be getting close?

Yeah. Doctor says due date is October
31
Go figure, Halloween twins

Yeah, go figure

Peg, I wanted to tell you that you got me through that night, too.

What night?

The night you texted me about Rick dumping you. His name was Rick, right?

Yeah

Well I had just got word from Julie about the MCAT and I was staring into the darkness and thinking about how nothing I've ever done has ever meant anything, like a total loser. I was trying to decide if pills would hurt too bad

Oh John

No it's okay. It was just Grand Canyon thoughts. But I'm okay now. Because you were there that night. I don't know how but you were. And then we got talking and next thing you know here we are

It was the same with me. If our threads hadn't crossed, I don't know where I'd be

Right. Because our threads crossed

You ok tonight?
Because the truth is if our threads hadn't crossed I never would have made it. Even without Rick, it was a pretty dark path I was on, and somehow this random word from a total stranger pointed me in a different direction

About that
I never asked you. Is Peg short for Margaret?

I've always hated Margaret, but yeah

You'll grow to like it, I think

I will?

Did I ever tell you that I'm a
Halloween baby, too?

Really?
Coincidence

Maybe. And that my biological
dad's name is Richard? Richard
Andrew Miller. My mom would
never tell me about him, except
once she mentioned he was
raised on a farm north of
Edmonton. Near the town of
St Paul. A hell raiser by all
accounts

What are you saying?

I don't know
But go ahead and ask me what
my mother's name is. I never
put it together before, because
she's always just gone by her
full name as long as I can
remember

Margaret

Are you there Margaret?

I guess you're ghosting me too.
Maybe for good. Or maybe you
always were. Either way it's
okay, because I think I've
gotten through now
Though if you can see this text
I want you to know that I think
it's going to be ok. Better than
ok. For you and for me. And
for what it's worth, I am so
glad our threads crossed the
way they did

6.

New Clothes

If you could somehow know, before it occurred, that something you were about to experience was going to leave an indelible mark on your soul, I suppose you'd make more of a conscious effort to absorb as many of the details as you could for later rumination. As it is, I remember very few, and those I do drift intangibly before my mind's eye, like grains of dust suspended and illuminated only briefly in the sunlight shaft of my memory.

I remember especially the heat. It had gripped me like a fist all that day as I waited for the evening's ballet. I'd whiled away the afternoon in the shade of the carefully manicured greenery of Vienna's Stadtpark, reading the last pages of Camus' *L'Etranger*. If I had not been working hard to effect that existential objectivity I so admired in its narrator, I probably would have indulged in the Bohemian something-or-other that the whole scene evoked: the drifting traveler in repose, detached and foreign, sitting and reading an existential French novel in the dappled shadows by the banks of the Donau, oblivious of the crowds rushing past him along the

Schubertring. In retrospect, I must admit that the majority of Camus' sparse prose was wasted on my ungainly schoolbook French, but the odd phrase here and there—"Do you wish my life to have no meaning?"—"I had no soul, there was nothing human about me"— whet my appetite for the profound just enough to keep me engrossed. I read and reread the final paragraph somewhat tremulously, trying to absorb the essence of those last sentences. Though I did not understand his *des cris de haine*, I knew well enough what he meant by *la tendre indifférence du monde*—a world which had ceased to concern me.

Perhaps this is why I was disappointed that evening to find that the two Americans so annoyed me. My annoyance bore witness to the failure of my contrived detachment. We were all crowded together in the dim light of the standing room only section of the Vienna State Opera House, these Americans behind me to my left, a stoic British couple just in front of me, to my right the Australian tourist who had chatted with me so affably while we waited in line for our tickets. A young woman was standing near me on the left.

The heat of the day had not waned at all with the evening, and in this crowd it swarmed oppressively. Many had already accordioned their programs into fans and were desperately trying to wave it away. My tour book of Austria had assured me that Stehplatz—standing room only admission—to the Vienna State Opera House could be purchased for a mere 20 Austrian schillings, and the cultured exoticism of it all had been irresistible to me. Perhaps I was not the only pseudo-bohemian traveler looking for a taste of the exotic after spending the day reading French nihilistic literature by the banks of the Donau, however, because the standing room only section was densely packed.

So it might just have been the heat and the crowds, but whatever the reason, as I say, I found myself greatly annoyed at these two Americans.

They had struck up a conversation of the most transparent kind with the woman on my left. She was a girl, really, perhaps twenty, and the tone of these two young tourists was particularly grating:

"Have you been to the opera before?" "Are you from Vienna?" "We've been traveling through Austria for two weeks now."

Without effort the image came to me of these two college kids back home in Connecticut, regaling their friends with stories of the good time they'd had with that girl they'd met in Vienna. The whole thing felt like a trophy snapshot in some sordid photo album, captioned with ugly words like "score" and "laid."

That the girl spoke English with an extreme brokenness, which she tried to hide behind averted looks, made the whole scene worse. They pressed her. "Are you Austrian?"

"No... not Austrian." Her accent was German. "I always have wanted... to see... ballet."

Because the crowds had pressed us all so close together, I could not help but notice her. She was quite lovely, in a timid way. Her skin was porcelain white, and the hair that fell in dark curls past her shoulders, together with the darkness of her eyes, made her fair complexion seem almost pale. She smiled faintly at their conversation, but something about the nervousness in the gesture, the furtive movement of her eyes as she did so, suggested to me a mother bird feigning a broken wing to distract a predator from the hatchlings in her nest.

Her figure, too, though graceful, had a fragility about it that was accentuated by her unusual attire. A simple white dress hung straight from her shoulders, curvelessly to her feet. Aside from the obvious newness of the dress—its stiffness and brightness—there was nothing remarkable in it alone. Even the platform sandals she wore, though they gave the impression of a child playing dress-up in her mother's high heels, were not especially unusual. It was the brilliant sash bound about her straight waist that caught the eye. A bright, lime green silk, it was almost gaudy, like a brazen star of green in a perfect night of white. On any other figure, in any other setting, this combination would have seemed eccentric, even clownish. In her it somehow gave her loveliness a bashful naiveté, pitiable perhaps, but not laughable. I could close my eyes and imagine this timid young innocent donning this plain white dress, her newest and best, for her first time at the ballet, scrutinizing herself before the mirror with a look of humble dissatisfaction, and then, with artless triumph, completing her ensemble with this garish green sash, blissfully ignorant of the glaring effect, and all the more lovely for that ignorance.

"You speak German?" one of the Americans was asking.

"Yes, German."

"We've never seen ballet before," the other was confessing. "Do you like it?"

Again the mother bird fluttered her broken smiles. "I always have wanted... to see... ballet."

"Well, when you're in Vienna, you have to go to the Opera House at least once."

"Yes. It is so... beautiful."

"I'm Josh."

"And I... I am... Sofia."

The British couple ahead of me was mumbling placidly to one another about the pending performance. "It says here that the show tonight, *L'Existence*, is an experimental modern ballet."

"Experimental and modern? I wonder what we should expect then."

"Something deep, I'd say. Interpretive, no doubt."

To my right, the effusive Australian started telling me some anecdote he'd read in his tour book about the emperor's commissioning of the Staasoper. "Look here, mate," he was saying. "It says the architects of the Opera House committed suicide after the Austrian emperor made some offhand remark about the building being too low to the ground. Can you imagine?"

Apparently, the foundation had been laid before the surrounding street was finished, and the street ended up being higher than planned. In his chagrin over his role in their deaths, the emperor sought to avoid the self-destruction of other artists by confining all subsequent aesthetic judgments to a simple: "*Es war sehr schön, es hat mich sehr gefreut*"—it was very nice; it pleased me very well.

"Not much of an art critic, was he?" laughed the Australian as he recounted to story.

All the while I listened to him, I kept the corner of my attention fixed on that strange girl and the two Americans. Before my annoyance could pin itself to a justifiable excuse, however, the ballet began.

The lights dimmed and the noise of the crowd faded. For a few moments my eyes gaped wide in perfect darkness while we waited for something to happen. Then, the faintest scratch of a bow on a violin moaned distantly and ceased. It scraped again, ceased again, and then the sound began in earnest.

To call it music would somehow fall short of conveying the chaos of tonal textures—staccato creaks, piercing wails and guttural groans—that escaped in irrational intervals from that unseen horsehair scraping wire somewhere in the darkness. It was not unmelodic. It was deliberately and calmly anti-melodic. Though no doubt these noises were all carefully contrived, the ear sought vainly in the sinuous bursts of sound for some pattern it might cling to and call rhythm. In the back of my mind, I wondered if this was what was called atonality.

Whether my eyes had begun to grow accustomed to the dark, or whether somewhere on stage a light had come up, I couldn't tell, but an image slowly materialized as I peered ahead. Two hunched forms occupied opposite corners of a large square platform, elevated some four feet off the main stage. In the hazy but growing light the platform appeared to be hovering there, suspended in a void of nothingness. It was lit, I now felt certain, from above with a grim grey light, but what made the scene hazy and indistinct was a transparent veil or scrim that hung in the darkness between us and the stage. In the centre of the platform sat a large, white cube.

For what seemed an unbearably long time, nothing happened. Then the figures rose and began their movements. Their black leggings and the shadows along the muscles of their naked upper bodies gave them a sinister look in that gloomy light. The music having no perceptible rhythm, it was somewhat difficult to discern a dance in their gyrations, but as they moved toward one another, the most unexpected thing happened. The platform began to tilt with the shifting weight of their bodies, pitching and heaving like some enormous, two-dimensional scale. As it did so, the white cube in the centre began to move, sliding slowly with it.

Once the movement started, it could not stop without threatening to dump one, the other, or the white cube off into the pit. And so the two figures drifted continually through the gloom, sometimes chasing, other times grappling with each other, or else twining together to form some subtly grotesque tableau before flinging themselves apart. And every movement was somehow punctuated with that eerie, formless sound.

Gradually the randomness of the scene wore off and a story—or perhaps more accurately, an implication—could be made out. The two men were in competition, but this was only clear from the way one would attempt to tilt the platform such that the other came precariously close to disappearing over the edge. They were also striving for control of the white box, and by manipulating the scale just so, one might cause it to slide to him, only to have it wrested from him by the machinations of the other.

At times the two would lock together, leaving the cube to slide dangerously close to the edge, only to be spared this just in time by further shifting the platform's angle. This continued through no clearly defined progression until, after a time, by some chance coincidence of friction and forces, the cube came to rest safely in the centre of the platform once more, the two figures balanced on opposite corners. There they hunched back to their original positions.

The violin heaved itself to a near-rhythmic tattoo, dropped darkly to a long-whispered sigh, and stopped abruptly. The faint light was snuffed out, darkness descended, and with it fell a palpable silence.

The lights rose and for the briefest glimmer of a pause, the audience digested what they had just witnessed. Then a knowing ripple of applause began. It was not enthusiastic, but neither was it obliging. It was an ovation of assent, not of approval, as if in one voice the audience was merely saying, "*Es war sehr schon, es hat mich sehr gefreut*," without passing any aesthetic evaluation on what had passed on stage. If the crowd had any enthusiasm for anything at all, it was simply to prove there was not an uncultured Philistine in all their midst.

I stood there for a while after the applause had died, suspended between consternation and bemusement.

"Well then," the Australian interjected at my right. "That was unexpected." His words brought me from my indecision and settled me squarely in bemusement.

In the row ahead of me, the British couple had begun to ponder the performance between them, their voices quiet with a taciturn, if somewhat cadenced detachment. "But what did it all mean?" she asked him, her voice betraying not the least hint of disquiet.

"I suppose that's entirely the wrong question," he answered knowingly. "Or a question impossible to answer. It meant nothing. Or rather, that there is no meaning."

She nodded uncertainly. "But it was experimental?"

"Indeed."

Indeed. The faintest hint of a thought glimmered in me. If it was so, with what could it have possibly been experimenting? Even as that revealed darkness dimmed, I stole a quick glance across the crowd and seemed to see the whole mass of humanity in a new light, blithely rationalizing the irrational. With mild interest they had already assented to it, nodding and consulting their programs for the next performance, as if to say, "Well, even so, life must go on."

Then she began screaming, the girl in the white dress.

"*Nein! Es ist eine Lüge!*"

And there is not a word sufficiently clear of cliché to convey that piercing cry. Frenzied, hysterical, lunatic, even bloodcurdling: it was all these things at once, and yet none of them. It was feral, to be sure, yet so precise, so oracular in its tenor that it came more as a clarion call than a howl of horror.

To make it worse, every word was garbled with that enigmatic ecstasy of an unknown tongue. "*Nein! Nein! Das kann nicht sein! Wie können Sie diese Spötterei schön nennen?*"

As often happens when the unconventional shatters the nice platitudes of manners that keep the pond water of society serene, it took a moment for the multitude to agree on an appropriate response. I could see people looking at one another with uncertainty and censure, and, concealed beneath that, the ancient terror of the weird.

At first, they gestured with their chins and condescending nods: "What is the matter with that one?" But like the pebble breaking pond water, a ripple spread concentrically from her, the standing crowds pressing back until there was a clearing around her of considerable radius.

And all the while she cried out. "*Es ist eine Lüge! Können Sie das nicht sehen? Es ist Hässlichkeit und Leere! Eine nackte Lüge! Es ist nichts drin!*"

Even those in the auditorium general, down below our crowded section, had begun to turn, look up, and murmur against the commotion.

But I found myself somehow paralyzed, frozen by the cry of this strange young sibyl, and I could not press back from her with the others. For a moment it seemed as if my whole consciousness had narrowed on her cry, or that the radius of the clearing around her and I had stretched out to infinity.

I looked nervously for those two Americans, but they had disappeared completely.

Then she turned her eyes on me, and as she did so, her body seemed to deflate, and she slid slowly to the floor. The look in her eyes trembled between pleading and defeat. I felt her reach up and clutch my hand. And those fingers, their strange flesh, felt like ice against my skin. She was babbling now, subdued, but her voice still had an inexorable urgency: "*Wieso? Warum können sie es nicht sehen? Das ist nicht Schönheit oder Wahrheit! Es ist ist nur eine nackte Lüge!*"

I could not escape the impression that her eyes were imploring something of me. Some response, some sympathy was clearly called for, but I stood there stupidly.

She sat up on her knees, still clutching my hand in that icy grip. She turned her voice one last time over the crowd and shouted a final indictment. "*Können Sie es nicht sehen? Das ist nicht Schönheit oder Wahrheit! Es ist nur eine nackte Lüge!*" Then she sank down again, her chin drooping on the breast of her new white gown.

The confused murmurs of the crowds trickled toward me. Part of me longed to shake my hand discretely free of her grip and join them in their condescending indignation. But I stood there, still stupidly.

"*Was ist denn mit Ihnen los?*" The voice of an usher broke the tension. Surely someone had summoned him to sweep away this impropriety.

Her face was ashen as she lifted trembling eyes to him, like one stirring from the dead.

"*Kommen Sie, lasst uns gehen. Sie sind wohl betrunken?*" The fact that he spoke in German could not veil from me the utter contempt in his voice.

"*Ich bin nicht betrunken.*" Her voice was subdued now, but her eyes still cast about with a hint of their previous wildness. "*Aber was war denn das? Ich dachte, es sollte schön sein.*"

"*Kommen Sie, Fräulein. Lasst uns gehen.*" He reached out his hand, a menacing invitation.

She rose resignedly to her feet. Her hand was still gripping my fingers, but it felt now like air, not ice. She let it slip away, and my fingers were left haunted by the frozen imprint it had burned against them.

"*Aber es war nicht schön.*"

The usher snorted. "*Nein, das war Kunst.*"

She left a kind of awed stillness in her wake. Slowly the crowd pushed back to fill in the void of her passing, as if in one mass they were trying to shrug off the memory of her. The hushed murmurs rose up again, but more subdued this time. "What was that all about?" they asked, expecting no real answer.

Behind me I heard one of the tourists who seemed to have a smattering of German translate for another. "She asked about the ballet... what it meant... why it was so ugly. He said it was just art."

Her knowing "Ah" at this information crept across my spine.

The lights were dimming a second time, signaling the end of the intermission and the start of the next performance. I tried to focus my reeling concentration on the music that was now rising as the darkness descended.

This was a ballet in the fullest tradition of that word. Taut bosoms and terse thighs pirouetted across the stage in tight silk, while the music washed over us all with a lush, fecund, somehow verdant sensuality, the gyrations of string and leaps of horn echoing and reechoing in the luxurious movement of those carefully honed bodies.

My ears rushed with it, until it became a roar. Even as I watched, I felt my body convulsing with the urge to vomit. The heat and the press of the crowds overwhelmed me. I groped for the exit frantically, burst into the foyer almost gasping for breath and rushed out into the moist night air. The traffic on the Opernring swirled around me. My hand still burned with cold.

When the retching finally stopped and I was able to compose myself, I began making my way slowly through the pressing night toward my lodgings. But every step was a labor, and the eyes of that girl in white—like the haunted eyes of one who has looked through a torn veil and seen a gaping void of nothingness behind—pleaded with me through the darkness. And in my burning ears, as if it would never leave me, rang that forlorn howl of execration.

7.

The Words of Zumisura, Priest of Ea

British soldiers discovered this strange text in 2005, while on routine minesweeping exercises in southeastern Iraq, west of the Tigris-Euphrates Delta. It was found on a strip of vellum, rolled tightly into an earthenware jar. Though the stratum of sandstone that it was discovered in dates roughly to the late Miocene era, the script itself appears to be an extremely primitive form of Akkadian cuneiform, suggesting a date of ca. 2500 BCE, at the latest. It has been tentatively translated by Dr. Alan Kircher, Ph.D., of Cambridge University.

And now that the rains have ended the waters churn with the great beasts of the deep, unlike any we have seen before. They leap and they fall with terrible noise and much foam. Ugurik has said they will bring down our wicker boat with the pound of their mighty tails, but I say that we have placed our souls already into the hands of the gods, and if this is how they wish us to end, there is nothing to be done.

Who can resist their will?

I cannot say how long the rain has fallen. Surely it has been more than a moon, but it has been so many days since we have seen a moon that none can tell. Elinumelek, who is high priest of Enlil and knows the meaning of sacred numbers says it has been forty days, because forty is a number of heaven. Ugurik, who is recorder for King Gilgudur and can do sums, says that it must be more, because our stores are nearly gone, and we had food enough to last a hundred days when we began. Elinumelek struck him about the ears when he said this, and when the blood no longer flowed, Ugurik could not hear on the side of his strong right hand.

Ugurik has done the count and says there is food now for three men to eat seven days, and then it will be gone. All the waters of high heaven and all the waters of the great deep have come together as one, I believe, and if we sailed for seven moons together we would not find rest nor land. If we are the last three men, as Elinumelek has said, then when we are gone there may be none to speak the praises of the gods, and so I write these final words now in memory of Ea.

When I was a scribe in the house of Gilgudur I wrote on the eternal tablets of stone used by the priests of Ea, but there is no stone to inscribe here. I use this, my leather cloak, as my stone, and soot from the lamp mixed with wine for my words. Ugurik fought me when I took the last of the wine to write these the final praises to Ea. He is afraid to starve, he says, but I say that we have placed our souls already into the hands of the gods, and if this is how they wish us to end, then there is nothing to be done. When the blood no longer flowed, I could not see from my eye on the side of my lesser left hand.

Ea, if you have brought this catastrophe upon us, as Elinumelek says, because the noise of the men you had made kept you from sleep and ate up your peace, who can question your wisdom? But who will offer you the sacrifices of smoke and fire that feed the gods and give them joy, when we are gone?

Can this be wise?

Elinumelek struck me when I asked you this, but even now that the blood no longer flows, the question burns within me. Will the gods not die with us, if we are swept away?

Utnapishtim, the builder of the great boat, said it was not so. How many hearings with king Gilgudur he had before the rains came, I cannot say, but as scribe in the house of Gilgudur I heard them all.

He served the great Shaddai, he said, whom he named king over all the gods, but Gilgudur subjected him to many lashings when he said it. Even when the blood no longer flowed still Utnapishtim spoke the same. It is because of the hurt that lurks in the hearts of men, he said, the lust for hurting that springs from being hurt. Shaddai will wash away the hurting with water, he said, until all the earth is clean.

Utnapishtim's boat was many years in the making, and often Gilgudur heard him. Utnapishtim urged the king to stop the hurting that hurts Shaddai himself and join him in building his boat. Elinumelek mocked. Shaddai's great builder of sand-sailing boats, he named him. Hurting does not hurt the gods, he said. Hurt is of the gods. We hurt because they made us to.

Utnapishtim said it was not so, but Elinumelek struck him and Utnapishtim returned to the building of his boat. Gilgudur said he would not join him.

The last day before the rain, Gilgudur gave a great feast for all his priests and scribes. He gave his daughter Niqutu to the King of Uruluk in marriage that day, and married Uruluk's daughter Hasis, at the same feast. There was much eating and much drinking, and many gifts of smoke for the gods.

And then the flood came out, roaring like a bull, screaming like a wild ass. Wind howled. Darkness thickened. There was no sun.

In the days when the first rains fell, before the water covered everything, Elinumelek said that if we offered sacrifices of smoke and fire the gods might relent. We slaughtered every beast of all the herds of Gilgudur, and still the gods did not relent. Elinumelek said that if we offered up the blood of men the gods might relent, and so we did. When the blood no longer flowed, still the gods did not relent. Elinumelek said that if Gilgudur gave his new wife Hasis and Uruluk gave Niqutu, then might gods relent.

After this, Ugurik, who could do sums, said that the deep would soon cover even the palace of King Gilgudur itself. He had formed a boat out of the wicker baskets from the storehouses of the king and provisioned it with earthen jars of bread and wine. The water had covered most of the land by then, but Elinumelek joined him, as did I.

The great waves swept away all the rest.

O Ea, mighty and inscrutable, did Utnapishtim speak true? Is there a god higher than the gods themselves, who sent this rain not to hurt but to wash the hurt away?

Elinumelek will not allow me to speak such questions, but if he is right, Ea the unquestionable, and you have done this, then why did you form these, the men you made, when first you did? Does Elinumelek speak true when he says that the gods are little more than the greatest of all the great men, and no thought of their hearts is better than the darkest thought of ours?

The deep now covers the whole face of the land. It floats with the debris of the house of King Gilgudur, and with the debris of all the great kings of the earth. But O Ea the inexorable, if every house of every king writhed with the same pain that writhed in the house of Gilgudur before the rains came, then I say the flood had wisdom in it. And if you, too, will pass away, because when the water is gone there will be none to feed you with blood and fire, then that is wisdom too.

Ugurik bleeds again from the ear that Elinumelek struck. He sleeps now more than he wakes and when he speaks his words are dark with dreams and fever. I myself grow weak and see only through a great darkness. The end, I say, comes near.

I have told Elinumelek that when I am gone, and the stores are spent, he is to keep himself and Ugurik alive with my body.

Eat it, I say, as bread.

If Utnapishtim spoke true, and the flood has covered the earth, this gift will not save Elinumelek and Ugurik from following me into the final darkness. But if Utnapishtim spoke true, then in giving myself like this, instead of hurting, I may find the hurt washing from me, at last, even as the flood has washed it all from off the face of the earth.

O Ea the terrible, I do not hope to speak your praise again, but if the Shaddai whom Utnapishtim serves has eyes to see, perhaps he will see this gift and be honored by it.

The wine is gone.

I will seal these words away in one of the jars that held our bread. We have no other need of it now. I will offer then the jar to the waters of the deep. None live now, I think, to find it, but if any do, know that these are the words of Zumisura, who served once as the priest of Ea.

8.

Test Day

The first difficulty Dexter encountered on the morning of the test was the unexpected reappearance of a nervous habit he used to have of giggling uncontrollably in stressful situations. This had caused all sorts of trouble for him when he was in high school. He'd barely made it through the social dance unit in Grade 9 phys ed, and more than one speech in his Grade 10 public speaking class had fizzled out in a fit of soprano tittering. He'd been such a mess during his Grade 12 biology exam on the human reproductive system that they had to send him from the room. The F he'd earned in that class had been well deserved.

But that was back when he was a pubescent teen, surging with anxieties and prone to all sorts of emotional incontinences. He hadn't had a giggling episode like that in years. He probably wouldn't have had one now, except that he urgently needed this job; that, and the unfortunate fact that the man at the front, who handed him the test paper, said he could call him Semi Truck.

"Name's Semeniuk," he said, folding beefy arms together and resting them on a great distended beer belly. "Mac Semeniuk. But everyone round here calls me Semi Truck."

The look on the man's face was inscrutable. Dexter couldn't tell if he was truly unaware of how apropos this colorful nickname was for a man of his girth, or if he was just daring him to make a comment to that effect. Whatever the case, the name certainly fit. Mac Semeniuk was a great juggernaut of a man, not especially tall, but wide enough that Dexter could see very little of the desk behind him as he leaned his fulsome weight against it.

Dexter could feel a fit of giggling brewing in him and tried to hide it behind a fake sneeze. He badly needed this job.

"Gesundheit," Semi Truck said gruffly. "Here's the test. You got three hours if you need it. And remember: it's pass or fail. There's coffee and dingdongs on the table over there." He nodded with a wobble of his chin. "Help yourself."

It had to be dingdongs, Dexter thought, trying to suppress another wave of giggling. It couldn't have been doughnuts or croissants. It had to be dingdongs.

"You need a pen?" Semi Truck was saying, giving him another inscrutable look. He motioned with his chin down toward the desk. There was a basket sitting there, full of pens emblazoned with the company name.

"I—um—you know, Mr.—er—Truck? It turns out I do."

Semi Truck didn't move at all, and Dexter was forced to reach around him for the pen. This brought him far closer to the man than he would have liked, even if he hadn't been on the verge of erupting into a fit of nervous laughter. He almost did erupt when he looked at the pen itself. He had known the company was called B & M Hardware Manufacturing, but he had no idea their slogan was "We go nuts for all your loose screws."

"You can turn it in on the desk here when you're done," was Semi Truck's final word of instruction.

Dexter nodded, unwilling to risk another sentence out loud, and turned to find a place to write. They were in one of the factory's loading bays. It had been haphazardly converted into a makeshift classroom, with tables and chairs set out in rows that gave Dexter unfortunate flashbacks to high school biology class.

The room was surprisingly full, for all it being just a few janitor jobs up for grabs. Of course, jobs were scarce these days, and when B & M Hardware had announced they were expanding their operation and needed to hire millwrights and line workers by the handful, guys had streamed in from across the region to apply. Dexter had passed on those first rounds of hiring. He'd never graduated high school and didn't really trust himself behind heavy equipment. But when the ad went out in the local paper that they also needed custodial staff, he figured something like that might be more his bag.

He hadn't expected so many guys would share the same bag. There were at least two dozen men here, twenty-four guys for three measly custodian jobs. The ad had said there would be a simple aptitude test, and the top five scores would be offered interviews.

The chairs were set out two to a table. Dexter found a seat next to a lanky, disheveled man with a lean, unshaven face.

"They have dingdongs," the man whispered as Dexter took his place. "Many as you want."

The tabletop around the man's test was scattered with crumbs, and his paper was smudged with oily fingerprints. He cast a tantalized look toward the refreshments table. "You want me to get you one? I'm going for another."

Dexter shook his head. "I'm good," he said. He placed the test neatly in front of him and set the pen carefully beside it.

"You sure?" The man was rising from his seat. "Free dingdongs?"

"Enough chit-chat!" grumbled Semi Truck from the front. He had taken a seat behind the desk and was scowling out over the room.

Dexter's desk mate shrugged, as if to say, "suit yourself," and headed off for his second round of dingdongs.

Dexter opened his test and read the first question.

In a class of "P" students, the average (arithmetic mean) of the test scores is 70. In another class of "n" students, the average of the scores is 92. When the scores of the two classes are combined, the average of the test scores is 86. What is the value of p/n?

Dexter stared very hard at the question for a long time. He turned back to read the cover of the test, just to be sure.

B & M Hardware Manufacturing, it read. Custodial Staff Aptitude Test.

There was no mistake. He had the right test. The nervous giggle began to squirm desperately in the pit of his stomach. He looked up in Semi Truck's direction, but the large man wouldn't—at least, he didn't—meet his eyes.

Maybe the questions started hard and got easier, he thought. He turned the page carefully, smoothed the test flat on the tabletop and read the next question.

The equation of a circle in the xy-plane is: $x^2 + y^2 + 4x - 2y = -1$. What is the radius of said circle?

The giggle began to feel more like a scream. Dexter tried nonchalantly to tamp it down by running his hand across his mouth. He looked toward the refreshment table. The dingdong man was still there, in no apparent hurry to return to their table. Dexter wondered if the guy knew something he didn't.

He rose, and Semi Truck threw a questioning glare in his direction.

"Dingdong?" Dexter said weakly. Semi Truck nodded. Dexter wandered over as casually as he could manage.

"Maybe I'll have one after all," he whispered to his tablemate, reaching for one of the pastries with a slightly trembling hand. He really needed this job.

"I would have left hours ago," said the other, "except, you know: free dingdongs."

Dexter nodded. He took a napkin and, using it as a makeshift plate, returned to his table, setting the dingdong down neatly next to the pen.

He cast a glance over at the table next to him. A middle-aged man was sitting there, hunched over his test paper like a cowering dog caught in the act of chewing a slipper. Next to him sat a young guy—possibly there for his first ever job application—staring at the test with saucer plate eyes, clutching desperate fistfuls of his own hair as he held his head in harried hands.

Maybe it's not all math, Dexter thought. He turned to the next page.

Translate the following line from the Old English epic, Beowulf, and comment on its significance to the overall theme of the poem: Gæða wyrd swa hio scel.

"For the love of all that's holy!" someone cried out from the back of the room. Dexter turned to see him crumple his test paper in furious fists and fling it to the floor. "What in the world does that have to do with being a stupid janitor?"

The man rose so abruptly his chair clattered to the floor behind him. He stormed from the room, seething bitterly, though not without stopping to grab two dingdongs on his way out.

Dexter looked down at his own test. He prayed feebly that it was the Beowulf question that had caused this outburst, and not some tougher monstrosity still to come.

He turned the page again.

Apply Einstein's special theory of relativity to solve the following problem: if a spaceship travelling 0.80c makes a nonstop journey to a distant planet and returns in 10 hours according to the spaceship's clock, how much time has passed on earth?

Dexter puffed his cheeks and widened his eyes, running his hand through his hair and trying to quiet his mind. A haunting realization passed over him that at some point in the last few minutes the urge to giggle had left him.

He looked around the room again. Three more guys had given up. Two had simply left their unwritten test papers behind and fled the room. The third had stalked up to where Semi Truck sat scowling behind the desk and flung the test paper toward him.

"What kind of a joke is this? It's a lousy janitor's job!" He threw his "Nuts for Loose Screws" pen onto the desk in disgust.

Semi Truck said nothing, but he gathered up the paper and pen. He placed the one on a pile of unfinished tests in front of him and returned the other to the basket on the desk.

"Two hours," he said to the room in general.

Dexter wasn't sure if this meant they were two hours in or had two hours to go—time had ceased to have much meaning for him—

but he gauged the thickness of the remaining pages in his test and realized it probably didn't matter.

The dingdong guy still hadn't returned to his place. He wasn't at the refreshment table either, and Dexter figured he must have finally eaten his fill and left. His test was still lying open on the table they had shared, littered liberally with dingdong debris.

Dexter turned to the next question.

Explain the Kantian Moral Imperative and apply it as a solution to the famous Thompson Trolley Problem.

It crossed his mind wildly to wonder just exactly what kind of janitorial work they'd be doing in this job.

The next question was worse.

Summarize the ontological argument for the existence of God as postulated by Rene Descartes, and contrast this to the classic cosmological argument postulated by Aristotle.

Dexter placed his head on the table and rested it there for a long time.

Descartes' ontological argument for the existence of God? The phrase echoed over and over in his mind. The cosmological argument postulated by Aristotle?

If there really was a God, this test was not an especially strong argument in his favor. He just needed a dumb janitor's job. The best proof he could imagine for God's existence would be some sort of divine intervention to get him through this ordeal.

He kept his head down, but somewhere near him he heard two more chairs screech back as two more test writers gave up the ghost and wandered from the room.

The question about Descartes flashed his mind randomly back to the earliest days, before test taking had this effect on him. He remembered the Sunday School class he'd gone to as a kid—of all things—and how they used to do—what were they called?—sword drills?

The whole class would stand in a row at the front of the room with their Bibles held over their heads. The teacher would then call out some random Bible verse—from among all 31,000 of them the teacher would pick one at random and call it out.

"Deuteronomy 4:7! Go!"

Then a room full of middle schoolers would dive into their Bibles, digging desperately to be the first to find the verse. "Done!" someone would cry. And then they'd read it out triumphantly, the race won.

Was that where all this anxiety had started? It seemed to Dexter like the worst possible time to do psychoanalysis, but Semi Truck had said there were two hours, and for all he knew there might be a question about Freud on the next page, so he followed the train of thought into the tunnel.

Sometimes the Sunday School teacher would call out verses that didn't even exist in the Bible. "Acts 30 verse 2!" he would say, or, "Hezekiah 19 verse 6!" And then he'd laugh as it slowly dawned on the children after minutes of frantic searching that there was no such place in the Good Book.

To the best of his memory, Dexter never won any of those sword drills, even when the verse in question was a bona fide text of scripture.

And now, here he was, being asked to summarize the ontological argument for the existence of God for the sake of a miserable janitor job in a screw manufacturing plant—he who had never even been able to find Deuteronomy 4:7 in time to win a Sunday school sword drill.

He lifted his head, and though he wouldn't have said he had been praying, there was a strange calm, almost a resolve, in his face.

He turned to the next question.

Johnny, Mia and Sam all have some apples. If Johnny has 8 apples, and Mia has 6 apples, and there are 27 apples in total, how many apples does Sam have.

Dexter breathed deeply and smiled. For the first time since opening his test, he reached for his pen.

"Time," said Semi Truck from the front.

Dexter looked up, mid-reach, his face falling. "Time?"

"That's time," repeated Semi Truck with a scowl.

Dexter looked around. All the other men, it seemed, had long since given up, and aside from Mr. Semeniuk scowling at him from across his desk, Dexter was alone in the room. He nodded with sad resignation.

Without a word he closed the test paper carefully, smoothing it flat on the tabletop. He picked up his uneaten dingdong, brushing the table clean with the napkin, and took his company pen, still entirely unused. Slowly and very deliberately he rose, pushed in his chair neatly and approached the front of the room.

The man who had told him to call him Semi Truck watched him the whole time, his huge arms resting idly over his belly. He didn't say a word.

Dexter stood for a moment in front of the desk. There was a stack of unfinished test papers—a full two dozen of them if there were three—and slowly he set his own on the pile, taking care to align his stapled corner with all the others, and pressing it down almost tenderly. The basket of pens was still there, too, and with only the slightest tinge of regret, Dexter placed his pen gently back among the rest.

"Thanks for your time," he said to Mr. Semeniuk, unable to meet his eyes.

The other man nodded curtly.

"You're hired," he said.

Dexter must have looked something like a deer in headlights because Semi Truck said it again, almost impatiently. "I said, you're hired. You got the job."

"But the test," Dexter began. "I didn't finish a single question."

It wouldn't exactly be accurate to say that Semi Truck smiled, but a wry look crossed his face.

"You passed the test. In fact, you're the only one who did."

"I passed? But how?"

"Look," said Semi Truck. "When this factory gets going at the height of production, things can be pretty chaotic around here. And we need janitors. Good ones. Janitors who don't get easily rattled and don't let the pressure keep them from doing thorough work no matter what." Semi Truck nodded in the general direction of the room. "Out of all those mokes, you're the only one who stuck it out to the end. And more importantly, you're the only one who cleaned up his workstation and returned his supplies to where they belonged when he was done."

Dexter was still confused. "My supplies?"

"Your pen. You're the only one who put the pen back in the basket like you were supposed to. A tidy man makes a good janitor. Now do you want the job, or are you just gonna stand there with your jaw hanging open like a broken screen door?"

"Thank you, Mr.—er—Mr. Truck." Dexter held out his hand, but the other man had begun putting the stack of useless test papers into an oversized manilla tag envelope, and he ignored the gesture.

"First shift starts Monday at nine. Don't be late."

"No sir, Mr. Truck, I won't. And thanks again."

Dexter wouldn't have said that he felt at all nervous as he left the warehouse that day, but even so, he couldn't keep himself from giggling uncontrollably.

9.

Songs of Deliverance

The first time David saw the guitar on display in the window of the pawn shop downtown, he felt as though it were calling to him. People say this kind of thing all the time without meaning it, but for David it was truer, maybe, than even he understood. Mike Baird, a friend of his dad who had played guitar for years, said that choosing a guitar was like that.

"If it's the right one," he said, "it'll call to you." Mike had known his dad back in the seventies, and whatever experimenting they had done together in those days—from Zen Buddhism to peyote dream visions—it still flared once in a while, like a distant light in Mike's eyes. He'd offered to teach David how to play, though he hadn't said anything so formal as that. "Get yourself a guitar and we can jam once in a while," is how he'd put it. He only played oldies stuff, but David had acquired a taste for Bob Dylan and the Stones from his dad, and learning "the classics," as Mike called them, helped it to hurt less not having Dad around anymore.

There was nothing especially remarkable about the guitar itself. It was an old Gibson acoustic. David knew enough about guitars to recognize the name, but it was hardly the brand that had attracted him to it. True, it did have a unique sunburst finish and an elaborately stylized pickguard, but David's preference was for understatement, and if anything, the look of the instrument put him off.

If he were forced to put it into words, he would have said that it just looked so worn. That's what drew him in. The finish was scratched and dented like some ancient artefact. The wood around the sound hole, where the pickguard didn't cover it, had been worn bare with strumming, and there was another bare patch on the back where it must have rubbed repeatedly against one belt-buckle after another. "Strummed down to the bone," is how Mike put it when he saw it. The fretboard was rippled with countless years of playing, and the frets themselves were grooved with a thousand different handlings.

The price was high, especially for a pawn shop, and David said as much to the guy at the counter. The man just shrugged and said that it was a vintage guitar, and he could always go down to Long and McQuade and buy a cheap Epiphone if he didn't like it.

David didn't have that kind of money, of course, but when they were dividing up his dad's effects after the funeral, they found a bunch of power tools in the garage. David hardly knew how to use a handsaw, let alone edge bander, but everyone agreed he should have something to remember his dad by, so they bequeathed the whole lot to him. It took a couple of weeks to work up the resolve to do it, but one day he finally pulled up outside the pawn shop in a borrowed pickup truck loaded with his dad's tools, and asked the guy at the counter what he could get for them. There was enough left over after buying the guitar that he picked up a battered case to go with it. The shop owner even threw in an elaborately tooled guitar strap, assuring him that he was now ready to rock.

Mike was nearly effusive when he saw the instrument, and his approval was unexpectedly gratifying for David.

"Dude," he said—he was pushing fifty, Mike was, but even so he still said things like "dude" without the least hint of irony. "Dude, that's a beautiful axe."

David smiled sheepishly. "You think? I thought it was priced way too high, but I couldn't get it off my mind."

Mike reached for the guitar with an arch in his eyebrow that said, "May I?" and David handed it to him.

"Nah," he said, inspecting it closely. He turned it over and looked at the back, and then down the neck as though he were sighting a rifle. "Worth every penny. This is a vintage Gibson Hummingbird. '68 I think, or maybe '69."

He set the guitar on his knee and played the fifth-fret harmonics, then the seventh, then the twelfth, each position quickly in a row. David wasn't sure what had just happened—he was still new to the instrument—but suddenly the room was awash with ringing tones.

Mike grinned. He started playing: random chords at first, then a few riffs back to back. The wash of sound became a meandering river, then a flood. He played through some scales, improvising phrases and lines with the ease of a fifty-year-old man who had been playing since he was David's age.

He grinned again when he was done, and there was a look on his face as though he were returning to the present from somewhere far away. "That's a nice-sounding guitar," he said, handing it back. "You got a really good instrument there."

"Yeah? I thought 'cause it was so old, you know?"

Mike shook his head. "Nah," he said. "Old guitars are the best. Old guitars kinda remember they've been played, you know?"

David cocked his head curiously, and Mike laughed.

"I don't mean anything too out-there by that. It's just that, as the woodgrain of a guitar opens up, it becomes more resonant. It starts to have all these subtones and colors in the sound. And the vibration of the sound waves in the guitar helps to open up the grain like that, so the more it's played the better it sounds. I like to think it's as if the guitar remembers all the music it's ever made, and it comes out every time it's played."

David nodded slowly and placed the instrument on his own knee. He had only learned an E-minor chord so far, but he strummed it clumsily and tried to hear all the musical memories of the instrument, swirling about in the melancholy sound.

Mike laughed again and picked up his own guitar. "Here," he said. "I'll teach you a C-chord, and then you'll be able to play 'Eleanor Rigby.' Did you know that's only a two-chord song? C and E minor."

He started stumming and singing along, his voice creaking a bit when it got to the wistful part about all the lonely people and where they all came from.

David did his best to play along, and when they were done, Mike said, "You know there's a real Eleanor Rigby? Paul McCartney claims he just came up with the name at random, that he got it from the name of some shoe store in London or something. But years later they found an old gravestone in a cemetery in Liverpool with the name Eleanor Rigby on it. She lived in the 1800s or something. That's weird, isn't it?"

David agreed it was strange, but he was too absorbed in the sound of the E-minor chord and his newly learned C-chord to say much.

Later that night he sat on the edge of his bed working away at it. His fingers got used to the stretch of the chords relatively quickly, but try as he might, he couldn't reach the high note of the song. That part about all the lonely people and where they all belonged was beyond him.

He gave up on Eleanor Rigby after a while, but he wasn't ready to put his guitar down yet. He kept strumming those two chords the way Mike had taught him, whispering his own words over the music. They were about his dad, at first, how little David really knew about him and how much he wished he did.

A simple melody came to him with the words. People say that kind of thing all the time, but looking back, David was quite sure that this is how it happened for him. He'd certainly never written a song before, but somehow, from somewhere else it seemed, a haunting phrase took shape in his heart, and he started humming it as he strummed. When he was sure he had it right, he began whispering the words to the tune.

Once the melody had arrived, however, the direction of the words seemed to change. His dad was still there, but as David played, he discovered that the song was really about Mike. There was some dark chapter in their friendship that David had never really understood, but for the sake of the song he made it about addiction and deliverance, a metaphor about the redemptive power of friendship.

It only seemed like a handful of minutes had passed, but it was, in fact, five in the morning when he finally set down his guitar, lay back in his bed with his newly written song lingering in his ears, and fell asleep.

He played it for Mike the next time they got together to jam.

"I wrote a song," he said shyly.

"Dude," Mike effused. "That's awesome. I think the best way to learn guitar is just to start writing. Two chords and the guy's already hammering them out. You want to play it for me?"

David hesitated, but Mike was so sincere in his enthusiasm that he took a deep breath and with slightly trembling hands started strumming. His voice grew stronger as the song proceeded, and part way through something poignant seemed to break open in David's heart, as though he were standing there in the midst of the scene his words were painting, or living it himself.

There was an almost palpable silence when he finished, so still, in fact, that David feared to look up. He assumed it meant that Mike didn't have the heart to tell him how bad the song was. "Well," he muttered, staring into the sound hole of the guitar. "It's my first try, anyways. It's about Dad, I guess."

But when David looked up, he was astonished to see that Mike had tears trickling slowly down his cheeks.

"I never knew he told you," Mike said softly.

A look of uncertainty crossed David's face. "Told me?"

"About our past. The drugs and the booze and all that. I mean, you were singing about it as if you must have known."

"No. Dad never said anything about—well—I mean—I knew you and he 'experimented,' is how he put it—but—"

"I don't think I ever would have made it except that he carried me through. Things were pretty dark for me back in those days. It's just like you said in the song, though. He pulled me through when pushing wouldn't do. That's probably how I would have said it, too."

"Mike, I never knew. I knew you and he were good friends, but I never would have guessed…"

Mike pushed a tear away with the heel of his hand. "David, I don't know if I ever had a friend love me the way your dad did."

Now David had tears on his cheeks, too. He nodded softly, caressing the neck of his new guitar distractedly.

"It's really good, David. Really. Keep playing. And writing."

That day Mike taught David a G chord, an F, and an A minor, to go with his E minor and his C.

"There," he said. "Now you basically got the key of C. See what you can do with that."

That night David was sitting on the edge of his bed strumming idly when another song came to him. It came in the same way the song about Mike had come, only far more vividly this time. The words caught him somewhat off guard, too, and as he mumbled them to the tune, it was as if he were hearing someone else's voice sing them. Of course, that was probably because it was the least likely thing David himself would have ever sung about, the story of a teenage mother forced to offer up her newborn baby for adoption. As he sang it, it felt like his own heart were breaking with her pain, though it was hardly any pain that David could have understood. But the words were so sharp, and real, that he couldn't help but feel as if it was his own child being wrenched from his arms, each time he got to the chorus.

The bridge, when it was finally written, felt a bit forced to him. It described this distraught girl finding a guitar of her own and singing out her grief with all her heartbroken strength. It wasn't a bad image, but he worried it felt contrived.

Mike disagreed. David played the song for him the next time they got together, but he apologized for the clumsiness of the bridge. "I'm thinking I should just scrap it," he said.

"Don't you dare," Mike said. "I love that part. I've seen some things myself that only a guitar and a sad song could have got me through, so I get it. It feels real, you know?"

David didn't know, but he trusted Mike's judgment and left the bridge the way it was.

That day Mike taught him how to play "Dust in the Wind."

"It's a classic," he said. "And I really think it'd fit your style." David wasn't sure he had a style yet, but he learned the chords and gave it a try. He loved the lyrics, that haunting elegy to the fleetingness of life, and he sat on the edge of his bed late into the night, trying to master the complex fingerpicking pattern.

At some point, however, he realized he wasn't really playing "Dust in the Wind" any longer, but the tune had transformed into another song of his own. It was another entirely unlikely theme. This time an old grandfather was singing a plaintive blessing over his grandchildren, singing from the depths of a life hard-lived, in the light of a wisdom hard-won. David wasn't even that sure what he was trying to say with the lyrics, but it was clear to him that the grandfather in his song had seen tragedy and was trying to turn that pain into a gift of life for his children's children's children.

Strangely—because he had so disliked the image when it had appeared in his last song—David felt sure that in the final verse the grandfather ought to pick up an old guitar and literally sing the blessing against the sound of gentle picking. That's how he wrote the words, anyway.

"I'm noting a pattern here," said Mike when David played it for him.

David stared at his guitar, his cheeks coloring a bit. "I know," he said. "It's silly."

"No," said Mike. "That's not what I mean. It's just—" and here, for the first time anyone had done so in a very long time, Mike placed a steadying hand gently on David's shoulder. "Your songs are about people dealing with their pain through music, right? Trying to come to terms with it in a song? Well, that makes sense, doesn't it?"

David fixed his gaze on his instrument, but only because he feared that if he looked up, the mist that was forming in his eyes would become real tears, and if they started, he did not know where they would end.

"Keep playing, David," Mike said. "It's good."

The songs started coming more freely after that. They were all as different from each other as they could be. In one, a new father sang a welcome to the world over his newborn baby. In another, a betrayed lover sought healing in song from the heartbreak of a bitter divorce. In yet another, a timid boy told the girl he admired how deeply he had fallen for her. They were all different, but they all shared two things in common.

For one, they all featured, at some point or another, a guitar being played. Sometimes it was the main image of the song, other times it just appeared in a line or two, strummed by a secondary character in the scene, but a guitar was in there somewhere.

More poignantly and powerfully than that, however, was the fact that each song, as it came to him, overwhelmed David with the full feeling of what he was singing about. When the song was about the birth of a child, the joy bubbling up in him could not have been more scintillating if it had been his very own son taking his first breath. When it was a rejected lover picking up the pieces after a betrayal, it was as if his own heart had shattered with hers.

Whatever the song, the emotion was nearly so intense as to sweep him away, and only by strumming and singing—almost dutifully singing along—could he keep his place in the torrent that washed over him.

It was Mike who finally suggested that he try his hand at busking.

He didn't say it as plainly as that, of course.

"Dude," is how he put it. "You should take this show on the road."

David blushed crimson at the thought.

"No, I'm serious," Mike insisted. "Not to make any money; I don't mean that. But a song isn't a song, I think, until it's had an audience."

"I have you for my audience," said David.

"Nah. I'm your sensei—your Yoda. I can't be your audience."

In an effort to convince him, Mike taught him "Down on the Corner" that day. He even taught him how to play the bouncing base line while he strummed the chords, so long as he promised to "take his show on the road."

"Just give it a try," he said. "Set up in Memorial Park, if you want, and see what happens."

To this day, David is still somewhat surprised that he took Mike up on his suggestion. The park bench where he set up was near a bus stop, and there were people coming and going all day. He didn't have the temerity to open his guitar case for loose change, though. And anyway, that's not why he was there. He just had this handful of songs burning in his heart's pocket, and somehow he knew he needed to spend them somewhere.

He was there all morning, and more than once someone would linger, enjoying the music or suggesting a song. A guy who looked about Mike's age told him to play Free Bird, then laughed generously, but David didn't get the joke. A kid on a skateboard who clearly had nowhere to go hung out with him for over an hour.

At one point the skateboard kid asked if he could try. "I haven't been playing very long," he said, "but I can do 'Smells Like Teen Spirit' pretty good."

He took the guitar and hammered out the chords awkwardly. Grunge wasn't really David's thing, but he nodded along, and when the kid was done, he took the guitar back. In exchange he played the song he'd written about the newborn father welcoming his son into the world.

That night when a new song came to him, it was more vivid than any had yet been. He was strumming his guitar randomly and thinking about the kid on the skateboard, wondering what his story was, when a melody appeared somewhere inside him. He imagined the kid as a homeless youth—there was no shortage of those hanging around Memorial Park—and wondered what might have happened to have left him without a place to go. The skater in his song, as he wrote it, turned out to be gay. His parents had kicked him out when they discovered the secret of his existence—that line really worked for him—and now he lived on the streets because he couldn't love the way they wanted him to—that line felt forced, but it seemed to fit, so he kept it.

Once again, a strummed guitar made an appearance in the lyrics. This time it was borrowed from a busker downtown, in a throw-away line toward the end, but David figured that only made sense, since that was what had inspired the song in the first place.

And once again, too, he felt the ache of what he sang about sweep through him as he played, so intensely this time that when he was done, he found he was weeping. It was as though he himself had been rejected by his parents, he himself with nowhere safe to turn.

He fell asleep that night with hot tears still burning in his eyes.

The next day he found his way down to Memorial Park again with his guitar. The skater was nowhere to be seen, and David would hardly have played the song for him even if he had showed up, but still he was a bit disappointed. The pain he'd felt singing his song last night was so real that he wanted very much to meet the kid again.

It was a Saturday morning, and the buses were running less frequently, so the park was pretty quiet. Even so David sat there for nearly three hours, strumming through his repertoire. Toward the end, a man wandered by. Life on the street had worn him so thin that it was hard to tell his age, but David guessed he was in his thirties or forties. He sat on the grass opposite David's bench, grinning broadly and lighting a cigarette.

"You can really play," the man said, when David paused between songs.

David muttered something about how he was still learning.

"No," the man said. "You got heart. I play a bit myself. At least I used to. Had an old guitar something like that, though mine wasn't so nice as a Gibson. You mind if I give it a go?" He stubbed out his cigarette in the grass and reached out his hand. David had the vague impression of a drowning man reaching for a life raft. He extended the guitar to him.

The man set it in his lap and started playing weakly. He stumbled through the first few bars of "Stairway to Heaven," then a few seconds of "Norwegian Wood." David had heard Mike play each of these, so he recognized them, however bad a job the man was making of them.

For his part, the man seemed less interested in playing than just talking, and the whole while he fingered the strings, he told David the heartbreaking story of his life. He was a vet, as it turned out, and had even seen action in Afghanistan. Not much, but it doesn't take much to leave a mark on you that won't go away. When he came home, he found his wife and kids had left him for someone else. No surprise there, since they'd been fighting for years—he'd learned how to do that well enough from his own old man—so maybe it was for the best, since chances were pretty good he'd have done to his son no better than what his dad did to him.

"The worst of it, though," he said, dragging his thumb across a couple of minor chords, "is that they sold my guitar. Maybe that shouldn't be the worst thing for me, but it was. We were just clearing out old junk in a garage sale, is what she told me. Can you believe it? Old junk, she called it."

The man passed the guitar back to David. As he took it in hand, he thought of the last six months, the dozen or more songs that this battered instrument had sort of given him, in a way, and all the heartbreak and hopefulness that had come along with them. He thought of Mike and then of his dad, and how hard it would have been without an old guitar like this to help him make sense of it all.

"No," he said softly. "I can't believe it."

The song that came to him that night was the most intense of all, and this time David had no doubt that it was indeed coming from outside him, that it was not his at all and was only being offered to him by someone else. It was about a discarded warrior living on the streets—a soldier come home from the fight to discover that the war had stolen everything from him, even his father's old guitar.

It hurt him almost physically to sing it, as it came, but he recalled something his teacher had told him about a guitar remembering how it had been played. He wondered what hands had so handled this guitar in the past that it was able to give him the song about the abandoned mother, or the fading grandfather, or any of the others that had appeared in his heart since the instrument had become his. As best he could he opened himself to this new pain now, this soldier's pain, and as he did, he felt as though the song taking shape was extracting something hard but necessary from him.

The room was dark when the soldier's song was finally finished, and the memory of his pain lingered long after the guitar had fallen still. Even so, when he finally lay back in his bed to sleep, there was an unearthly stillness in David's face. He wouldn't have put it this way, but as he drifted off, he looked for all the world like an injured soul, nestling in at last under the shadow of a strong and healing wing.

10.

My Mother's Eyes

I have my mother's eyes. That's what they've always told me, anyway.

I've never really understood why, because she's been blind since childhood and I can see perfectly well, but that's what they say. She was only four years old when the doctors diagnosed her with a rare case of infantile glaucoma, but by then the disease had already advanced so far that the optic nerve was irreparably damaged. In every memory I have of her, her eyes have that impassive gaze of the unseeing: wide, and dark, and still.

It is true that my eyes are dark, too, and brown like hers. But that's the only similarity I could ever see.

Still, they always said it, that Iris has her mother's eyes. Her father's sense of humor and her mother's eyes.

I have to take their word on it for my sense of humor, too. If my mother is blind in every childhood memory I have, my father does not appear at all. There's some secret about him that no one would tell me, but since growing up, I've sort of pieced it together that his relationship with my mother was something of a whim for him.

When the realities of being with someone who couldn't see became real inconveniences, he moved on and left us to fend for ourselves. Whenever I thought of him leaving, I always imagined him writing it all out in a letter, how it wasn't her it was him, and then realizing she could never read it anyway and crumpling it into a ball. He left shortly after I was born, and I've never met him.

So I was raised by a blind, abandoned, teenage mom. We lived with her parents for the earliest years of my life, but as soon as I was old enough that I could help to make it manageable, we moved into an apartment of our own. I didn't pick up on all the nuances of my mother's relationship with her parents at that age, but even as a young girl I knew that they bickered a lot. I've since come to wonder if they blamed themselves for my mother's blindness, or if not that, then perhaps she blamed them. Whatever the case, my earliest memories of knowing real happiness seem to coincide with my earliest memories of us beginning to live on our own, my blind mother and her nine-year-old girl, together against the world.

Mom never got a service dog, though she could have, and when I was old enough to know the difference it might make, I begged her repeatedly to do so.

"Alison," I'd say—I don't know why but I always called my mother by her given name—"Alison, I'm sick of having to rush home from school to take care of things around here. And I worry like crazy about you while I'm at school. Why can't we just look into getting a dog?"

"Very funny," Alison said. "You can look. I can't." She was not at all shy about resorting to that kind of tactic when strict reason failed her in an argument. "Why don't you look, and tell me what you see?"

"That's not what I meant, and you know it."

"I'm just saying that I don't need a Seeing Eye dog. I've got you. You're my Seeing Eye girl."

"Very funny yourself," I said. She's used that line before, and I've always hated it. "I just think that we'd be happier—that you'd be happier—if you were more independent. I mean, I won't be around forever."

We were having the debate this time in the kitchen, preparing supper. I had the water for the spaghetti boiling and a pan on the stove ready for the sauce. My mother could use the can opener entirely by feel and had opened a can of pasta sauce for me. I was managing the stove top, of course, but she was wonderfully adept with a kitchen knife, and had started to dice up an onion. She had this way of curling her fingertips in and holding the onion down with the top of her knuckles, so she could guide the blade by running the flat of the knife up and down along the front of her knuckles with no risk of cutting herself. I've never been in a professional kitchen before, but I like to think she was as good as any bona fide chef.

"You mean you don't *want* to be around forever?" she said. Her blind eyes still watered like anyone's would, from the sting of the onion.

"It's not that," I said quietly. "I just want you to be independent."

"I'm plenty independent," she said, and it almost seemed as if she was slicing the onion with a bit of extra vigor as she said this. "Didn't I raise you on my own? Didn't we move into this apartment as soon as we could? Haven't I been working a real job all these years to pay for it?"

"Yes, yes, and yes," I said. Her tone reminded me a lot of the one she used when she argued with my grandparents. They were regularly pressuring her to move back home. "I'm not saying you're not independent. I just think that a lot of blind people find that Seeing Eye dogs help. That's all."

"Iris," my mother said, in that steady voice she used when she needed the debate to be over. "Honey, I know you're saying this because you love me. And I love you too. But I don't need any help." Her face was pointed stoically forwards as she spoke; though she knew exactly where I was standing, she did not turn toward me. "Now," she added. "Be a dear and help me put this onion in the sauce. I don't want to burn my fingers."

I stared at her blankly for a second. And then, because we had reached this dead end often enough that I knew we'd come back to it again at some point, I dropped the matter and finished making the sauce.

That evening, when the dinner was done and the dishes cleaned, we were sitting together in the living room of our tiny apartment. I was on the couch, working on my calculus, and she was plunking away at the piano. It was an old apartment size piano that I'd helped her find on Kijiji a couple of years ago. She worked at a call centre, one of the first blind operators they'd ever hired, and though the pay was steady, it was hardly princely, so it had taken her over a year to save up for the piano. It was no Steinway, not by a long shot, but then, she was no Ray Charles, either. She had a good ear, for sure, but her playing was still pretty halting and random. I had a really important test coming up, with college applications on the way and all, but there was nowhere else in the apartment to study, so I just put my head down and did my best, with Alison plunking away blindly in the background.

Suddenly she stopped playing and looked straight ahead.

"There's one just stepped into the room," she said softly. "He's standing near the couch, on your left." I didn't look up from my book or say anything, but after a moment she said, "he's a glorious one, too. A real warrior of light."

This is as good a time as any, I guess, to explain that my mother sees angels. I don't know if "sees" is quite the right term, but she has, or at least she thinks she has, some sort of spiritual gift for detecting the presence of these heavenly beings. It's been like this since I was a very little girl, mind you, so it doesn't spook me out or anything. She'll be busy doing something, or sitting quietly thinking, and suddenly she'll announce that there's an angel present. There's one standing at my elbow, she'll say; there's one sitting on the front stairs watching the street; there's one sitting in an empty seat across from us on the bus.

She never talks to them, mind you. She's actually quite strict about this, that we shouldn't ever address them directly, and the only time her angel-detecting gift caused any real grief between us was once when I tried to speak to one. This was a few years back, when I was at the height of that bratty stage of being a teenager, and I only ever felt embarrassed about my mom and her "gift." So one time when she told me there was an angel watching us from the kitchen table, I turned in that direction and asked if it would like to stay for supper. She scolded and told me that I ought never speak to an angel like that. "After all," she said, when the wave of alarm had passed, "they are only ministering servants like ourselves."

Grandma and Grandpa are Pentecostal. At least, I think they used to be when Alison was young, and maybe this is where she gets her superstitious side from. I know for sure that when Alison was first diagnosed, her mom and dad took her regularly to Pentecostal prayer meetings, healers and miracle workers and what not, praying that she'd have her eyesight restored. By all accounts they visited revival meetings from one end of the country to the other, hoping for a miracle that would make mom see.

For all I know, they actually found what they were looking for and never realized it, because, like I say, as long as I've known her, Alison has seen angels, and that's something. It's never spooky or creepy when she acknowledges one standing in our presence, either. Usually, I'm aware of a profound calm and a deep assurance sinking into me, whenever she points one out.

This particular night, though, with that ominous calculus test looming over me and the argument about the service dog still lingering in my thoughts, I didn't feel I had the patience for it. "Hmmm," was all I said, still buried in the pages of my book. "Maybe I should slide over and make him some room on the couch?"

Alison sat perfectly motionless at the piano, though, and in the silence it really did feel like an illuminating presence had descended over us, or was revealing itself to us. At the very least, my nerves about the coming test were suddenly soothed, and even the tension between us over the dog seemed to have evaporated.

"Mom," I said, after a long moment of pretending I was still studying. "It's just: I'm scared. I'm almost done high school, and who knows what's coming next? It's hard enough for any kid my age to figure all that out, without…" I trailed off.

"Without having to worry about who's gonna take care of their blind old mom?"

The calculus book in my lap had become blurry to me. There were times when I was sort of grateful she couldn't see. I wiped my eyes and hoped the tears wouldn't sound in my voice.

"Well," I said. "I just want us to be prepared for the future."

She sighed deeply. It wasn't a sigh of resignation or condemnation. If anything, there was a note of contentment in it, though it was mingled with a great sadness, like the color of autumn leaves.

"I know, sweetheart," she said. And then after a moment: "Well, he's gone now. They never stay long."

The next day on my way to school, Alex sat down next to me on the city bus. He didn't always take the bus, but he didn't have gas money enough to drive his car to school all the time, so every fourth or fifth day he took public transit with us lowly mortals.

Alex is a year older than me, though he's doing what used to be called Grade 13, and now, I think, they call it a victory lap. There's some rumor that makes me feel uneasy around him, about the real reason he's back at J. Milton Collegiate for another year. But even so, the honest truth is that I'm always wondering if he'll be there when I get on the bus each day. And I'm always a little disappointed when he's not, even though he hardly ever says anything to me.

Today was the exception. "Hey Iris," he said, settling in comfortably as we lurched away from the bus stop. "I was wondering if you're coming to Heather's tomorrow night?"

Heather is in Grade 12, like me. We were pretty close friends when we were younger, though as we grew up, I was so busy helping Alison live on her own that I didn't have much time for her, and we drifted apart. I'd heard from friends of friends that her parents were away or something, and she was throwing a party, though she hadn't invited me.

"Nah, I don't think so."

"Don't think so?"

"I'm not really interested in all those typical teenager clichés, you know?" I wanted to sound cynical, but the truth is that Friday night was when Alison and I always did our grocery shopping for the coming week. She worked all weekend and there was no way I could leave her to do that by herself. "House wrecking parties when the parents are gone? What is this, a bad episode of Riverdale or something?"

"Maybe so. If it is, you'd make a pretty good Veronica."

I rolled my eyes. I was trying to look utterly disgusted at this transparent—and honestly pretty pathetic—stab at flirting, but really, I was hoping the look I gave him would hide the deep-down sadness that was welling up in me.

"And you'd make a great Reggie. Isn't he the jerky one?"

He laughed effortlessly. "Okay, okay," he said. "I get it. You're not a fan. Fine. It's just—" and a very subtle change slipped into his tone as he said this part. "It's just, I see you, you know? Missing out on life and whatever? And I don't want you to look back with regrets. I mean, you only get to live your high school years once."

"Unless you come back for a thirteenth year," I said allusively, looking straight ahead and fighting down the faint smile that was dancing at the corner of my mouth.

There was a grey-haired lady with one of those old-fashioned scarves—I think they call them babushkas—on her head, sitting across from me. I hadn't noticed her before, but she must have been there the whole while, because the bus hadn't stopped since I'd got on. When our eyes met, she grinned at me, her wrinkled face folding up around the eyes, until the many sharp creases looked like beams of light shining out from a dazzling sun. I grinned back.

"Shots fired!" Alex was saying next to me, with another one of his effortless laughs. "Well, suit yourself, but I'm not gonna give up on you."

That night over dinner Alison noticed another angel. This time it was standing in the doorway of the kitchen. "He's got his hands raised in prayer," she said. "And there are tears in his eyes."

I took her word for it. It's true, I did feel the peace sweep over me that so often accompanied Alison's angelic visitations, but at just that moment I didn't feel I had the emotional energy to speculate about a supposed celestial being that I couldn't see. And anyway, I had more important things on my mind.

"Alison," I said tentatively. "Do you think we could do our grocery trip Saturday when you get home from work? Or maybe I could go on my own Sunday afternoon?"

For all her being blind, Alison was uncannily perceptive. "You want to go out Friday?"

"Well, there's this thing happening with some of my friends, and I thought…" I hesitated. I had so many thoughts rushing through my mind that I couldn't decide which to say first.

"You thought you'd like a night of freedom for a change?" It wasn't said passive-aggressively, I don't think, and it was true, but I was still young enough that I jumped on the opportunity to be offended.

"How could you say that, Alison?" I let my fork clatter on my plate and pushed back from the table. "What do you mean freedom? I just want to go out with some friends on a Friday night, like any normal kid my age. Why do you have to make this into a thing?"

I wondered if the angel had taken a step into the room, or if he had buried his hands in his face, because Alison had turned her attention in the direction of the kitchen door and held it there.

"I don't have to make this into a thing," she said steadily. "I'm working late Saturday, so that won't do. Sunday might, but we're out of just about everything, so it might be hard to wait till then."

"Fine," I said with an exasperated exhale. "It's fine. I'll be home Friday night like a good little girl, and we can go get your groceries."

She was still looking with that piercing gaze in the direction of the angel, but with a very soft voice she said, "Just so you know, I made a call to the Canadian Guide Dog Association today. I've got an appointment with them next month to see about finding a dog that's a good match."

She said this so softly, and my mind was swirling with so many other thoughts, that even though I nodded slightly, the comment barely registered.

"Good," I said at last. "But it won't be here by Friday night, so I guess I'm still stuck getting groceries with you."

I don't know if I had meant it to be as hurtful as it sounded, but my mother just sat there in meek silence. After a long moment she rose from the table gingerly and quietly left the room.

Alex was on the bus the next morning, waiting for me. This was the first time I'd ever seen him take the bus two days in a row. He was sitting on the bench that's normally reserved for seniors and pregnant moms, though the bus was pretty empty and no one needed the seats. It surprised me though, because he was sitting next to the old lady in the kerchief, the one that I'd noticed yesterday. He was sitting quite close to her, in fact, in that indolent way guys sometimes have of taking up far more room than they need to. It was if he didn't even notice she was there.

"Hey, Veronica!" he said with a bit of a laugh. "You comin' to Archie's party tonight?"

"Gee, Reggie," I said, and I hoped my tone sounded dismissive, not playful. "I don't know."

The old lady didn't seem at all shy to listen in on our conversation, though Alex was sitting so close to her that she hardly could have helped it. In any case, she grinned at me gently when I added, "Do you think Betty will be going too?"

Alex got up, steadying himself against the lurching of the bus, and made his way over to me. He didn't sit down, but held on to one of the overhead handrails, standing right in front of me and swaying slightly as the bus rounded a corner.

"Seriously, Iris. Have you had second thoughts yet?"

I kept my gaze lowered, but a burning memory of the angel my mother had seen at the dinner table the night before—those infuriating, embarrassing angels—flared up in my mind. I squeezed my eyes shut against it.

"Sure," I said. It was like I was listening to someone else, speaking through me. "Only, the buses don't run after midnight. So how would I get home?"

"Hey, if that's your worry, no problem. I can take you. You want? I could pick you up at nine."

I inhaled deeply. "Could you make it six? My mom gets home at six-thirty and I kinda wanna be gone before she gets home."

"Your mom 'gets home'? Isn't she—"

"Yeah, she is. I usually meet her at the bus stop to walk her home. But I'm sure she can manage with her cane." I looked at his face for the first time. "At least, she has before. She won't miss me."

He didn't seem to feel the gravity of what I was saying. "Yeah," he said with a flippant laugh. "Yeah, sure. Six o'clock it is. I'm sure we can find something to do till the party starts."

The rest of that day was a bit of a guilty blur for me. Whenever I let my mind wander, I would see this image of Alison stepping off the bus, and me not being there. Alison standing on the curb and calling, and me being not there. Alison, when she finally accepted that I wasn't coming, unfolding her cane and tapping her tentative way home, and me not being there.

I did very poorly on the calculus exam that day.

That evening, however, I was dressed for the party and ready to go by five-thirty. It was way too soon, I know, but I was full of nervous energy, terrified that Alison would come home early for some reason and catch me. So I waited by the door, staring at the knob and breathing unevenly.

When the knock finally came, I checked the clock and was surprised to see that it was only ten to six. Alex didn't strike me at all as the kind of guy who arrived early; if anything, I was worried he would arrive too late to sneak away.

I was even more surprised when I opened the door, and instead of Alex standing there, it was the old lady from the bus, still wearing her babushka. The light in the hall was dim but I recognized her the instant that gentle smile dawned across her face.

"I'm sorry to bother you, dear," she said, "but are you Iris Sullivan?"

"Yes? But… how did you—?" Though I had every reason to be unsettled, it occurred to me that my breathing had quieted down for the first time that whole anxious evening.

"You dropped this on the bus this afternoon." She was holding out something that I didn't recognize right away. "It had your address on it."

It was my driver's license; I'd gotten it last summer. Alison didn't have a car, of course, but in one of the only real bonding experiences I'd ever had with my grandpa, he'd let me learn on his car. He even drove me to the driver's test. I haven't driven anything anywhere since getting that license, but at the time it had seemed like the most triumphant achievement of my life.

I didn't take the license from her right away, though. I just stood there, staring at it.

"Thanks," I said at last. "I hope you didn't go out of your way, though. I don't suppose I'd have missed it. I don't need it. At least, I never use it."

"Oh," she said quietly. "Maybe not. But you will." There was a strange note in her voice. It was unsettling, but only because it was so reassuring. Somehow, as she spoke, I had no doubt that what she said was true.

I took the card from her hand and looked at it hard, as though I were seeing it for the first time. The photo on it was hideous, even for a driver's license. I'd hated it the moment I'd seen it, and I hated it all the more as I looked at it now. The look on my face in the picture was just so haunted, like a deer in the headlights. The flash on the camera must have caught me off guard, too, because the eyes were dark and wide and blank.

"Thank you," I said, but the old lady had already turned and was moving down the hall. At the sound of my voice, she stopped and turned back.

"It may not be my place to say," she began. "But about that boy on the bus…"

"Alex?"

"Yes. Alex. I just want to say that I don't think he's right for you, dear." And again, the quiet assurance that what she said was true broke over me, and into me, driving away all doubt the way light drives away shadow.

She turned again, but I didn't see her go. I was staring with unseeing eyes once more at the driver's license in my hand, knowing for certain that one day I would use it.

When Alex arrived some twenty minutes later, he found me sitting at the threshold of the open front door, still staring blankly.

"Hey Veronica," he said, not noticing the look on my face. "You ready to party?"

He only paused when I lifted my haunted face and shook my head at him heavily.

"No."

"No?"

"I can't." I said, blinking my eyes finally and grasping for resolve.

"Can't? Why not?"

"It's just—oh, you wouldn't understand. It's just like they've always said. I have my mother's eyes."

11.

The Day's Last Dance

No one could have predicted, the year of Bethel Academy's first and only high school dance, that it would have ended as spectacularly as it did. But then, given the number of people so set against it, few could have predicted that it would have happened at all. The administration only entertained the possibility of a school dance because that year the president of the PTA, the one who had actually proposed the idea, was the wife of a member of town council. Even that would not have been enough to have swayed the decision in any ordinary year, but the school had petitioned the city to install a traffic light on its intersection, to keep the kiss-and-ride for the elementary grades moving more smoothly, and they needed all the help they could get. Consequently, they had agreed to let the PTA add the item to the agenda of their next meeting, trusting holier heads to prevail.

The PTA was split, however, into a number of distinct camps. There was the old guard, of course, who wouldn't dream of letting something so unseemly as a school dance sully Bethel Academy's long legacy of providing quality education in a pure Christian environment. And even within that camp, the tents were not all pointing in the same direction. Some simply dismissed dancing as a frivolous waste of time that would distract students from more godly pursuits. Others wondered what seductions of Jezebel the school would be proposing next. Would we be opening a tattoo parlor? Teaching classes in yoga? Mrs. White, who kept the meeting's minutes, was in fact the leader of this camp, so there's no guarantee that anyone in the meeting actually used the words "abomination that causes desolation," but certainly the term is recorded, to this day, in her account of the heated debate that was had that night.

There were other camps, however. The most vocal of these was a group of younger parents, many of whom were relatively new to the Bethel Academy PTA. The PTA President, Heather Smythe, had been wanting to see Bethel move in a more "progressive"—this was her word, though again, the official minutes of the meeting read "worldly"—direction for many years. It would make the school more attractive to prospective students, she argued. It would build camaraderie among the student body. It would be good old-fashioned fun. No one questioned her sincerity, though one or two of the moms did mention it between themselves, after the meeting, that recently the pastor at Heather's church had censured her for enrolling her daughter in dance class—and jazz dance, of all things—and they wondered—just wondered, is all—if she wasn't pushing this crazy dance idea to prove a point.

Whatever merit there may have been to this speculation, it turned out Mrs. Smythe had enough support to win the day. One mom, who had enrolled her daughter Emily in Bethel after Emily had been expelled from public school, stood and asked if someone could please explain to her where was the harm in boys and girls of a certain age dancing together? A few knowing glances flitted about the room when she claimed, innocently enough, that she had actually fallen in love with her first husband at a high school dance; and it didn't help when she laughed and added that she had also met her second while chaperoning a dance for Emily's older sister. These unfortunate admissions notwithstanding, Mrs. Smythe felt that, on the whole, her speech had helped the cause considerably.

Of the teachers on the PTA, only Mr. Windsor supported the idea, but the support he offered was warm to the point of being effusive, and it carried much weight with those who had not yet made up their minds. It was about time, he insisted, that Bethel stepped into the new millennium. The kids these days can do worse in a half hour, alone in their rooms with their cellphones, he argued, than they could ever do at a high school dance. And anyway, he couldn't remember reading anywhere in the Bible where it says thou shalt not dance! Mrs. White did note down that Mr. Windsor taught English literature (one of the more liberal disciplines) but still she recorded his comments in the minutes as faithfully as she could.

In the end the dance was approved, by a vote of seven to six.

For our part, the student body of Bethel Academy was not quite as factious as our parents, but there were still very definite, and, indeed, polarizing opinions about the coming event. Aaron Clarke, the president of the Student Council, also happened to be the son of Heather Smythe's pastor, so publicly he toed his father's line, that dance was simply a gateway sin into much more sensual debaucheries. Emily, the one whose mother had met her stepfather at her older sister's prom, kept dropping suggestive inuendoes about the kind of things that might happen behind the bleachers or in the far corner of the gym's mezzanine once the lights went down.

These only represented the far ends of the spectrum, however, and most of us landed somewhere between these two extremes. Rebecca Smythe was also on the Student Council, and because it was her mother who had hatched this plan, she was a natural pick to serve on the planning committee. As such, she scowled whenever Emily regaled us with stories about finding herself alone with some boy at a dance she went to at her last school.

Rebecca insisted that this was not going to be like that, that it would be a classy affair, and whatever else, wholesome. She festooned the hallways of Bethel Academy with all kinds of handmade posters promoting the dance. The planning committee had chosen the theme "Bethel Beach Ball." They went with this primarily because Mr. Windsor was on the committee, and he couldn't resist the alliterative pun, but also because the beach theme generated no end of ideas for décor.

Rebecca was totally chagrined when, a few days later, someone had surreptitiously modified all her posters so that they read "Bethel ~~Beach~~ Bikini Ball!" Her chagrin grew to horror when, later that day, the principal issued a stern announcement over the intercom reminding everyone of Bethel's long-standing dress code and warning them that absolutely no swimwear would be permitted at the upcoming dance. The planning committee worked late into the afternoon to replace the vandalized signs.

By the next afternoon, however, they had been modified again. This time they read "Babylon ~~Bethel~~ Beach Ball?"

Around this time, someone started up an Instagram group chat, where the student body discussed the coming dance in terms far less reserved and considerably less filtered than they ever used with their parents or teachers. Here Emily was much more graphic in describing the things that she was looking forward to at the dance. In general, the students took much more interest in discussing this than they did when she brought it up in public. One or two of the boys, in fact, messaged her to find out more. Here, too, the student body discovered Aaron's real feelings about dancing. He was only saying all that stuff about a gateway sin, he explained, because he had to. There would be hell to pay if his dad thought he felt otherwise, though he'd be damned if he was gonna miss out on the first school dance ever to happen at Bethel. He even used the words hell and damn, though outside of Instagram he only ever spoke like that when he was discussing doctrine. Other students weighed in. Some were nervously looking forward to it, others were going to boycott, others still were wondering what all the fuss was about.

The only two students who said nothing—and since it was a private school, the student body was small enough that their silence ought to have been noticed, even though it wasn't—were Star and Autumn Cardinal. They were just starting their first year at Bethel, the Cardinal family having recently moved to the city from a place out in the country. Mr. and Mrs. Cardinal had been prominent members of their church back home and had wanted their girls to get a good Christian education, so they'd enrolled them in Bethel, the only faith-based school in the neighbourhood.

Looking back, no one thinks they had been intentionally excluded from the Instagram group chat. It's just that they seldom said much of anything, so it was easy to overlook them. They kept to themselves and tended to speak only when spoken to. No one meant to avoid them, either; at least if asked, no one would have said so. It's just: no one wanted to make anyone uncomfortable asking awkward questions about the new kids and where they were from. As a result, whatever Autumn and Star thought about the flurry of high school politicking and adolescent theologizing that was raging around the school's preparation for the big Bethel Beach Ball, no one could say.

Not that anyone much cared. There was enough politicking and theologizing going on to keep us all busy for days. Rumors started on Instagram that Emily had already snuck a bottle from her stepdad's liquor cabinet and was planning to bring it to the dance. Rebecca started a disastrously ill-advised poll about what kind of music ought to be played. It might have been better if she had done this in person, but as it was, her poll exploded into a veritable minefield of controversy. Some insisted that only contemporary Christian music should be played. Others still said that the last thing contemporary Christian music should be used for was a high school dance. Many requested the latest Taylor Swift and Ed Sheeran releases. One or two parents somehow got ahold of the suggested playlist and threatened not to let their kids attend if "trash like that" was going to be played. Someone even sent Mrs. White a YouTube link to the video for Ariana Grande's "7 Rings." Aaron Clarke took the blame for this, but he denied it on Instagram in the saltiest language a pastor's son could have possibly known. At any rate, Mrs. White wrote a stern letter, as secretary of the PTA, to the principal of Bethel, and as a result she received executive veto power over the music selection.

The Instagram group chat was lit up for days over this development, and everyone wondered what kind of gospel jamboree their first dance was going to devolve into, now that Mrs. White was head DJ.

There comes a point in the unfolding of any epoch-making moment, however, when the best-laid plans of everyone involved cease to matter much, because some inexorable force, greater than the sum of its individual parts, seems to have come into being, driving events forward to an outcome no one individually would have chosen. Looking back, that's what seems to have happened the night of Bethel Academy's first ever Beach Ball.

Despite the constant threats to boycott the party, the entire student body did attend in the end, and for the most part, everyone was dressed appropriately. The closest anyone came to wearing a bikini was Rebecca Smythe, who wore a strapless summer dress. It is true that Aaron Clarke wore shorts, but he also wore a shirt and tie.

When the final playlist had been thoroughly vetted by Mrs. White, there was far more Gaither music in the rotation than anyone could bear, even the chaperones. As a concession, however, she had permitted a handful of ABBA songs, though Dancing Queen was not among them.

The rumors about Emily turned out to be mostly true. She had snuck a bottle in with her, though when she revealed it to a group of us, up on the mezzanine of the gym and beyond where the chaperones could see, it turned out to be a bottle of her stepdad's homemade wine. Despite our disappointment, though, one or two of us did stay on the mezzanine to drink it. Someone even produced from somewhere a contraband package of cigarettes, though no one had ever smoked before.

This was not the biggest surprise of the night, however.

To this day, everyone agrees that this honor goes to the moment when Autumn and Star arrived. No one knew for sure if they were even coming, though we'd all made our assumptions. What none of us expected was that when they did arrive, they would be dressed so stunningly in their traditional Cree dance regalia.

Few of us even knew that Star and Autumn were, in fact, Cree. No one had bothered to ask.

There was no need to ask, though, when they walked through the gym doors, dressed in two shimmering jingle dresses, brilliantly colored and beautifully crafted, tasseled and beaded and plumed. The music of "Because He Lives" that just happened to be playing over the PA system when they arrived kept playing, of course, but other than that a kind of hush fell momentarily over us all. They stood there, these two unassuming girls whom we'd been passing in the halls for months unnoticed, looking now so striking and dignified and strong. It's not that we didn't want to welcome them. It's just that no one knew what to say.

It was Mr. Windsor who finally broke the tension of the moment, though for all his being an English teacher he was unusually clumsy with his words. "Autumn! Star!" he said. "You two look—well—it's fantastic—I'm so glad you—those gowns—are they?—dresses?— they're fabulous!"

"It's our dance regalia," Autumn explained. "For when we go to powwows back home. We're not supposed to wear them out like this. Not to something like this. But dance—" She looked hesitantly at her sister, but something larger than any of us was at work in that moment, so she pushed past whatever it was that had given her pause. "Dance is very big deal for us—and we thought—maybe—"

"We hoped it would be ok," said Star.

"Of course! Of course it's okay!" said Mr. Windsor. "You two look wonderful." He made a wide sweep with his arm, as if to welcome them onto the dance floor.

There was no need for anyone to make space for them, though. There were very few students doing any actual dancing that night. This might have been because very little of the music that had passed Mrs. White's exacting scrutiny was even danceable, but more likely it was because very few of us had any real idea how to dance. Even Rebecca Smythe, despite all the hubbub it had caused in her church when she'd started taking jazz dance, was all toes when it came to doing anything graceful out there on a bona fide high school dance floor.

One or two of us made a timid attempt at pairing off when a slow dance came along, but it was more than awkward, trying to sway together in time to "Something About that Name," of all tunes. A couple of Taylor Swift songs had made the final cut (mostly because Mrs. White had been made to see the wisdom of "shaking off" the world's "hate"), but even when these came up in the rotation, no one really knew how, in fact, to shake anything. Whatever the quality of the Christian education we'd received at Bethel, it had not taught us much at all about what to do with our bodies. The eternal destiny of our disembodied souls—we all knew how to guarantee that—but to move at peace with the limbs and the lungs the good Lord had given us—not even Mr. Windsor's poetry class could teach us that.

For all our clumsiness with each other, however, Autumn and Star seemed to have no doubt what was needed that night. Regardless the tune warbling from the PA speakers in any given moment—Abba, Gaithers, Jesus Culture or Hillsong United (though only a few of their songs had passed the Mrs. White smell test)—the Cardinal sisters danced their hearts out at the centre of the gym, stomping and leaping and soaring and spinning as though they'd done it all their lives (for, in fact, they had), and all the while jingling with the glorious noise of a hundred scintillating bells.

If most of us gave up dancing and stood simply to watch, it was really only in awe. Not even Aaron Clarke, who was the preacher's son and had inherited his father's theological acumen, could find anything to say. It was like a world was suddenly opening up before us, one that we had no right to enter but were hospitably welcomed into, where the body and the spirit both are celebrated as gifts from the Creator, and together they can become instruments of healed healing. No one knew—except perhaps Mr. Windsor, but he only theoretically—and I myself have only learned it since, through many hard trials and false starts—that this truth had been there in our faith all along, that the body and the spirit both are indeed gifts from the Creator (otherwise why would he have taken on flesh?) and only together can either be instruments of healing. But none of us could have said so that night, at seventeen. The best we could do was to stand there silently and watch the dance, deeply aware that we were standing on the threshold of a great grace, and as clumsy in our awe as we would have been had we tried to join in.

The moment was not to last, though—such moments seldom do—and toward the end of the night, as the last dance approached, Autumn and Star slowly realized that they were at the centre of the room and intently being watched. There was a moment of silence while the final song of the night was being cued, and the silence grew palpable, as everyone became aware that everyone else's attention was fixed on these two girls.

Autumn was a bit short of breath, but Star found the words. "This dance," she said, "is a healing dance. We used to dance it at powwows."

It wasn't clear at that moment if she had given some cue to the person at the sound system or if it was simply a coincidence, but whatever the case, the final song of the night suddenly started. And if Mrs. White had personally chosen the tune, it couldn't have been better suited, because at that moment the Hallelujah Chorus of Handel's Messiah roared out over the gymnasium. And the last dance began.

Autumn and Star began soaring once more, inaccessible to all of us and awe-inspiring to most, and then in the very next moment, completely forgotten by everyone.

Because right at that spot in the song where the choir belts it out, how the Lord God Omnipotent reigneth, two teens who had made themselves ill on Emily's stepdad's homemade wine slipped coming down the stairs of the mezzanine and got sick again trying to right themselves, sending up a squeal of disgust from those closest to the mess. At the same time, a garbage can up on the mezzanine that had been smoldering unnoticed for hours suddenly burst into flames— we found out later that Emily and her friends had stuffed their cigarettes into it in a panic when one of the chaperones had happened by and almost caught them smoking—and the brilliant orange flame leaped up suddenly like the wings of a hundred burning seraphim.

That's how it seemed in the ensuing chaos, at least, because the fire set off the alarm. It was an old-fashioned hammer-and-bell type fire alarm, and it started blaring deafeningly over the gym. No one thinks the DJ intentionally turned up the music to be heard over all that blare; more likely he was at the controls when the alarm sounded, and as he leaped into action, he probably just bumped the volume slider up as loud as it would go, accidentally. Regardless the reason, however, suddenly the sound of a thousand human voices declaring the truth that He shall reign forever and ever began thundering like the end of days over the alarm.

And at that very moment came the flood. The alarm had activated the school's archaic sprinkler system, and it sprang to life, raining down a shower of water over the whole assembly. The inquiry that the board of directors conducted in the aftermath of the dance concluded that the administration had been negligently lax in keeping up with regular inspections of the fire sprinklers, but for all of us there that night, this sort of went without saying. Because right at the crescendo of the song, as the music was swelling to that final, glorious *Hall-e-lu-jah*! and the whole student body was scurrying about in utter pandemonium, suddenly, six or seven of the sprinkler heads burst off their fittings beneath the pressure of the water, and the shower became a downpour.

In a matter of seconds, the gym floor was pooling everywhere with water, and every student in the place was looking for all the world as though they ought to have worn swimwear to the dance after all, they were so sopping wet. Except for—and I was there, so I can confirm this was the case, though the commotion in that moment was so great that no one can be quite sure of anything—but even so I will swear to my dying day that this is true—there was a spot in the centre of the gym where the sprinklers inexplicably had not started up, and even when the other sprinkler heads had burst, this one spot had stayed mysteriously, miraculously dry.

And there in that spot at the centre of the room, perfectly dry and oblivious, it seemed, to the chaos all around them, Autumn and Star Cardinal finished their healing dance, entirely removed from this world of rain and fire and thunder and flood—or perhaps more a part of it than anyone there could ever know.

12.

The Paper Crane

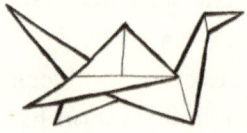

Evelyn might not have met the old man except that she was running late for work that morning and had to cut through the park to make it to her bus stop on time. Even though this route shaved a full eight minutes off her walk, she almost never took it. She preferred the chaos of the city streets in the morning—the roar of garbage trucks, the jostling of taxi cabs, the general pandemonium of everyone getting to where they had to be before eight a.m. It was why she had moved downtown in the first place. Something about the stillness of the city park, its serenity and its verdure, left her vaguely unsettled, so she usually took the long way around.

It had been so long since she'd cut through the park, in fact, that she'd underestimated how much time it would save her. As it turned out she had nearly five minutes to spare when she reached her stop. There was a bench set among some unkempt willows near a straggling inlet of the park's duck pond, hemmed in by a stand of cattails on one side and a low stone wall on the other. She had only come to the bus stop from this direction a few times before, so it didn't especially surprise her that she'd never noticed this bench till now.

What did surprise her—though she couldn't exactly say why—was the old man sitting there by himself. She'd certainly never seen anyone at this stop so early on a Monday morning before, though again, she didn't usually come from this direction. And there was nothing especially remarkable about his appearance, unless it was the strange air of tranquility that seemed to hang about him. His attention was fully absorbed with something mysterious in his lap, too, though this was more curious than surprising.

She had time to spare, however, so she lingered to see what he was working at so intently. He became aware of her almost instantly and looked up from his lap. He had the thinnest whisp of a white beard, and deep-set, almond-shaped eyes that narrowed when he smiled at her. Almost as if he understood her curiosity, he nodded quietly and motioned with his chin to the mystery he held in busy hands on his knee.

It was a paper crane, or at least a square of coloured paper in the final steps of becoming one.

The wizened fingers worked deftly at the folds, turning and creasing and pulling and pressing. Evelyn had the unexpected memory of an origami unit from a grade school art class flash across her mind. She had done very poorly in that unit, though she had learned to fold a passable paper crane before it was through.

This old man's crane, however, was a much more intricate design than any she had done as a child, and his fingers moved with such ease that she found herself mesmerized to watch him. The crane looked as if it were finished, at least the wings were fully spread and the neck gracefully extended, when he lifted it unexpectedly to his lips and breathed a puff of breath into the centre of its flat origami body, gently but surely. The whole paper form puffed out and took full shape.

Then he fixed his dark eyes on Evelyn with another silent smile and lifted a finger—either to ask her to wait, or to hush, she could not tell which. He rose from his bench and moved to the edge of the pond, kneeling among the cattails. Without a word, he placed the paper crane in the water and pushed it gently adrift. Then, still smiling, he returned to his spot on the bench.

He nodded at her again.

"I used to make paper cranes when I was a kid," Evelyn began, but the man lifted his finger again and she knew this time for sure what it meant. She fell silent.

The paper crane had just drifted out of sight behind the cattails, the little ripple of its wake falling still on the surface of the water, when two things happened simultaneously. Behind her on the street her bus arrived with a cacophonous cough of its airbrakes. Evelyn was so absorbed by the old man's origami that the noise startled her greatly.

And at just that moment, gloriously—and all the more glorious for being so unexpected—a beautiful blue heron stepped out from among the cattails, wading through the water on delicate legs. With a sudden flourish, it fully spread its wings and gracefully extended its neck, and then it folded itself up again, tucking its head low against its body the way herons do, and staring impassively at her with its bright black eye.

Evelyn was too startled by the arrival her the bus to absorb it, how rare it was to see a blue heron in the city, though once, long ago, they had been far more common.

"Oh," she said, feeling a strange urge to apologize. "I'm sorry. That's my bus."

The man said nothing, but he nodded faintly as she turned to go.

That day at work, Evelyn tried to stay focused on the site plans for the new subdivision her firm was developing, but somehow her mind kept wandering back to that wizened old man and his beautiful origami crane. The fact that she was so new to this job made it all the harder to concentrate—there was so much she didn't understand yet about the work—but this was her first real job as a civil engineer, and she couldn't afford to screw it up.

And yet she couldn't get her mind off it. What were the chances that a real blue heron would happen along at just that moment? And that tranquil smile of his when it did: had he been expecting it to appear?

Evelyn took the long way home from the bus stop that night, west along Central and south down Riverside.

The next morning, she took longer than she usually did over her coffee, though she couldn't have said if this was entirely accidental, or if it was her unshakeable sense of curiosity that made her linger. Whatever the reason, she ended up leaving the apartment so late that the only way to make the bus was to cut through the park again.

For the whole of her walk, she fully expected no one to be there, but when the path came at last around the duck pond and down along the overgrown stand of cattails, she saw him, a serene old man moving earnest hands deftly over a square of paper in his lap.

She was strangely relieved.

He looked up. His smile was different this time, as though he had been waiting for her. He nodded again and held up his finger to forestall anything she might offer by way of greeting. He nodded toward a patch of grass a few feet from the bench. There were five grey pigeons there, fussing about for something to eat.

The man turned his attention back to his origami, and when Evelyn looked, she saw that he was folding a delicate paper bird, something like a sparrow maybe, though it might indeed have been a pigeon. It was considerably rounder than yesterday's crane. Its wings were swept back, and it had the most finely folded paper beak Evelyn could have imagined. When it was done, the man held it to his lips, as he had done the crane, and puffed, causing the body to fill and the wings to stand out as if it were about to take flight.

"Watch," he said, and it was the first time he'd spoken to her. He reached into his pocket and pulled out a bit of dry bread, breaking it into crumbs and tucking them into the folds and crannies of his beautifully-folded bird.

Very carefully he slipped from the bench toward the flock of pigeons, getting as close as he thought they'd dare to let him. They must have been quite used to people, because this was remarkably close. He set his origami pigeon down and crept back to the bench.

As soon as he was seated, the pigeons seemed to have noticed the paper bird for the first time. They descended on it together, rushing to be the first to get the breadcrumbs it contained. With a whorl of wings and a cacophony of cooing, all five pigeons jostled eagerly with each other, pecking furiously at the origami offering. It didn't seem to Evelyn that they were fighting, but still there was such a chaos of feathers that it was hard to make out what happened next.

Because all at once the pigeons scattered, swishing their wings out over the duck pond in a panic. It was so sudden that they left Evelyn somewhat startled in their wake. The paper bird was gone—the pigeons must have pecked it to bits for its breadcrumbs—but there was something more startling still. Evelyn figured she must have miscounted, because there, all alone where the flock of pigeons had been squabbling together a second earlier, sat a single white pigeon that she hadn't noticed originally among the others.

Evelyn turned to the old man, who seemed to be chuckling to himself.

"Where did—?" She began, but again, the gasp of airbrakes interrupted her, announcing the arrival of her bus.

That day at work, the mystery of the white pigeon was even more distracting than the paper crane had been the day before. At some point someone came by and told her that the survey for the development was ready, and she could begin working on the grading. She got started on this somewhat mechanically. There was a drainage slough on the site that would have to be filled, and storm sewers were needed to handle the runoff. She made these notes as she went, but the whole while the mystery of the old man and his origami bird haunted her.

The next morning was a Wednesday, and she left the house a full twenty minutes early, arriving in time to see the old man putting the finishing touches on a stunning origami fish. It was not the simple triangular thing they had taught her to make in grade school, either, but a fully formed catfish, with serrated fins and intricate scales, a drooping, lifelike mouth and two delicate whiskers.

"It's beautiful," she said.

"Namazu," he said, with a wry smile, his dark eyes twinkling.

"Namazu?" she repeated.

"Yes," he said. "Namazu. Now watch."

He crept from the bench to the water's edge, and this time he motioned for Evelyn to join him. She knelt beside him, ignoring the soiled print it left on the knees of her slacks.

The man did not breathe into the paper fish this time, but he placed it into the water and blew gently, causing ripples all around, so that the namazu took on water faster than it otherwise might have. Evelyn was taken aback at how quickly it grew heavy and sank.

"Why work so hard on something so beautiful," she said, "only to throw it away like that?"

The old man lifted his patient finger. "Watch."

In a moment—and it shouldn't have surprised Evelyn by now, but still it did—a large, lethargic catfish nosed its way to the surface, a little way from where the origami fish had sunk, but close enough that Evelyn's jaw fell open.

"Did—" she stammered. "Is that the—?"

The old man's smile deepened as he turned dancing eyes toward her. "Namazu," he said.

The roar of the bus, arriving as usual at the bus stop behind them, roused the catfish from its stupor. Its tail slapped the water suddenly and it disappeared with a plop.

"Your bus," said the old man.

"Yes," said Evelyn. "My bus."

Thursday morning Evelyn left her apartment in time to find the old man folding the third of three finely detailed origami mice from a square of grey paper. The underside of the paper was white, so that when he turned the belly of the folded animal up, it showed soft and bright like any real mouse's belly might.

The other two mice he had already placed in the grass near the bench. She could see their pointed paper noses peeking up through the green.

"Nezumi," said the man gently, looking up briefly from his work. His fingers kept moving, folding and turning and smoothing down the edges, and when he looked back to the paper in his lap, it seemed to her that his breathing rose and fell in time with his hands, as if each crease was a breath.

For such a small figure, the origami mouse was one of the most intricate creatures she'd yet seen him make, with perfectly formed paws and delicate ears. When at last it was finished, he held it up in the palm of his hand with a benevolent grin.

Evelyn looked down to where its two brothers had been set, and this time she was not at all surprised to see that the paper mice were gone and in their place were two soft, warm, live grey mice, nosing the grass at the foot of the bench and altogether unalarmed to be so close to the old man's feet.

"See?" he said, nodding gently in their direction. "Nezumi."

He reached down very slowly and placed the origami animal next to the two live mice. Evelyn had no doubt that if she watched closely, it would only be a matter of seconds before there was a third live mouse scuffling about with the other two.

She had no time to see it happen, though, because at just that moment the roar of a diesel engine announced the arrival of her bus, and she had to turn away.

That day at work she lingered for a long time over the grading designs for the new subdivision her firm was developing. She had only recently signed on with Eden Group, and this was the first real project they'd given her free reign on. The last thing she wanted to do was to botch it, but every time she laid out a new lot on the site plan, the image of that third paper nezumi kept coming to mind, and with it the namazu, and of course, that gloriously unexpected blue heron.

She must have been some time sitting there and staring idly at the screen, because all of a sudden Adams was standing over her desk, looking down with a frown. Adams was the head of her department, and even though Evelyn was new at Eden, she was quite familiar with his reputation for impatience.

"How're those drawings coming?" he asked.

Evelyn tried to disguise her distractedness with a bustle of activity. She leaned toward her computer screen and started opening and closing windows with a great show of purpose.

"Coming along," she said, not looking up from the screen.

"Can you have them by tomorrow afternoon? They're already a day behind."

"I can. Sure. That's no problem."

Adams watched her click a few more random windows, then turned to go.

"I was thinking though," said Evelyn suddenly.

Adams turned back.

"There's no green space," she said, glancing up at him for the first time. "Have you noticed? It's all monstrous condominiums with no yards to speak of. I was thinking maybe we could redesign a bit and leave some of this green space in the centre, turn this drainage slough into more of a pond. No need to bulldoze everything, is there?" As soon as she'd voiced the suggestion she turned away timidly, back to clicking pointlessly on her computer screen.

Adams sighed, though she couldn't tell if it was in thoughtfulness or exasperation.

"We've been over this, Ev," he said. "Condos sell, and green space costs. The developers aren't interested in green space, and most homeowners don't want it. And anyways, a strip of land like that, in the centre of the city? There's barely room to put what we're trying to put in there, let alone adding green space."

Evelyn nodded without looking up.

"Look: do the grading for the plans as is. And have it ready by tomorrow, or I'll give it to someone who can get it done."

Adams left without another word, but long after he was gone, Evelyn continued to open and close windows randomly, staring blindly at the screen, with the haunting image of a beautiful blue heron burning in her brain.

The next morning, she left the apartment with enough time to take her old route to the bus stop, north along Riverside and east down Central. She timed it very carefully, so as to arrive at the stop just as the bus was pulling up. She had to run, actually, to reach it before it closed its doors, so she couldn't spare even a second to look over her shoulder in the direction of the bench, to see what the old man was creating for that day.

She had to get those drawings done, she told herself as she settled into her seat, and she'd be utterly useless today if she had another encounter with him.

In the end, the grading took far longer than she had expected. It was past five o'clock before the oversized Teriostar printer spat out her grading plans. She spread the paper on a drafting table and looked at them for a long time, inspecting every line and thinking more deeply than she had in ages.

The slough was gone. In its place was an elaborate system of storm sewers, routing the water away. It was actually a very elegant solution to the flooding problem that area was prone to, and she knew Adams would be happy with it. She should have been proud.

Even so, she couldn't shake the memory of that blue heron—or the white pigeon, the three grey mice, the languid catfish—the old man and his gentle nod, his mysterious smile, his warm breath.

She rolled up the drawings to turn them in on Adams' desk, and with every bend of her wrist she felt she was rolling a heavy tombstone into place.

The next day was Saturday, and Evelyn slept in far later than she usually did. Even when she woke, she lay in bed for a long time, staring blankly at the ceiling and thinking about the old man. She had a great urge to go down to the park and see if he was there, but she knew she could never bring herself to do it.

When lying alone in bed became unbearable, she finally sat up in a bit of a flurry, flung the bedclothes aside and stalked out to the kitchen of her tiny apartment.

She hunted through a drawer where she kept odds and ends until she found a writing pad. It was one of the custom notepads that Eden Group had printed as promotional material, and Evelyn had brought one home the day she'd been hired, as a sort of memento of her first job.

She tore out a page and set to work, trying as best she could to remember the steps from her childhood: first fold the square in half, diagonally, then turn and fold along the other diagonal. Bring in the two side corners to meet the corner pointed toward you. And on it went.

The paper crane was pathetically lopsided when she finally finished it, but she was surprised at how quickly her fingers remembered the steps. She tore out another page and tried again.

Three or four paper cranes later, she could almost imagine one or two of them bursting to life and stepping into her living room on real, delicate legs and folding open their wings with a flutter, like the heron in the park had done.

Of course, her cranes were laughably facile compared to the intricate art she had seen the old man produce. She reached for her laptop and searched up other origami patterns.

She was almost alarmed to discover how many different paper animals there were: frogs and fishes, birds and rodents, foxes, bears, dragons and deer. She tried one or two of them, but quickly found herself swimming in a sea of mountain folds and rabbit's ears that was far beyond her depth. She did manage a passable mouse, in the end, but it was much too mangled to ever suppose it might actually start scurrying about the green grass, alive with curiosity.

By the time the Eden Group notepad was spent, evening had come, and Evelyn went to bed, emotionally exhausted. The floor of her apartment was littered with crumpled balls and aborted attempts at paper animals.

She set out for the park early the next morning, while the first groggy light of dawn was still breaking over the city. It was a Sunday, and the streets were still sleeping off the week that had been. No garbage trucks roared; no taxi cabs jostled. No one stirred, and no one bustled. She had little hope of finding him so early in the morning, but she made her way to his bench, nonetheless.

She had never noticed the park thriving with life the way it did this bleary-eyed Sunday morning. A flock of pigeons muttered bemusedly at her, huddling together by the side of the path as she passed. Overhead two squirrels bickered furiously for squatting rights to the gracefully-arched limb of an ancient elm tree.

A fish plopped contentedly out in the water of the duck pond, though it occurred to her for the very first time to wonder how a fish could manage in such a small bit of water—it was really little more than a drainage slough.

She breathed deeply and wondered if the air had ever tasted so soft and verdant as it did in that moment.

The bench was empty, of course. The drooping tendrils of the weeping willows seemed to drift dreamily about it, and Evelyn was tempted to wonder if he had ever really been there at all.

Just then, however, a soft sound came from the water behind her. She turned and saw a glorious blue heron stepping out from the cattails. It reached with its elegant neck, cocking its head and opening its wings, testing the air once or twice with a great sweep of its feathers. Then, with the faintest splash and an even fainter whisper of wings, it rose from the water.

Evelyn watched as it lifted itself through the trees, following it breathlessly for as long as she could. Every reach of its wings seemed to wring a drop of blood from her heart, and when it was finally out of sight, she felt a great, creaking emptiness yawn inside her.

She walked home along Central, and as she turned south on Riverside, she noticed for the first time a billboard that had been erected at the corner of the park, facing out toward the street. It must have gone up Friday, she thought, and though she couldn't bring herself to look at it, she knew exactly what it said:

Future Home of Parkland Condominiums
Luxury Living in the Heart of the City
Designed by Eden Group Developments

13.

All is Bright

How it possibly could have come down to this was still beyond Nathan's ability to explain. He swore every year that things would be different, swore that he'd do it right next year, start sooner, plan better.

He swore.

Literally, he swore, as an oncoming car jerked in front of him and lurched into the parking spot he'd been aiming for. As he rolled past the holiday motorist who'd just stolen that prime piece of real estate out from under his nose, he muttered ominously under his breath about decking somebody's halls.

Looking in vain for a new place to park that was still within trekking distance of the Walmart entrance, he came to rest at last at the furthest corner of the lot. Flinging his scarf over his shoulder with all the bravado of a WWI pilot, he stepped out into the blinding blizzard.

It would have been lovely, really—haloes of coloured Christmas lights shimmering just barely through the thick white haze—lovely, if it weren't December 24th.

It would have been breathtakingly beautiful—pure drifting sheets of silent snow—beautiful, if it weren't 10:39 pm.

It would have been picturesque, even, if he wasn't a last-minute Christmas shopper on his way to Walmart, of all places, on Christmas Eve; Walmart, because they were now open until midnight on this Most Wonderful Night of the Year.

So he squinted into the blinding white wind and swore: things would be different next year.

By the time he reached the doors, the blizzard had piled a good couple of centimeters on his shoulders—the dandruff of heaven, he might have mused, if his mission hadn't cleared all fanciful sentiments from his heart and replaced them with one single, clear purpose, burning like a Christmas candle in the window of his soul. He had to find the perfect gift. At 10:42 p.m., Christmas Eve.

He'd need some wrapping paper, too, he noted as he pushed his way through the bottle neck of beleaguered boyfriends, desperate dads and harried husbands who, like himself, had left this one male shopping duty of the year to the last possible moment, and were now muttering ominously under their breath about showing *them* who's naughty and who's nice.

He stumbled past the happy-faced badge on the chest of the sad-faced greeter at the door and squinted at last in the florescent glare of the store.

A robotic Santa Claus boomed a metallic "Ho! Ho! Ho!" at him, from a display of last-minute Christmas decorations. The vaguely evil undertones of this animatronic belly laugh mingled with a vaguely threatening rendition of "Santa Claus is Coming to Town," pouring down from invisible speakers somewhere overhead. For just a moment, the Christmas candle in his soul flickered, allowing him the briefest of whimsical thoughts. He remembered sitting in church with his buddy Eddie, during a Christmas Eve service they were ignoring as kids, and Eddie had showed him how you could rearrange the letters in the name Santa to spell "Satan." He had even written it out on the back of the bulletin while they both giggled under their breath.

Nathan squinted suspiciously at the robotic Santa. "Ho. Ho. Ho."

But then his mission was burning in him with full flame again, and he pushed past Santa on his way toward the perfume-baubles-and-other-things-generally-romantic section of the store. Surely if the perfect gift existed, it lay to rest under those gleaming posters of radiant young women in jewelry or makeup, photos hung like so many summoning angels over the respective products they announced.

Nathan shuffled his way toward them.

Before he reached the place over which these posters shone, however, a frantic looking dad had knocked him sideways, on his eleventh-hour mission to get the last Holiday Barbie in the store. A man with a dull gleam in his eye jostled him to the right, pushing past him on his way to the pet supplies because, Nathan could only assume, little Fido had asked for a box of liver Puppie-Yums for Christmas, and they'd accidentally bought chicken.

By this time, however, the perfume section itself was but a faint legend from the distant past, like stories about frankincense and myrrh washing up on the shores of Christmases gone by, and he found himself standing instead in the electronics section, of all places, trying to convince himself that nothing said Merry Christmas like a spool of re-writable CDs made in China.

In the distance he could hear Robo-Santa laughing at him. The florescent lights battered him mercilessly.

"You'd better watch out…"

Maybe if he threw in a gift card for iTunes?

"Ho. Ho. Ho."

The two centimeters of snow had soaked through his coat now and had begun to trickle, like cold regret down his spine.

"You'd better not pout; I'm telling you why."

The WWI flying ace scarf sagged as his shoulders drooped. He turned to go.

And then, if Nathan's life had a soundtrack, the noise of a record needle scratching abruptly on vinyl would have blurted out suddenly, strangling the Walmart muzak to silence. The Ho! Ho! Ho! would have dullened to a slow, echoing pulse, like an anxious heartbeat. And choral music—the angelic humming of children, maybe, or silvery seraph song—would have begun softly, swelling into a single, throbbing "Ahhh!" that drowned out all else.

Because there it was: the perfect gift. She'd asked for it every day of the last 364. In one way or another she'd been asking for it maybe all her life. Not with words, of course—never in any audible speech—but with every gesture. That slight tilt of her head when she said, "You know what I wish?" That faint droop at the corner of her mouth when she said, "You know what I hate?" That soft sigh that escaped her when she flumped in front of the TV after a hard day at work.

All of it—everything—had really been about this: this glorious gift, this perfect present. The candle in his soul burned with white hot light as he reached for it.

And then the lights went out.

The store plunged into instant darkness. A miraculous darkness, he would later learn, because the blizzard that had been piling snow on the power lines all day knocked out Walmart's backup generator, just at the exact moment the wind finally brought down the power poles, and, with a sudden flash at the fuse box that stank worse than a Radio Shack on fire, it plunged the whole world of Walmart into pitch and utter night.

Nathan stood there, frozen in darkness, his hand still reaching for that now invisible, perfect gift.

And in the dark, whimsical thoughts rushed at last through his mind. He saw visions of Pompeii caught in the ash of Vesuvius, frozen forever in the everyday act of buying and selling and giving in marriage, until the bitter end. In the black distance, Robo-Santa's laugh ground down to silence, and he thought of air escaping a long-discarded accordion.

"Ho.... ho.... o..."

For a surprisingly long moment nothing happened, the dark was so thick. And more miracles: no one cried out, no one shouted, no one said anything at all for just a moment. You could feel them all, that hot press of humanity, still and silent, but close. And no one dared to move.

And then somehow more whimsical thoughts rushed at Nathan in the dark. He remembered snippets of those stories in church that he and Eddie had giggled their way through—stories about a little child who broke into the brilliant chaos of this world with a light no one could see—and about some who could see it, but could barely recognize it as light, because it hurt their eyes.

He remembered vaguely about an old man up at the front who'd said something about how this child had come to upset the status quo, to turn things on their heads, to name our darkness for what it is.

And give us real light.

And he remembered lighting a candle—quite vividly, this—while a chorus of rusty singing voices lunged for the top note in Silent Night.

Holy night.

All is calm.

All is bright.

And in the darkness his hand fell to his side with heavenly peace.

Of course, because it was Walmart, of all places, on Christmas Eve, someone in a back room fired up the backup, backup generator. Florescent light blared out over the store once more, and the cogs of the machine started to move again.

But Nathan was already on his way to the door. As he stumbled outside, into the halos of coloured lights that shimmered just barely through the thick white haze, he checked his watch. It was almost midnight.

14.

Kangaroo Care

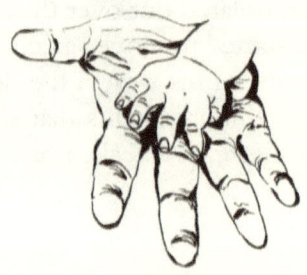

We all agreed that they were in over their heads. It wasn't our place to say, of course, and everyone was working hard at staying professional, but the rumor among the nightshift nurses was that she was barely holding things together, and he didn't have the foggiest idea how to handle the situation.

This isn't uncommon, at least not in a neonatal unit like ours. But what made this couple stand out was the kid's earnest, if fumbling effort to get it right. More often than not, the dad's the problem in situations like theirs, abandoning the mom, or neglecting her, or worse. We've had plenty of deadbeats we've had to call security on, one even that had to be hauled out by hand.

But this guy was different. He was barely past boyhood for one thing, far too young to be a dad. And there was a kind of timid tenderness about him, like a frightened baby chick, that made us all want to take him under our collective wings. Esther had been working the dayshift when their baby came wailing into the world, and she saw the whole thing. She said the mom wasn't much older than him, but she was falling apart with fear and pain, and more than once the boy was used as a sponge for her emotional spills. Her labor had been dreadful, mind you, dreadful enough that the doctor wanted her to stay in the hospital an extra week or so to recover. So it might be understandable that she was miserable, but the boy was so compliant through it all that you couldn't help but root for him, however ill-equipped he seemed for the job. Those are Esther's words, mind you, but it's saying a lot. Esther was the one who'd called security on the troublemaker and had him dragged out in handcuffs, and rooting for the dad didn't come naturally to her.

The boy's name was Isaiah, though his girlfriend called him Izzy. After we'd got to know him a bit, we took to calling him that too, and he didn't seem to mind.

Their baby wasn't named yet. She was only a bit premature, but she had some alarming irregularities in her heartbeat and the worst cholic any of us had seen. She was dangerously underweight, too. The notes on her chart said that she was suffering from NAS, and though everyone was working hard at staying professional, it was hard not to jump to conclusions.

None of us will ever forget the day he showed up in the NICU, though, and not just because of how the whole thing turned out for the three of them.

He was just getting off work. He worked the nightshift, cleaning an office building downtown, so it was just past four in the morning when he finally got there, dressed shabby and worn thin. His girlfriend was still asleep, and he didn't want to wake her, so he'd come directly down to the neonatal unit. That baby chick look in his eye was so pathetic that you almost wondered if he might give a terrified little peep at some point. He lingered by the nurse's station nervously, wringing a toque in his hands and waiting for someone to notice him.

It was a slow week on the unit. There was only one other baby in the nursery, a relatively healthy little soul who, like Izzy's baby, had been born a bit too early. She was almost as underweight as Izzy's girl, too, though she had no other issues. She might not even have been in the NICU, except that her mother had abandoned her and there was no father to speak of. Really, we were just helping her put on some weight while the powers that be decided what to do with her. So it was a slow night, but even at that it took a long time for anyone to notice him.

It was Gail who finally looked up from her screen and asked if she could help him.

"I'm here to see my baby," he said nervously. He nodded in the direction of the neonatal cribette. "I think that's her over there. The doctor said she was born underweight." He trailed off a moment, and then, as an afterthought: "She's not named yet, but I'm the dad."

Gail's own husband had walked out on her not long after the birth of her first, so she was always cautious around the dads. She eyed him coldly for a second, but the frightened baby chick in his eyes cowered so timidly that she softened in spite of herself, like a brooding hen opening her wing.

"Come on," she said. "I'll show you."

We've seen lots of parents meeting their babies for the first time, but looking back, all of us agreed that something especially beautiful happened when Izzy met that little bundle of heartache that day. A slow light dawned in his face, for one thing, like a frail but determined sunrise on the foggiest of fall mornings. And the sigh that escaped him was the purest mixture of yearning and fear you could imagine. He even raised a hand to his lips, in a gesture that would have seemed premeditated if it wasn't so gentle and tentative. One of us said that seeing him peer over the railing of the cribette like that made you think of a child peering into a well, trying to catch a glimpse of his own face peering back up at him.

He looked at Gail hesitantly, who was watching him with a strange grin on her face.

"Is it okay if I—can I—" Something somewhere between fear and shame kept him from finishing the sentence.

"You want to hold her?"

He nodded.

"Sanitize your hands," Gail said, nodding in the direction of a dispenser, "and put on one of those gowns. I'll get her ready for you."

He did as he was told, and a few seconds later Gail was placing into his arms the smallest, tenderest living thing he'd probably ever held. If Gail had given him a soap bubble to hold, he couldn't have handled it more carefully. Another sigh escaped him, and this one almost did sound like a chick's peep. When he looked up from gazing into that wrinkled face, there were hot tears in his eyes.

"She feels safe," said Gail softly.

"Yeah?" One of his tears found its way down his cheek.

"Just look how quiet she got. She's been fussing all night, but as soon as I put her in your arms, she nestled right in. You can tell. She feels safe." It was mostly true, too. The baby did seem uncannily at ease in the arms of her boy-dad, though Gail was clearly playing it up a bit, to put the frightened chick in him at ease.

A weak smile passed over his face, and he moved to give the baby to Gail again.

"You'd better put her back," he said. "I don't want to hurt her. And anyway, I can't stay long."

Gail placed the baby gently back in the cribette. "You can come back anytime," she said. "You won't hurt her at all, and you'll probably do her a lot of good. Babies need their daddies." Gail probably didn't mean that last part to sound as recriminating as it did, but we all knew she was saying it from a place of experience.

He did come back the next night, though. It was after his shift at work again, sometime around four in the morning. We all remembered him from the night before, and perhaps because we were so much warmer toward him, he seemed less nervous.

But only slightly so. The tears still appeared when we put the baby into his arms, and he still handled her as though she might disintegrate in the slightest breeze. He needn't have, though. It was obvious this time that what Gail had said the day before was true. The baby felt safe in this boy's arms, falling still and peaceful in a way she hadn't been all night.

"Her mom's not doing well," he said in a whisper, after a long moment staring into that placid newborn face. He stroked the forehead gently with two fingers and even clucked his tongue instinctively.

"She was struggling a bit even before this, but she's in a real rough way now. I think the doctor said she's got—what do you call it?—post-parental?"

Gail was watching him with the same strange grin as the day before.

"Do you mean postpartum?" she asked. We all worked nightshift, when Izzy's girlfriend was sleeping, so few of us had really met her. It was the day shift that would bring her down to the neonatal to spend time with her baby, or, on occasion, wheel the baby into her room. So none of us really knew if she was as gentle as Izzy was with this fledgling little life. Except for Esther, none of us had seen them together, and she'd been away on holidays since the birth. From the rumors we'd heard, though, we weren't surprised to learn that she was in a rough way.

"Well, she's lucky she has you," said Gail in a whisper. "They both are."

None of us can really remember who it was that first suggested he try doing some kangaroo care with the baby. It might have been Gail—she'd warmed up to him that much after a couple of visits—though it might have been me. I'd been thinking about the other little resident we had on our ward that week, the little abandoned preemie. No one ever came in to see her, and aside from us nurses, no one ever handled her. She didn't seem to be suffering too much from it, mind you—her only real concern was being so underweight—but it got me thinking about how important that kind of contact was.

"What's kangaroo care?" he asked when we brought it up.

"Skin-to-skin contact," Gail explained. An utterly terrified look flashed across his face, so vividly that Gail started laughing very softly.

"With the baby," she said. "You open your shirt and let the baby rest on your bare chest. It does wonders for both of you. Releases all kinds of healing hormones in your baby, helps her regulate her heartbeat. It's good for you too. Helps you bond."

He still looked terrified, so Gail added: "They've done studies. It's super helpful for babies in her situation especially."

He nodded and let Gail take the baby out of his arms. "I'm not wearing a shirt with buttons," he said.

"Just take off your sweatshirt. We can cover you with a nursing blanket."

He pulled the sweater over his head uncertainly while Gail undressed the baby. Someone pulled up a chair for him and he took a seat.

"Here you go," said Gail, as Izzy leaned back awkwardly and let her place the infant on his chest. The peace that washed over that little soul in that moment was so palpable that you might have thought we could feel it, too. The baby had been deeply unsettled all evening, aching and yearning the way only an NAS baby can, but the instant Gail placed its hot, soft skin against the boy's bare chest, it gave, for the first time since its coming into the world, a genuine, satisfied whimper.

Izzy still looked very awkward, but the same peace we were all feeling seemed to be working on him, too, and you could see his muscles relaxing. "They call this kangaroo care?" he said.

Gail nodded. All of us were trying to stay professional, but she raised her hand furtively and quickly wiped away a tear. "You're doing great," she said.

And it was mostly true. The skin-to-skin contact seemed to help him as much as it helped the baby, and over the next few days you could almost see the confidence growing in him. He started to share more and more of his story with us, as he sat there nestling the bare body of that little baby as close to his heart as he could: how he and his girlfriend had met in high school, and though he loved her, this pregnancy wasn't anything either of them had expected, and it had thrown them both for a loop; how he'd had to drop out of school and take that lousy job; how he didn't really know how it was going to work, but he was determined to do whatever it took.

When I was in nursing school, they taught me that kangaroo care can help a preemie regulate its heartbeat, but there was one evening, listening to Izzy talk, that it occurred to me it may have the same effect on the caregiver. At any rate, I kept in touch with Izzy for a bit after they left the hospital, so I know how he went on to make good on his word. Despite the obstacles that came, he saw it through, and his own dear baby girl never lacked for a whole-hearted father.

One night, Gail told us, when it was just her at the station and just him in the nursery, she could hear him whispering a soft promise over the head of his precious child: "Wherever you go, I promise my love will always go with you..."

It was something like that, anyway. This happened more than once over the next three nights.

And no one ever told him, but that baby probably never would have made it except that he came in, every night, right around four, and opened his heart to her little newborn life, placing his skin gently against hers and letting her draw warmth from him. We knew, of course, because we could see in the chart notes how her weight increased, and her cholic faded, how her heartbeat stabilized, and the rhythms of her life grew steady. But it wasn't our place to tell him all that, especially not after what happened to them, in the end.

Because the day came at last when his girlfriend was well enough to go home, and his baby's grip on life was strong enough that she could join them. They were all going to be discharged late in the morning, but we had grown so fond of Izzy that a few of us had swapped with the dayshift just so we could be there to see him off.

Gail had even got him one of those shiny foil congratulations balloons and passed around a card for us to sign. She was holding it happily when he arrived to get their baby. He wheeled his girlfriend into the neonatal ward with the proudest grin we'd ever seen on his face. For her part, Izzy's girlfriend seemed far less miserable than any of the rumors had led us to believe, though perhaps the change we'd seen in Izzy over the last week had touched her too. She did seem weary, of course, and not nearly so confident as he was.

He left the wheelchair at the nurse's station and went into the nursery to get their little bundle of joy. The place was quite familiar to him by now, and though Gail helped him pick the baby up, he was hardly nervous anymore, to cradle her in his arms.

He walked back to his girlfriend. "And here she is!" he said triumphantly, a week's worth of kangaroo care buoying up his confidence as a new dad.

Izzy's girlfriend had been watching him closely the whole time. She looked at him oddly when he held their daughter out to her, folding her brow into a quizzical furrow.

"Izzy?" she said. "That's not our baby."

Izzy stared at her blankly.

Gail's hand sprang to her mouth, as if suddenly realizing something she should have known all along.

"What are you talking about?" Izzy said. "Of course she's ours!" He was blustering incredulously, but some inexorable knowledge was rising up in him. "Of course she is. I've been with her every night this week." He looked anxiously to us for help.

"Izzy," she said again. "I know our baby. They've been bringing her to me every morning to feed." There was a warm note in her voice, but it was also strangely calm, and all the more strange for the rumors we'd heard about her postpartum. Looking back, I even wonder if a little laugh didn't escape her.

"I know our baby," she said, "and that's *not her.*" She nodded with her chin over Izzy's shoulder, to where the second neonatal cribette was standing, our second ward on the NICU that week, the healthy but underweight preemie whom everyone assumed had been abandoned.

His eyes followed the motion, and an odd light dawned in his face. "You mean," he stammered. "All this time I was kangarooing with the wrong baby?"

"Kangarooing?" she repeated. "Izzy, have you been—"

It may be that the commotion had grown louder than any of us realized, or perhaps there was something at work in the NICU that morning that was bigger than any of us. Whatever the reason, at just that moment the second baby, Izzy's real daughter, squirmed lightly and then woke with a wail, the first wail we'd heard it make, as hearty a wail as any baby had ever made.

Realizing what had happened, Gail bustled forward and took the mistaken child from Izzy's arms, giving us all a sideways glance awash with mortification. "Izzy," she said softly, returning it to the cribette and picking up the other child. "I think your daughter needs you."

Izzy reached for the little bundle of life that Gail held out to him, and though he was quite dumbfounded, his hand was practiced as he took it in his arms. A sheepish grin dawned at the corners of his mouth. He tried at first to suppress it, but it spread quickly, until, for the first time since they had come to the hospital, the baby's mother and father together began to laugh.

15.

The King's Virgin

All that night the king had been uncontrollably cold. On previous nights when the shivering seized him, he would reach for me in the dark, drawing my body against his chest till he was warm and it had subsided. That night, however, he lay alone on the far side of the royal bed for a long time, shaking violently beneath the great mound of furs and throws they had heaped on him.

Whether because he would not, or because he could not, I do not know, but he did not reach for me.

Silver starlight fell in through an open casement, washing the bedchamber with a soft grey light. It was a gloriously bejeweled night, and a crescent moon as sharp as a khopesh hung low on the horizon.

I lay motionless for a long time, staring blindly at the ceiling, where the finely carved cedar beams joined unseen in the darkness. I could feel the tremors of his body beside me, but however well I knew my duty, I did not move.

The shadows of the room blurred as a mist of tears burned my eyes. Images long buried, of the day the king's officials had arrived in my village, rose unbidden in my mind. They were seeking the loveliest virgin in Israel, is how the rumor went, and so I ought to have been flattered they had chosen me, that my mother had adorned me and my father had presented me to them.

The body of our lord the king, they said, has grown cold. No amount of covering can console him, so we've been sent to find a maiden who can lie her beauty next to him and keep him warm throughout the night.

That had been back when the firstfruits of the field were just starting in.

Adonijah, the king's own son had led them. He had insisted that it was a great privilege for a village girl as lowly as I to be chosen for this task; he had insisted that my parents would gain in honor what they lost in a daughter; he had assured them that I need not come if I wished not to go—though he'd made it known in ways other than words that his will could not be resisted.

When he was done, the shame I would have carried had I refused left me no choice but to consent. And though he did not steal me away, still I cannot say I went willingly. But I came.

And here I was, months later, lying awake in the silver-laced shadows of the king's chamber, sensing him shiver in the bedclothes beside me and knowing I must lend him my warmth.

"Abishag," he said unsteadily.

I said nothing, and after a moment he repeated it. "Abishag."

I could not tell if he was calling to me or simply muttering in his sleep, but I blinked my eyes clear and shifted my body toward him. I reached beneath the pile of fur and cloth that covered him and found his flesh lifelessly cool. My palm felt hot against it, and he seemed to shake all the more as I touched him, as though a desert wind were passing through him.

"I'm here, my lord the king," I whispered at last, keeping my eyes averted lest they should meet his in the shadows. "Please come and be warmed."

He was shaking so violently that he could not move, so I shifted my body again and brought my bare form against him. I eased my left arm beneath his head and draped my right across his chest. It was still broad with a warrior's girth, but it felt alarmingly frail. He was colder than I had ever found him to be before, and I could feel the warmth passing palpably from me to him.

"See: the winter's past and over, and gone are the rains at last," I sang softly, more breathing out the tune than singing it. It was a lullaby my mother had once sung to me, and her mother to her. "Flowers break up from the earth and a season for song has come."

I sat up slightly against the pillows and cradled his head against my breast, pressing my lips gently against the hoary crown of it, the way I might have done had he been my newborn child and I his maiden mother.

"Arise my darling, my beautiful one," I sang. "Arise and come with me." His shivering had begun to still and I could feel his weight sink against me as his sleep returned. He groaned softly once or twice from the depths of a dream, but soon even that had passed and he was warm at last.

I knew what his groaning meant, or at least I could guess. One night early on in my time with him, a similar fit of cold had swept over him—the first really violent bout of shaking I had seen since coming to the palace—and he'd groaned in a similar way.

I was still new to him then, and he to me, and the honor of lying next to the LORD's Anointed was still sacred to me. So after I had soothed away his shivering with my body's warmth, I'd asked him what had caused him to groan so desperately.

"I was remembering the Philistine dead," he'd said after a long pause, his voice far colder than his flesh had been. "When Saul demanded a hundred Philistine foreskins as the bride-price for his daughter."

I'd heard the legends and knew the story well. "Saul has killed his thousands," is how they'd sung it in those days, "and David his tens of thousands."

I'd always known he was a man of blood and valor, but still it had given me chills to hear him tell the story like that, against the darkness of his chamber in the dead of a cloudless night.

"A hundred Philistine foreskins for Michal my first wife," he'd said in his faltering voice. "And I in my youthful arrogance brought him double, two hundred Philistine warriors slain."

With a quivering hand I'd reached and stroked his grey head softly. "Shhh," I whispered. "Please my lord the king… shhhh… and be at peace."

A few nights later, he woke with a sob and a start, clutching at my body like a drowning man reaching for something to keep him afloat. "Every two lengths!" he'd cried out that night. "Every two and spare each third!"

"My lord the king!" I said in alarm as he drew me almost violently against his shivering side. "Please my lord, be at peace."

"But you weren't there that day," he said when the chattering of his teeth had stilled, and he could speak at last. "After the conquest of Moab, we lay their warriors along the ground and measured them off with a cord. And though they pleaded with me for mercy, still I gave the word. Every two lengths—slaughter every two lengths of them and spare every third. Twenty thousand men fell by the sword that day at my command."

He'd buried his face in my hair that night, sobbing silently, though I could not tell if he was shaking with cold or wracked with grief.

"You are hearing things no peasant girl from Shunem ought to hear," a voice in that moment had whispered from the shadows at the edge of the room. I'd recognized it almost immediately as that of Adonijah, the king's son, and that was the first night I realized that he was given to watching his father while he slept. Or so I had assumed he was doing, standing unseen among the tapestries near the entrance of the bedchamber. His voice was placid, but there was a hunger in it that reminded me of the day he'd taken me from my village, and a cold chill passed over me.

"There will be secrets you must carry," he said. "Secrets you will encounter in this chamber that should not be yours to keep." And here he'd stepped from the shadows so I could see him fully for the first time. Even in the dim light, I recognized something menacing in the shape of his silhouette. "But keep them you must, Abishag. Remember Tamar? It would not do if they were known."

Adonijah had spoken truly; there were more secrets to come. And more than once after that the dead of night was shattered with the king's groaning, as some horrific memory wrenched us both from sleep. Sometimes when it happened I could feel Adonijah watching us from the shadows, though he never again made his presence known. Other times—and this more often as the days went by—we were alone in the room when the nightmares woke him.

On one such night, he'd woken trembling from a dream about Uriah and his wife.

"Gone," was all he'd been able to say as he quaked in the dark. "I told Joab to pull back in the heat of battle and abandon him at the wall. I had him murdered, Abishag, to hide my sin and take his wife as my own."

I cradled him to myself, shuddering with the horror of what I'd heard, for this secret was darker than any he'd cried out to me before. It crossed my mind to wonder if I was the only one who knew it, though when his groanings were quite gone and the room had grown still, I was sure I could hear the sound of stifled breathing, coming from among the tapestries.

That had been weeks ago, now, and there had been many such nights since, so I could guess what his groanings meant this night, tonight, as I lay in the soft starlight with his head sunk deeply against my side. I let my hair spill down to cover his cold shoulder and whispered soothingly over him, trying to warm him with my breath.

"Shhh, my lord the king. Shhh… and be at peace."

Even after I knew he was deeply asleep and sure not to wake, I sat there, propped up by the royal cushions. I held him to my bosom as I might have done had he been an infant, and indeed there was something childlike in the steady rhythm of his shallow breaths now that the cold had passed from him to me.

But I did not move. I could not. His head pressed me down, and I knew I'd wake him if I shifted my weight even slightly. I listened intently in the direction of the tapestries by the bedchamber's entrance, my ears gaping wide for any sign of breath or movement, but it was perfectly still. I held my breath and listened even more intently, until I knew that we were alone.

Then I exhaled and stared sightlessly at the ceiling.

"Saul has slain his thousands and David his tens of thousands," is how they'd celebrated his exploits so long ago. Even I had sung the words, back when I was a young girl in Shunem, though no one knew then how cold that life of slaughter would leave him.

"Seven sons of Saul," he murmured suddenly in his sleep. "Given over to the Gibeonites to be avenged."

Another strangled groan escaped him, though he did not wake. "To bring the famine to an end... put to death in the first days of the harvest... just as the barley was beginning."

I'd heard this story before. Three years of famine had decimated the land, and when the king had inquired of the LORD, they told him it had come on Saul's account, because of the Gibeonite blood that still stained his house. And so they'd slaughtered Saul's seven sons in vengeance, hanging their bodies on a hill to rot.

It was said that Rizpah, Saul's concubine and mother of the slain, had mourned their death in sackcloth and ashes, chasing the carrion birds away from the bodies till their bones were bleached and the rains poured down.

The king whimpered weakly in his sleep a final time and sank more deeply still against my skin.

I wondered for the first time about Rizpah, if her misery for her lost sons was at all like mine, and if David had shared it with her. They say that when he heard what she had done, David came and took the bones, burying them together in the tomb of Saul, their father.

I wondered if his bloodstained hands had stung him that day, and if they stung him still.

It even occurred to me to wonder if there might have been a different way for him to reign than all this spilled blood and agony. But I dared not.

For the first time since coming to the palace, I looked down on him tenderly—I only did so because I knew he was fully asleep and there was no chance our eyes might meet—and gazing on his pale, fading face, I pitied him for the first time, this frail man of blood and valor. With my pity came a surging desire for the justice that was said to be the foundation of his throne.

"My lord, the king," I said softly, when I was sure from his breathing that he'd sunk so deeply asleep that he would not hear. "I am your handmaid, and I lend you my warmth willingly, with all my heart." I hesitated, listening as intensely as I could, until I was fully satisfied that I heard nothing. "But my lord the king, I call on you for justice—if there is such a thing as justice still in Israel—because your son…"

I trailed off, knowing how futile it was, my confession, and too horrified to say the truth out loud. "He disgraced me," I whispered at last, and it was all I could manage, to put into words the secret I carried: that I was not, nor could I ever be, the virgin of the king.

"Adonijah has shamed me, my lord. Please do not let him shame me further when you are gone."

My voice trailed off. My heart was racing, roaring in my ears with the admission I had made, but I did my best to listen over the noise of it, to be sure we were still alone.

The king said nothing. The room was serenely still.

"O LORD," I prayed after a long moment, wiping unseen tears from my eyes. "O LORD, our Lord, have mercy."

I don't know how long we lay there, warming each other in the darkness, but suddenly, so suddenly that I gave a little gasp, he opened his eyes wide—startlingly wide—and sat rigidly upright in the bed.

"Abishag."

I would say that I had never heard him say my name with such compassion before, but it did not seem that he was the one saying it. His voice was coming from somewhere far beyond us both, deeper and more resonant than anything I'd ever heard him say. And he did not look at me as he spoke.

"The LORD is with you," he said, "highly favored handmaid of the king." There was a tone to his words so ethereal as to be terrifying, but even so I felt a great peace fall over me, almost smothering me with its weight.

"Your mercy to this man of blood will bear fruit," the voice prophesied. "Your warmth has kept him alive long after old age should have taken him. And because it has, he will not die now before placing his son Prince Solomon on the throne; and Solomon will be a father of kings, the one through whom the LORD will establish the covenant he has cut with his Anointed One."

A wind breathed in at the open casement, and I could feel it on my face, though still the night was perfectly calm. I closed my eyes against it, and as I did, I could see kings, generation after generation of them rising and falling, and vying for power and begetting heirs, reigning and striving and warring with each other through the ages, all of them flowing from the issue of this cold and withered man.

"And so will come at last the one who will redeem every gift of sacrifice and every self-surrender. Every drop of blood spilled and every tear shed will be made right in his coming." A long silence came, but finally the voice added, "Even yours, Abishag. What you have suffered will not be wasted."

The king turned to me at last and raised his hands in a gesture like that of the priests before the altar. He placed heavy palms on my head, and I bowed beneath them. "May the LORD bless you," he intoned. "And keep you."

Against the darkness of my closed eyes, I thought I saw a child cradled in virgin arms, somewhere ages away from us, something maybe the way my arms had cradled his senile head so often. I knew I ought to fear, but I could not. Such a deep and lasting peace had enveloped in that moment that all fear had been driven out by a glimpse of perfect, burning love and what it would accomplish.

"I am the servant of the LORD," I said at last. "May it be to me as you have said."

"And I promise you, my handmaid, you will not be given to Adonijah." The wind shifted one more time, and I knew the voice had left the bedchamber. The king sank back suddenly to the bed again, lying so still that I might have doubted it had really happened, if the words of his prophecy were not ringing still so clearly in my soul.

I reached to stroke that senile head a final time, assured beyond question that what he had whispered over me was true. And as I did, I found my heart opened and willingly offered to magnify the LORD.

16.

Llewellyn's Story

Grandpa Llewellyn was a deeply religious man and had been for as long as I'd known him. There were rumors, of course, legends swapped between my uncles about the dark days before the Lord which hinted at something wild in his youth. But the Lord had got a hold of him, the tightest hold I've ever known the Lord to have on a man's heart, and if anything, those rumors about a dissipated adolescence only lent him a vaguely biblical air, like the story about Jacob wrestling the angel before getting his new name.

Growing up, I never got a glimpse of the darkness that was said to have shadowed Grandpa's past, unless you count the merciless way he teased us grandkids when the mood struck him. He had a full set of dentures by the time he'd become my grandpa, and he'd learned to rattle these on his tongue, in and out with the ghastly chuckle of some B-grade horror movie mummy. Sometimes he'd hide at the top of the stairs when all the grandkids were staying for a visit, and as we came up for the night, he'd jump out of the shadows, clattering his death's head teeth and chasing us off to bed with squeals of terror.

He was a great storyteller, too. He may have learned this art from the steady diet of biblical lore he'd been feasting on since coming to Jesus more than half a century ago, those rich tales about the God of Abraham and the Fear of Isaac honing his taste for a story well told. His family was of Welsh extraction, though, on his grandmother's side, and another rumor had it that she'd been the great, great granddaughter of a bona fide Welsh bard. Grandpa Llewellyn certainly took great pride in his Welsh heritage, and if nothing else seemed intent on proving the stereotype of the Welsh way with words.

Summer nights when all the grandkids were visiting the old farmhouse and there was nothing to do in the morning so there was no reason to send us to bed early, he would gather us together in the living room and entertain us with fantastic stories of his own invention. These tended to be something like what you'd get if Beatrix Potter met Foxe's Book of Martyrs: the childish adventures of anthropomorphic animals with names like Randolph Rabbit or Billy the Beetle, whose winsome forest hijinks somehow bore faithful witness to the Lord Jesus Christ when they were all said and done. They were probably more preachy than I remember, but even so they kept us utterly enthralled late into the night.

Toward the end of one such summer, just as the first auburn of autumn was beginning to tinge the tips of the trees, Grandpa Llewellyn gathered us together for a final story time. We were expecting a typical tale about How Billy the Beetle Learned the Power of Prayer, or some such yarn, when he asked us unexpectedly, "Did I ever tell you kids how I came to know the Lord?"

I was old enough to have heard some of the rumors but still young enough that their more sordid details were lost on me. My older cousin was much more a man of the world than I, however. He said, "Wasn't it at an altar call at that old church down in the meadow? Weren't you out tipping cows that night when the preacher's son caught you? And didn't he make a deal with you, that he wouldn't tell if you came into the meeting till it was over?"

Grandpa Llewellyn grinned. "I know that's the story that gets told, but it's not exactly how it was."

"What's tipping cows?" I asked.

"It's when you sneak up on a sleeping cow and push it over," my cousin explained. "Cows sleep standing up, and if you can catch them asleep you can tip them over with one good shove."

"Is that true?" I asked grandpa.

He started laughing. "Well, it's true that's what cow tipping is, but it's not true that it really works. I've never known a cow to sleep standing up. And you ever try pushing one? It would take more than a good shove to get one over. No. Cow tipping must have been invented by a bunch of city folk who knew no more about a cow than you can learn from the highway, zipping past it at sixty miles an hour."

His laugh faded and a faraway look came into his eye. "Unlike this story," he said, "which is, I guarantee you, as true as I am sitting here today."

We recognized his storyteller's look, though there was a distance to his gaze we'd never seen before. I hugged a cushion against my chest and sank back into the couch. My older cousin was on the floor and settled in comfortably on his belly. Another cousin sat near me on the couch, draping himself with an old Afghan and nestling in.

"You see," said Grandpa Llewellyn. "It's true the preacher's son was there that night, but he didn't catch me. He had joined me. Me and him, and Owen Thomas, the son of the mechanic in town. And we weren't out tipping cows. Owen had pinched a bottle of—" He paused, seeming to weigh something in his mind before nodding to himself and proceeding— "a bottle of hooch from his old man, who probably wouldn't miss it because it was a Friday night and he'd be sleeping off one of his own by then. And anyway, even if he noticed it was gone, he'd probably just figure he drank it himself and lost count."

My cousin shot the briefest glance in my direction, as if to say: "This is juicier than anything Randolph Rabbit ever got up to." But I was younger than him by a good two years and was having trouble with all the details. I had a vague understanding of what hooch was, but the word struck me as far too playful to be anything sinister.

"We met in the churchyard because it was halfway between town, where Owen lived, and my place on the farm. And the preacher's son was there because his dad was holding a revival meeting that night, and Alister—that was his name—Alister Underwood had no use for that kind of thing. So he slipped out to meet us first chance he got.

"Reverend Underwood had only been preacher there about a year, but he was an old-timey Pentecostal from the hills, and that whole week a group of travelling evangelists from his church back home had been visiting, leading revival meetings. And they were snake handlers from the back woods, mind you. Said that if the Holy Ghost was really with a man, he'd be able to handle all manner of poisonous serpent and not be harmed. Which is what the Good Book says, to be sure. Mark sixteen, verse eighteen.

"So the rumor was going round town that these snake handlers had brought in a box of rattlesnakes and were set to bring them out toward the end of the week. If anyone wanted to prove their faith by taking them up, they said, they'd discover what the Holy Ghost can really do.

"That's what Alister told us at school that Friday afternoon, anyway. He swore he'd even seen the box. Said there were seven of them, all coiling together and dripping with venom. Owen said it was plain nonsense, that you'd need rocks for brains to be taken in by something like that. But I'd been afraid of snakes since one crossed my path as a kid, so I didn't want anything to do with them.

"It was Owen who said we should visit the church that night. Alister told him that the last thing we'd want to do was go to church during a revival. 'My dad'll snatch you up and convert you before you've fully crossed the threshold,' he told him. But Owen said we could just sit out in the yard and share a drink. 'We could watch through the windows,' he said, 'and if nothing else, we'll be able to hear the whole thing.'

"He was right about that. It was a warm night, for fall, and they had all the windows open for air. There was an old dead apple tree in the yard, just far enough from the church that we'd never be seen sitting under it, but close enough we could still make out the shape of what was happening through the windows.

"The tree must have been dead for decades, though. It was all naked and gnarled and the last time anyone had eaten an apple off it might as well have been back in Adam's day. Certainly no one could have done so in recent memory.

"But Owen's dad made awful hooch, and I couldn't manage more than two or three mouthfuls of the stuff. Alister's dad preached pretty regularly against drinking, so I figure Alister took an extra swig or two just to spite him. Owen had always been hell-bent on following his old man's footsteps, and he seemed to drink as much by himself as the two of us put together."

Grandpa Llewellyn paused again. The faraway look in his eye had a glint to it that I'd never seen in all the story times we'd ever shared before, and though I still had great difficulty with the grownup details, I could sense that he was unearthing something from his past that had not seen the light of day for a long time.

"Anyways," he said, "we sat out there under that ancient apple tree, watching the revivalists move back and forth across the windows. The sun had set, and the church was lit with oil lamps, so we could still tell pretty clearly when the snakes came out. One of the preachers was standing in the centre of the place, just beside a window, holding it up over his head in full view.

"He was saying how the Lord held the power of life and death in his hand, and unless it be the Lord's will, this creature that the Lord God had created wouldn't hurt him—couldn't do—and then he was saying how when Jesus rose from the grave he took away the sting of death, just as surely as this serpent had no sting for him—and then he started chanting the Psalm that says he will give us power to tread on serpents and scorpions and they will neither harm nor destroy on all God's Holy Mountain.

"Of course, I hadn't stepped foot in a church since they'd baptized me as a baby, and I had no clue what any of it meant. But the preacher's voice was almost hypnotic, and even though we were at the other end of the churchyard, we could see him clearly through the window, swaying all trance-like and holding that rattlesnake over his head.

"Owen scoffed to hear it, and Alister rolled his eyes. They passed the bottle of hooch between them and each took a pull. But I had been scared of snakes all my life, and I'd never heard anything like this.

"Owen was four sheets to the wind by the time the revival was over. At least, he sure wasn't any good for walking in a straight line, and Alister was terrified to let his dad see him, the state he was in. 'He'll just know we've been drinking,' he kept saying. And so, long after the church was empty and the night was fully black, we sat under that old dead apple tree, talking.

"Owen told about how his old man was getting worse and worse now that his mom wasn't with them anymore. He took another pull at the bottle when he said this. I said maybe he'd had enough, and he said maybe I should shut up if I wanted to live to see the morning.

"Alister had been staring up silently at the stars for a long time—they were sharper than razor blades that night—and he said something about how on nights like this, when the world's so quiet and the sky's so stunning, it's hard not to believe, but then he remembers all the hell his dad's put him through, and if that's what God's like then his dad can keep him; how he'd rather see the whole church burned to the ground than believe like him.

"We must've drifted off at some point. Or maybe Owen's hooch finally caught up to us. Either way, what happened next couldn't have been anything other than a dream—only—"

"Only what, Grandpa?"

"Only if it was, we all three of us dreamed it together, which is something I've never been able to figure out."

"What happened?" I asked, and as I did, it felt as if the shadows in the room were lengthening, reaching toward me.

"That old apple tree started to shake," said Llewellyn softly. "And it was the stillest autumn night you could imagine, mind you, not a gust of a breeze blowing. But it started shaking from the trunk up. And violently, as if the very ground it was rooted in was quaking, though again, everything else—everywhere—was as still as the morning it was made.

"I sat bolt upright, and Owen, too, stiff as a corpse, and he turned his eyes all wild in my direction. And then something fell. It hit Alister in the face, which sat him up, grunting about what in hell was going on.

"But we never did learn what in hell it was, because at just that moment—and if it was a dream, it was the most real thing I ever dreamed in all my life—suddenly that shaking tree started to drop apples from its limbs. One of them hit me on the shoulder and to this day I'd swear it was a real apple. And dozens of them started dropping down all around us, while that withered tree kept shaking, fit to raise the dead.

"Owen was the first to bolt, and Alister was on his feet and running ahead of me. I was running, too, but not before turning back to see it one last time, that old apple tree shaking like it was the end of days, and apples dropping off its lifeless limbs, hundreds of them if there were a handful."

My cousin gave me another look. In all the years of story time with Grandpa Llewellyn, we had never heard anything quite like this before.

"Then what, Grandpa?" said my younger cousin in a hushed voice from beneath the old Afghan.

"Well," said Llewellyn, swallowing drily, "the next day I went over to see Owen. It was a Saturday, and his old man was still recovering from his bender the night before. Neither of us could agree if what we thought had happened in the churchyard really had. Owen insisted it was nothing, that too much of his dad's hooch made a fellow see things that weren't really there. But I was sure of what I'd seen and told him so.

"He told me don't be ridiculous, and I told him he could say what he wanted now, but I saw him running from the churchyard last night just as fast as I was.

"He'd finally had enough. He went into his dad's shop, and I could hear him rummaging in there for a long time. When he came back, he was carrying a big bushel basket. It was stained with oil—I

think his old man had been using it to hold discarded engine parts—
but long before that, his mother had used it for picking apples.

"'Here,' he said pushing it into my chest. 'If it really did happen
like you say, then we'll have our pick of apples to bring home, won't
we?'

"There was a playful glint in his eye, like the whole thing was just
a big joke to him, so I pushed the basket back. But he insisted, and
pushed it at me harder, shoving me back a step.

"'Dammit, Llew!' he said. 'I'm telling you it was only my dad's
hooch, but if you want to settle it, then let's settle it.'

"I looked at him closely and wondered if the glint in his eye
wasn't really a welling up of tears. At last I nodded, and took the
basket gently out of his hands.

"The ground beneath the tree when we got there was bare as it
ever had been. Not an apple in sight, and the branches were just as
withered as they'd been the night before.

"Owen looked at me as if to say I told you so, but I shook my
head at him. 'I know what I saw,' I said again, as I turned and
followed him out of the churchyard.

"On the way home, we stopped at Reverend Underhill's place
and asked for Alister.

"'He's upstairs in his room doing his Bible reading, boys,' said the
Reverend as he let us in. 'He wasn't feeling so well this morning, so
he's spent the day in bed with the blinds drawn.

"He squinted one eye and looked at Owen sourly.

"'How's your dad doing, son?' he said abruptly. 'I haven't seen
him for some time, not since your mom—'

"'As well as can be expected,' said Owen quickly, looking away.

"'You know, you might think about coming down to the meeting
tonight,' said the Reverend. 'Maybe get things right between yourself
and the Lord? It says that the Lord visits the sins of the father on
their sons to the third and fourth generation. But there's no reason it
has to be that way.'

"I could see red fire creeping up Owen's throat from under his
collar. 'That may be, sir,' he said. 'But don't it also say that only the

soul that sins shall die, and the sons don't share in the guilt of their fathers?'

"The Reverend wasn't used to being contradicted, especially when it came to the Good Book. He pursed his lips tight and didn't say anything for an awkward second, so finally Owen added, 'That's Ezekiel eighteen, isn't it?'

"The Reverend nodded, his one eye still squinting at us, and then with a curt motion he gestured up toward the staircase. 'Well,' he said, 'I guess Alister will be glad to see you.'

"We turned to the stairs, but just before bounding up them, Owen turned back. 'By the way, Reverend Underhill,' he said, 'what do you know about that old apple tree in the churchyard?'

"The Reverend snorted. 'That old thing? As far as I can tell it's been dead for ages. Only reason we haven't pulled it up is because folks say the farmer who gave the church the land to build on—this is going back generations, mind you—they say he's buried under it. Story goes that his wife planted that tree after they'd put him in the ground.'

"He gave Owen another close look. 'Story is he died of cirrhosis of the liver.'"

"What's that, Grandpa?" my younger cousin asked. Grandpa Llewellyn must have been lost deeply in the memory, because the question seemed to startle him into the present.

"It's when your liver stops working cause of too much drinking," said my older cousin. "Isn't that right, Grandpa?"

"I suppose it is," said Grandpa Llewellyn vaguely. "But the way Reverend Underhill said it, you would have thought that Owen himself was personally responsible for that farmer's passing. When we heard the story, though, Owen and I looked at each other as if we'd seen a ghost. I opened my mouth to say something, but Owen shook his head, very, very faintly, so I closed it again.

"'Anyways,' said Owen, turning back to the door, 'thanks for the advice, Reverend Underhill. We'll find our way to Alister's room.'

"Alister couldn't stop laughing when he saw me holding that battered old apple basket. He was sitting in his room with the blinds drawn, just like his father had said, though there wasn't a Bible in sight.

"'What were you thinking?' he said between gasps for breath. 'That you'd bring home a bushel of haunted apples or something? Bake them into a pie?'

"I tried to change the subject. 'Your dad says the old farmer that owned the land is buried under that tree.' I lowered my voice. 'Says he died of the drink.'

"'If he did, it must've been some of Owen's homebrew. A single shot of that stuff's enough to kill a bull. My head's still throbbing from it.'

"'Listen Alister,' I said. 'I'm not so sure what we saw wasn't real. Owen thinks it was the hooch, but I just don't know.'

"'He'd know better than you, wouldn't he? You were running so fast outta there I'd be surprised if you were sure of anything at all.'

"'You were running, too!'

"'I'm telling you,' said Owen tersely. 'My old man's hooch can make a fellow see things that aren't real.'

"'Well,' said Alister with a grin, 'I can think of one way to find out. Why don't we head down there tonight and see if it happens again? It'll beat the devil out of sitting through another night of revival meetings, if nothing else.'

"I wasn't so sure, but Owen spoke up right away. 'Suits me fine,' he said. 'Not that I think it makes any difference who's buried under that tree—it could be the good Lord himself for all I care—but I'm game to give it a go.'

"'What do you say?' Alister asked me. And even though the thought of it sat like molten lead in the pit of my stomach, the thought of the shame Alister would heap on me if I didn't go burned even more.

"I nodded faintly. 'Sure,' I said. 'I'll go.'

"We'd arranged to meet at eight o'clock, but I was afraid I'd be seen by folks heading into the church if I arrived too early, so I didn't set out until I knew the revival would be well under way by the time I got there.

"I found Owen by himself, hiding in the tall grass beneath the twisted tree limbs.

"'Where's Alister?' I asked.

"Owen shrugged and nodded in the direction of the church. 'His dad caught us out here,' he said, 'and dragged him inside, kicking and screaming. Al was none too sober, neither, and was threatening murder. Said that no way in hell would he go in. But his dad grabbed hold of him real tight, and said he'd do whatever it took to drive the devil out of him. Tried to make me go in too, but no way was I gonna step foot in there. Not after what they did to my mother.'

"'Have they brought out the snakes yet?' I asked crouching into the shadows next to him.

"'Shhh,' he hissed. 'I think they're just getting to it.'

"They'd lit the oil lamps, and by their greasy glow we could see the preacher stalking back and forth at the front. The windows were closed this time—it was a cooler night than it had been night before—and I couldn't make out what was said. I could see the shapes of the congregation though, silhouettes at the windows swaying in time to some rhythm I couldn't hear.

"'And here we go,' said Owen. Through the big window at the front of the church I could see the shape of the preacher stop and stoop, then rise again, holding a writhing shape aloft. We were quite far back so it was hard to be sure, but I think the congregation was swaying slower, more gently than it had been a moment ago. I could see one or two silhouettes move toward the front, taking the snake from the preacher and holding it up in trembling hands.

"I hadn't stepped foot in a church since they'd washed me as a baby, mind you, and it was really hard to tell what was happening way off like we were. Even so, something seemed to well up inside me in that moment, and though I barely even knew the Lord's prayer, still I wanted more than anything else to join what was going on inside that church. I could feel the memory of what I'd heard the previous night, about authority to tread on serpents unharmed, beckoning me.

"I must have looked twice the ghost as Owen did, because suddenly he put his hand on my forearm. 'You okay?' he asked.

"I nodded, but I couldn't speak. Neither could he; at least, he didn't. We just sat there in the darkness, watching silently till the snakes had all been put away and the last revivalist had left the building. The churchyard was dark—there were no stars out this time—and everyone had wandered home.

"We stayed there, crouched in the grass for a long time. It had grown so quiet that I could hear my breath coming and going uneasily. I was just about to say that maybe we should head home, when it started."

"The tree?" my cousin asked.

Llewellyn nodded and dropped his voice to barely above a whisper.

"The tree started shaking again, like it was being throttled by a madman. I was on my feet and bolted wildly in the direction of the church. I had almost reached it when I heard frantic screaming behind me, so I pulled up. And even though my heart was in my throat and every ounce of me was saying don't do it, I turned and looked back.

"It was Alister. And he wasn't screaming, he was laughing, only wildly enough to raise hell.

"'Look at him run!' he hollered. Through the half-light I could see him standing by the tree trunk, holding it with both hands and heaving on it with all his weight. He gave it another shake, as though he were strangling it. 'Where's your haunted apple tree now, sissy-Llew?'

"'Damn you Alister!' I hollered back. I was burning with shame for having been taken in, and with something hotter, too, fury and fear mingled together. I picked up a stone and hurled it at him.

"It missed by a good couple yards, but when he saw me do it, something seemed to break in him, or come over him, some kind of an unholy fit.

"He stooped and grabbed a stone of his own and hurled it. But not at me. It was clear I wasn't his target. The stone flew far over my head and clattered off the roof of the church. He grabbed and hurled another, then another. One struck the side of the church with a loud clap. Another rattled on the roof again. The third went through a windowpane with a crash.

"'What's wrong with you, Alister?' I shouted, but whatever it was, it had taken full hold of him. He was screaming bloody murder, some of it at his dad, some of it at the church, and some of it, to this day I can't say who it was at.

"After the fifth or sixth stone, Alister gave up on throwing rocks and flung himself bodily in the direction of the church, legs pelting with all his might. He pushed past me, screaming something about wanting to burn the place down. I saw him reach the door, heaving on the handle, and to my great surprise, it flung open. It could be that Reverend Underhill had forgotten to lock up, though it was an old church and maybe it was just that easy to burst the lock. Whatever the case, the door opened and Alister rushed inside.

"Owen ran up beside me.

"'What's gotten into him?' I asked.

"'I don't know. He's been saying stuff like that about his dad for months,' said Owen. 'But I've never seen him in such a fit as this.'

"'Should we go get him?' I asked.

"'Probably. He was talking about burning the place down again, and he's so far gone this time, I'm not sure he won't follow through.'

"We ran up to the church door and found it swinging half open, like a broken jaw lolling down. For some reason, I couldn't bring myself to touch the handle, and instead tried to slip through the gap without brushing the door at all.

"The church should have been pitch dark, but outside the moon must have finally broken through the clouds, because the greyest light imaginable was falling through the big window at the front. In the gloaming I could see Alister's silhouette standing perfectly still before the altar.

"He didn't speak, but I could hear his breathing, rugged and heavy in the silence, and under that, softer and more sinister, a shivering sound that I vaguely recognized but couldn't place.

"'Alister?' I said. He didn't answer. I could see his head move just slightly in the shadows, as though he hardly dared to shake it.

"We took a step closer.

"'Alister,' said Owen softly, 'why don't we head off now? No sense making real trouble for ourselves.'

"We took another step forward, but Alister lifted his hand slowly. 'Don't move,' he breathed through clenched teeth. With the slightest nod of his chin he gestured to the floor at his feet. I followed the motion with my eyes and saw it: a coiled rattlesnake sitting in a patch of moonlight. It was wound tightly and ready to spring, whispering death threats at us with the quivering of its lifted tail.

"But I had moved. I'd stepped right up to him and was standing less than a yard from the poised snake. Its head hunched down into the coil of its body, tightening the spring, and the hiss of its tail crescendoed.

"The next three things happened so quickly in turn that they seemed to be happening all at once. Alister leaped back, away from rattler's reach. The snake sprang, its head flashing faster than a lightning bolt falling from heaven. And my hand shot out, just as suddenly, so quickly that to this day it feels like it wasn't me, but something reaching out through me—quicker than it ever had moved, my hand struck—and when my mind caught up to what my body had done, I saw that I was holding that snake fast by the head. Miraculously, my fingers had landed just behind its jaw, and my thumb was somehow pressed across its throat, far enough back that its sting couldn't reach them but close enough that it couldn't twist its head around and touch me.

"All three of us stood frozen, staring in disbelief at the writhing body I held out at arm's length. It whipped its tail about my wrist in rage and fear, but I was holding it by the throat for dear life and its bite never landed."

Grandpa Llewellyn paused, as if he were standing even now in that church before that altar, holding a twisting serpent by the head in frozen fear. He didn't speak for so long that finally my cousin whispered, breathlessly, "What did you do, Grandpa?"

"Well," he said, seeming to come to. "It's one thing to take hold of a snake like that. It's another thing to know what to do with it. I was overcome with the urge to crush it, and maybe if I had tightened my grip I could have, but I've heard stories of snakes biting even after they're dead, and anyway, I was terrified that if I moved my fingers even a hair's breadth, that snake'd be able to reach them.

"So I didn't know what else to do, but very slowly I carried it from the altar, keeping my arm as stiff as a corpse the whole time. I reached the door—it was still swaying free from when Alister had wrenched it open—and I slipped outside.

"The clouds had passed, and the moon was out in full now, flooding the whole church yard with a ghastly light. I stepped across the yard to where the grass had grown tall. The whole time the snake was whipping me mercilessly with its tail, and in the pale light I thought I could see its death-black eye, fixed on me fatefully.

"When I reached the tall grass, I crouched as gently as I dared, and with all the courage I could muster, I loosened my grip, dropping the hissing head and leaping back. I slipped when I landed and fell on my side, but it may be that the snake was just as terrified as I was, because when I sat up, it was gone.

"I sat there in the moonlight for a while, I think, and when I could find my breath again, something seemed to come over me—for all I know it was the same thing as what had reached through me to grab the snake—and I started laughing. It came quietly at first, but soon my whole body was wracked with it, great heaves of laughter, relief mingled with wonder, though not without a tiny bit of terror, too, like a long exhale, or a desperate gasping for breath.

"I was still laughing faintly when I finally got up and made my way back to the church. Alister and Owen had followed me out and were standing on the porch in terror. Alister said something about how sorry he was, and Owen about how lucky, but I didn't really hear it. I pushed past them and entered the church. They didn't follow me. It would be some time, actually, before I would see them again, but it didn't matter. I knew I was not alone in that place. It was streaming with a presence that pressed in on me, almost crushing me with its weight.

"So I knelt at the altar. And even though I had no real idea how to do it, I prayed, maybe the first time I had ever really prayed in all my life. I tried as best as I could to say the Lord's Prayer. I'm sure I missed most of the words, but when I got to the part about his leading us not into temptation but delivering us from evil, that laughter started to well up inside me again. It wasn't desperate this time, or even relieved, but something different. Assurance, maybe, a kind of happy holiness, I don't know, but I laughed in sheer amazement. My shoulders shook until I couldn't tell if I was laughing anymore or crying, though maybe it was a bit of both. And when I finally rose, I knew that I was no longer my own, and that nothing would ever be the same."

Grandpa Llewellyn stopped talking. The room had grown very still, and in the dim light I could see my cousins' eyes staring widely, mouths hanging open. But no one spoke for the longest time.

"And that's how you found the Lord, Grandpa?" I whispered at last in wonder.

Grandpa looked at me, and for a moment it seemed he was seeing me from across a great distance; then the moment passed and he smiled faintly, present once more. He leaned over and kissed me gently on the head.

"Not exactly," he said. "But that is how he found me."

17.

The Binding

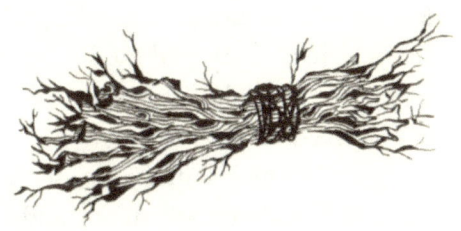

When James got the call that night, he still hadn't finished his sermon for Sunday morning. He didn't usually leave it until the night before, but between an unexpected funeral earlier in the week and a series of denominational meetings scheduled all day Friday, he hadn't found time to sit down with his text until late Saturday night. Add to this the fact that the passage he was working with—the Binding of Isaac—was hardly straightforward, and he was already feeling on edge when his cell phone rang.

He continued to stare at the open page of his Bible as he reached for the phone, and he didn't look away even as the officer on the other end explained the situation, though at some point in the call his gaze went blurry, then blank.

"I'll be there as soon as I can," he said quietly after a long pause. He asked the officer to repeat the room number, and he scrawled it down.

He ended the call, switched off his desk lamp, and rose to leave. His gaze lingered for just a minute on the Bible and notebook lying open in the shadows of the desk, and at the last second, perhaps by force of habit—or maybe prompted by some deeper impulse—he took them up and shoved them into his bag.

The officer met him in the lobby when he arrived at the hospital. After talking it over with him at length, she directed him up to the nurses' station in the J Wing. It was quite late, and the halls were only dimly lit at this time of night. A single desk lamp filled the station with a futile yellow light, and the attending nurse did not look up from her charting when he stepped to the counter.

"Hello," he said softly, not wanting to jar the silence. "I'm here to see a patient named Jas—" He caught himself, pushing against the force of habit. "That is… Jem. They told me I'd find her here."

"Visiting hours aren't until eight tomorrow morning," the nurse said curtly, her eyes still fixed on her charting.

"No, I realize that, but I'm his—I mean *her*—father, and they said to come." The nurse still hadn't looked up, and the silence that followed this admission felt to James like an accusation.

"I spoke with Officer Paul downstairs," he added. "She sent me up."

When the nurse finally lifted her head, there was a weary look on her face which James found difficult to read. Was it exasperation, or simply exhaustion? The ghastly yellow light gave her a menacing air, and something in her eyes seemed to be appraising him.

"Jem's mother has already been," she said. "And there was no mention of her father."

"Well, we're not exactly talking, Jem's mother and I aren't." James's voice came unevenly, and he wondered if it was necessary for him to admit so much to a perfect stranger. It occurred to him that Sarah might have already poisoned this nurse against him, but he did very much want to see Jem, so he added quickly: "But Jem and I are still close."

If this admission made any difference to the nurse, she gave no indication of it. She began flipping pensively through some pages on a clipboard.

"With patients in Jem's situation," she said, "we have to be very careful who we allow to see her. We wouldn't want anything triggering her, now would we?"

The nurse continued flipping through her clipboard for a moment, then finally let out a soft sigh. It sounded very condescending to James. "Well, Mr.—"

"Richard," he offered. "James Richard."

"Well, Mr. Richard, there's a waiting room down the hall. Why don't you wait there? When I go in to bring Jem her medication, I'll see if she's feeling up to a visit."

"Jem's on medication? Is it for her anxiety? Or for her—"

The nurse gave him an arch look. "I don't think I'm at liberty to discuss her treatment with you, Mr. Richard. Why don't you take a seat, and I'll find you after I've spoken with Jem?"

The waiting room was only two doors down from the nurse's station, but it felt like the longest walk James had ever taken. He flicked a switch when he entered, and a buzzing florescent tube sputtered half-heartedly to life, throwing an unsteady pallor over the room.

A pathetic stack of obsolete magazines littered an end table next to a dreary-looking couch, and in one corner a plastic plant did its best to add a note of color to the austere décor. The walls were hung with PSA posters about mental health awareness and suicide prevention, no doubt intended to encourage people in James's position with words of wisdom and support. These had the opposite effect on him, however, and he drew a shaky breath against the turmoil of despondency rising in him.

He sat down wearily, reaching a three-year-old Sports Illustrated from off the end table. It was dated July 2016, and the cover story happened to be a feature on Caitlyn Jenner. He flipped through the pages quickly, so as to make a good show of it, but just as quickly tossed it back on the pile. It felt a bit more than he could handle at that particular moment.

The posters seemed to be staring him down, so to escape their glare he reached into his bag and pulled out his Bible and notebook. He didn't know how long it would be until the nurse came for him, and he still had his sermon to preach in the morning, so he turned to a fresh page and opened his Bible to Genesis 22.

"Then God said, 'Take your son, your only son, Isaac—whom you love—and sacrifice him on a mountain I will show you.'" The words seemed bitterly ironic, given the circumstances, but he blinked through his cynicism and scratched out some tentative thoughts.

"Early the next morning Abraham got up and loaded his donkey," he noted, scribbling down some commendatory words about Abraham's silent acceptance of God's command, however painful it would have been for him. He circled the phrase "whom you love" in his Bible, underlining it twice, and then in his notebook he put down something about Abraham's willingness to give up Isaac, despite his deep love for the boy.

He put a tentative title on the top of the page: "Faith that Surrenders All." He squinted at it, trying to imagine it printed in tomorrow's bulletin, and then tried a second: "The Sacrifices of Faith."

He pressed his eyes with his thumb and index finger and gave a furtive glance through the door toward the nurse's station. She was still sitting at the counter, stooped over her clipboard, so he rubbed his face vigorously and turned back to his work.

He scratched out a few more thoughts when he came to Isaac's hesitant question: "The fire and wood are here, but where is the lamb for the burnt offering?"

He closed his eyes to visualize the scene—he found this often helped in preparing a sermon—and saw the child, almost cowering—why had he never imagined the boy cowering before?—in the shadow of the stoic patriarch. The bundle of wood placed across the boy's shoulders seemed to dwarf him, and though in times past James had been taught to imagine it as a cross, tonight, strangely, the comparison seemed almost obscene to him. If it really were a cross Isaac was bearing up that hill, surely neither he nor his father could have understood it to be one. And anyway, tonight the bundle seemed far too menacing to have been a symbol of salvation.

He opened his eyes and read the next line in the story, Abraham reaching out his hand without a word, lifting the silent knife inexorably, poised to slay his son. And there lay Isaac bound—

inescapably bound—however hard he strained against the cords and cried out for desperate mercy.

Why had he never heard those cries for mercy before, James wondered, as the knife reached its apex, and the devout father held it there for the most terrible of pauses?

"Abraham!" cried the Voice from heaven. "Abraham!" James wondered if the muscles of the patriarchal arm had already contracted when the divine interdict finally broke the silence, if the blade had already begun its dreadful descent.

"Do not lay a hand on the boy," said the Voice. Normally at this point James would have rushed on to the end: the Lord's affirmation of Abraham's unwavering obedience, the reiteration of the promise, the heavenly oath to bless the chosen family.

But there, in the uncertain light of that hospital waiting room, something rose up in his throat and stopped him dead. His eyes narrowed, and he stared unseeing at the verse: "Do not lay a hand on the boy!" The words, once so consoling, seemed for the first time like an accusation.

"I swear by myself," said the Lord, "because you have done this and have not withheld your son, your only son."

The flotsam of a memory surfaced briefly and submerged just as quickly, but not before it crossed James's mind that the phrase, "because you have done this," was hauntingly familiar. Hadn't the Lord said the same thing, or something very much like it, to the serpent who deceived the woman in the beginning?

He reached to scratch down a note, that he should look this up at some point. He punctuated the thought with a series of question marks; and even as he did, he noticed it for the first time, glaring so starkly that he wondered how he'd never seen it before: the Lord did not call Isaac the son "whom Abraham loved" in verse sixteen.

A drop of sweat appeared, just above James's eyebrow, and his forehead was furrowed in thought. The rest of the phrase was identical to verse two, where God had initiated Abraham's dreadful test. "Take your son, your only son, whom you love." James underlined the phrase again with a trembling hand. Then he reread verse sixteen: "Because you have not withheld your son, your only son..."

There was no further mention of Abraham's love for Isaac.

James stole a glance toward the nurse's station. She was no longer at her post, and he wondered vaguely if she'd gone in to see Jem at last. The drop of sweat became a bead, and it broke free, sliding slowly down his temple like a trickle of blood.

"Why did the Lord not call Isaac the son 'whom Abraham loved' this second time?" he scrawled out in his notebook. He noted it down, too, that the phrase had also appeared in verse twelve, when the Lord called out at the last possible second to still the trembling patriarch's hand. And James noted now, just as tremulously, that the words "whom you love" were also missing there.

Like a burst of white light against an impervious darkness, a searing thought etched itself into James's mind. He couldn't quite put it into words yet, but he scribbled down a question at the bottom of his page: "What was the Lord really testing in Abraham?"

"Mr. Richard?"

James shut his notebook and Bible quickly and looked up. The nurse was standing in the doorway, and when she saw the closed Bible, she arched her eyebrow again.

"Mr. Richard, Jem is awake now, and she says she'd like to see you." Her eyes met his squarely for the first time since he'd arrived that night. "If," she added slowly, "if you can promise that nothing will happen that might trigger her."

James nodded, choking down the huge lump of shame rising in his throat.

"Can you—" He felt miserable to ask it. "Can you just give me a minute?"

Her eyes held his for a moment more, and she seemed again to be weighing him carefully. "Okay," she said at last. "But I don't want to keep Jem up for long. Come find me in the station when you're ready."

When she was gone, James opened the Bible on his knees once more, not for study this time, but for strength, like he used to do when he was a young man, before everything had become so complicated. However hard he tried not to, he thought about the little congregation he led, which he'd be preaching to tomorrow morning, and he wondered what they'd think to see him here. A parade of images passed unbidden across his mind: of Matt, who had just yesterday sent him a link to the latest YouTube clip he'd found decrying the modern sexual ideology; of Thom, who'd come to him last year with his recently outed son in tow, and who, despite James's pleadings, had turned him out; or of young Pete, who'd confided in him last month and was wondering if the Lord would still have him; Mary who'd asked him to sign that petition about sex ed in the schools; and old Andrews, who'd cornered him that Sunday morning after his sermon on Romans 1:27, because he didn't think James had said it as clearly as he should have.

And there was Jem at the end of the hall, his own cherished child, lying harmed and half-poisoned in a psych-ward bed.

He became distantly aware that his hands were shaking, and when he could focus his eyes, he realized that he'd opened the Bible again to Genesis 22, the Akedah, the testing of Abraham. There were, of course, a hundred other passages that might have helped more in that moment, assuring him that the Lord was his shepherd and that he was near to the broken hearted, but he blinked through his tears and stared sightlessly at the story lying open and exposed beneath him.

What was being tested after all, he wondered, that day on Mount Moriah?

It occurred to him that at the end of the story, only Abraham returned from the place of sacrifice to the waiting servants, no mention of Isaac with him. He looked closer and realized that Abraham chose to live in Beersheba after this dreadful encounter with the Lord, even though, to the best of James's memory, Isaac would go on to live in the Negev, and his mother in Hebron.

He remembered vaguely, too, something about Isaac's son referring always to the Lord as the Fear of Isaac. If this were a sermon, he'd have to look that up to be sure, and then say something clever about Isaac learning to fear the Lord through the testing on Mount Moriah.

But this was no sermon. This was an aching father longing to go to his heart-hurt child and hesitating for nothing more than tremulous faithfulness. What if—and the thought came so unexpectedly that it sounded in his heart like someone else's voice—what if the test was simply to know if Abraham really loved his child enough to cry out for him in protest?

A stifled sob punctuated the thought. What if the test was to teach Abraham that he needn't sacrifice his son to prove his faithfulness, the voice said more fervently, that if he had simply cried out, "No! Lord, I know you too well to think you'd ask this of me!"—if he had simply protested—he'd have passed the test with his family intact?

It was past James's strength now to keep the sob submerged, and it broke from him with great force. Somewhere at the far end of the hall, the nurse heard it and turned her head, though mercifully, she didn't rise or come near. James swallowed it down as it rose up a second time, and he passed a trembling hand across his streaked face. As he did, the Voice in his heart spoke again and then fell deathly still. "Neither do I require you to sacrifice her," it seemed to say, like a gentle hand unloosing something tightly bound in James's heart, setting it free at last with an immense pain of aching loss.

James closed the book, nodding, though he hardly knew why, or to whom, and rose from his seat, squeezing his eyes tight against his tears. He turned down the hall, to where Jem lay alone in a psych-ward bed. As he did it seemed to him, in that moment, as though he were climbing a steep road to the lonely top of a holy mountain.

18.

A Scent of Smoke

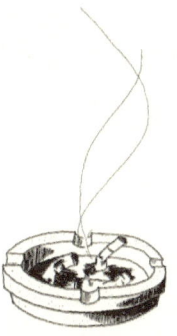

The first time it happened, I was sitting in my cubicle at the office, so deep into my work that it would have taken a crisis, maybe, or a miracle to pull me out of it. It came over me so strongly that I was sure someone must be smoking, though the office has very strict rules about that sort of thing, and Alice, who sits in the next cubicle over, polices them militantly. As soon as I realized what I was smelling, I looked in her direction, half expecting her to be up and on the hunt for the culprit. The smell was very intense, so I was surprised to see her still at her desk, hunched over some paperwork.

It was a scent of smoke. Not aromatic, necessarily, but not unpleasant either: warm and woody, the smell of a campfire when it first takes hold and invites everyone to gather round, or of a cigarette just after it's been lit and it's not yet become stale and choking. My father had smoked for as long as I'd known him, and a sad memory of him drifted over me with the smell.

I wrinkled my nose and tried to return to my work, but the smell persisted, until I began to wonder if something was burning. I stood and looked around me, but no one else seemed to have noticed anything. They all droned away in a muted hum of collective busyness.

I turned a slow circle, sniffed deeply, and though the smell was as intense as it had been when it first started, I still couldn't tell where it was coming from. At the far side of the office, Ed finally noticed me standing. He didn't really lift his head from his screen, but I could see him arch an eyebrow and throw a quick glance my way.

I stepped from my desk and walked the aisle. I took quick, deep sniffs, searching for the smell as best I could without it becoming audible. I glanced in each trash bin I passed and stopped briefly at the opening to each cubicle, pausing and sniffing as long as I thought I could before it became awkward. But though the smell never subsided, it seemed to have no source. I found no one furtively finishing a final drag in the corner of a cubicle, and none of the wastebaskets were secretly smoldering with smoking paper.

I reached the window and looked out. Our office is on the third floor of a downtown complex, and a new, government funded safe injection site had recently opened across the street. When word had reached us that ACC Financial would soon be sharing the block with a safe injection site, mild waves of grumbling washed back and forth over the office staff. Would we be safe if the street was overrun with their clientele? we wondered to one another; would we have to step over passed out junkies just to get to work? Alice had been especially vocal about it, and had even circulated a petition, though I couldn't bring myself to sign it.

It was 10:30 in the morning. Looking down I could see two or three of the clinic's clients sitting on the steps outside their door. A woman dressed in scrubs and wearing blue latex gloves was speaking with them. It was impossible to say for sure from that distance, but her forward-leaning pose, and the slight tilt of her head as they spoke struck me, even from the third floor looking down, as profoundly gentle.

My nose was suffused with the scent of smoke now. I was still no closer to figuring out where it was coming from, but it was so strong that I was seriously beginning to worry.

Ed's desk was near me, right next to the window, so at last I took a real audible sniff, so loud that he'd hear it and notice. He didn't look up from his work, so I snuffed again, louder than before.

"Do you smell that?" I asked.

Ed glanced my way, and when he saw I was looking out the window he scoffed unkindly.

"I think it's disgusting, too," he said, misunderstanding me. "But I doubt you can smell them from here."

"No," I said. "I don't mean the S.I.S. I mean… um… smoke. Do you smell smoke? Like, wood smoke, maybe, or something burning?"

A quizzical look crossed Ed's face and he grinned. "Smoke?" he asked. He leaned back in his chair and took a deep breath. He held it a moment, then exhaled with a sigh.

"I don't smell anything." He threw me a dismissive look. "You keeping it together, Terry?"

I took a deep breath of my own, but the smell had started to fade, as strangely and suddenly as it had started. There was just a faint hint of it in my nostrils now, and I wasn't sure if I hadn't imagined the whole thing.

"No," I said. "I'm okay. I could've sworn, though. It was like, I don't know, like incense, maybe. Or a cigarette."

"You think old Alice would let someone last fifteen seconds with a lit cigarette around here?"

I tried to laugh, though Ed's tone betrayed the bully that always lurked in the corners of his pointed sense of humor, and it made me profoundly uncomfortable.

"I could've sworn," I said.

"You sure you didn't stop in at the Junkie Shop yourself this morning, Ter?"

I gave another forced laugh. The smell was gone now, as if it had never been there, though the memory of it still haunted me. I turned from the window and found my way back to my desk. I stopped at Alice's cubicle and briefly considered asking if she smelled anything—if anyone could, she would—but I was starting to feel ridiculous and decided in the end just to sit down and get back to work.

Three weeks later it happened again. I'd just sat down at my desk to start the day, and while I was waiting for my computer to spring to life, my mind had wandered to the interaction I'd just had with Adrian at the front door of our building.

He had been lying across the front step, huddled under a soiled parka and entirely blocking the threshold. The S.I.S. hadn't opened yet, but looking across the street I could see a handful of bodies strewn along the sidewalk waiting languidly for 10:30, so I assumed this derelict soul had found its way here to wait in peace, away from the rest. I reached for the door but quickly realized that there would be no way through without disturbing his sleep.

Alice's remarks about stepping over junkies to get to work flashed through my mind abrasively, and with it the memory of her petition. I cleared my throat and crouched down.

"Excuse me," I said tentatively, and when there was no response, more boldly: "Pardon me."

The man stirred, raising bleary eyes in my direction.

I gestured toward the door with my chin. "I'm sorry, but you're blocking my way."

The man said nothing, but turned his eyes to the door and looked at it blankly for what seemed a long time. At last, he heaved his weight drearily and shifted so that there would be enough room for me to squeeze past if I hugged the door jambe.

I didn't rise immediately, though, and looked at him for a moment more. He hadn't closed his eyes again, but I couldn't tell if he was looking at me, even though his gaze was pointed my way.

"I'm Terry," I said at last. And though something trembled terrified within me as I did, I held out my hand.

He blinked blankly and shifted his gaze across the street.

"I'm Terry," I said again. "What's your name?"

A long pause, and then at last: "I'm Adrian," he muttered, keeping his eyes averted.

"Adrian," I repeated. "It's good to meet you." Out of a sense of obligation, or habit, I reached into my pocket and pulled out two twoonies and a quarter. It was all the change I had on me, but it would have been more than enough for a coffee. I held it out.

"Can I buy you a coffee?" I asked.

Adrian looked at my hand and then lifted his eyes to my face, offering me a faint nod. He reached and took the coins.

I was still thinking about this exchange some twenty minutes later, sitting at my desk and waiting for my computer to power up, when suddenly the same scent of smoke filled my nostrils. It was as strong as before, not especially nice-smelling, but neither was it pungent. A languid wood smoke smell, it wafted over me unmistakably, though again, like last time, no one else in the room seemed to notice it.

I took a deep sniff, but I couldn't decide if I found it fragrant or repulsive. It reminded me of the day I was going through my father's effects and I came across an old sweater of his, rank with his many years of smoking in it. I'd held it to my face, and though I could hardly bear to breathe it in, still there had been something deeply comforting about it.

I was just about to take another tour of the office, hunting for the source of the smell, when Alice appeared at my desk.

"Can you deal with this one?" she said, holding out a manila file folder. "I've called the loser five times this week and each time he just tries to push me around. I think it's because I'm a woman."

"What does he owe?" I asked.

"It's over twenty-five."

"Hundred?"

"Thousand. The deadbeat. And it looks like he's got half that on a Visa card, too."

I nodded and took the file from her.

"Hey Alice," I said as she turned to go. "Do you smell anything?"

Alice sniffed deeply. "Like what?"

I hesitated. "I don't know, like smoke? Like someone smoking, maybe. Cigarette smoke?"

"There'd better not be," she said abruptly. She sniffed again, almost viscously. "Though I don't smell anything." She swiveled in a slow circle, stalking a smell that wasn't there, until I began to feel embarrassed.

"Nope," she said at last. "And I'd know it if there was." She looked at me sideways. "You okay, Ter?"

I tried to laugh it off. "Yeah. Maybe. I don't know. Maybe I didn't get enough sleep last night."

When she was gone, I opened the folder and looked at it blankly. I took a final furtive sniff, but the smell was gone, vanishing as suddenly as it had appeared. I cleared my head with a shake and got to work.

The third time it happened, about a week or two later, I finally decided to make an appointment to see my doctor.

I'd just gotten off the phone with Alice's client. We call them clients, though I've sometimes wondered if prey might be a better word. It had taken me a full week to track him down, and when we finally spoke, he did try to bluster in a way that, if I had been Alice, I would have taken as an attempt to intimidate me.

Unlike Alice though, who always punched back savagely at even the slightest bump, I'd learned to take a gentler approach. My father liked to say that you catch more flies with honey than with vinegar, and I've always taken him at his word.

"Listen Frank," I'd told the man on the line. "I know you feel backed into a corner. I would too. But we all want the same thing, don't we? To make this debt disappear? Why don't we find a way to work together on it?"

"You don't understand," Frank had said. "It's not like I blew twenty-five thousand on a beachfront in Tahiti or something. I lost my job."

"Debts can really pile up when you're out of work," I said. "I get it."

"But then my wife got cancer, and I couldn't look for work because I was taking care of her, and…"

"Your wife got cancer?" This time my empathy wasn't just a tool of the trade.

"She died of it."

"What kind?"

"What do you care?"

"My dad died of cancer, too. Just a few months ago."

"Bone." A single word, spoken after a long pause.

I squeezed my eyes shut. "His was lung," I said.

We'd talked for a bit more, and by the time we'd hung up, I'd offered to request an extension for him, and he'd agreed to sit down with me in the coming week and work out a debt repayment plan. I stared at the phone for a thoughtful moment after I'd returned it to the receiver, which is when the smell flooded my senses, the same smoldering but not unpleasant scent of smoke.

It was familiar by now, though no less troubling, and I sniffed deeply two or three times, just to be sure. I didn't get up and go looking for it this time, however. I knew enough, by now, not to do that. My hand was still on the phone, and I picked it up again. Because of my recent ordeal with my father, my family doctor's number was scrawled in the front of my daybook, so I looked it up and dialed.

Three weeks later I was sitting in his examination room, sheepishly explaining the whole thing. I'd had two more episodes since booking the appointment, so it seemed to me that they were getting worse.

If Dr. Cohen thought I was going insane, nothing in his tone gave it away. He flipped very calmly through my file and asked a handful of gently probing questions.

"How often do they come?" he asked.

"I don't know. Maybe once a month. Maybe more."

"And are you aware of anything triggering them? Blinking lights on your computer screen? Increased stress at work?"

I thought of Frank, though I would hardly have called that exchange stressful, and then, unexpectedly, I thought of Adrian.

"Not really," I said.

The doctor seemed to hold his breath and scanned my file some more. "Any history of epilepsy in your family?" he said at last.

I hadn't thought of this until now, but it suddenly occurred to me: "My grandmother had epilepsy," I said. "Or so they told me, though I never saw her have a seizure."

Dr. Cohen nodded.

"Am I going crazy, Doc?" I asked, trying to pass my worry off as a joke.

"Probably not," he answered in a matter-of-fact tone. "Though we can't be sure." He looked up from my file when he said this, and I couldn't tell if he was joking, too.

"Phantosmia isn't necessarily a serious concern," he said at last. "But we'd better rule out the more serious causes."

"Phantosmia?"

"Phantom smells," he explained. "It's not uncommon and usually harmless, though it can be a sign of something more serious. We should book you in for some tests at the epilepsy clinic, an MRI maybe. And you should probably see an otorhinolaryngologist."

"Easy for you to say," I mumbled, still trying to wrap my worry with humour.

"A nose, ear and throat specialist," he said, smiling for the first time. He looked at me and then asked abruptly: "You say it's a smoky smell?"

"Yeah. It's not sweet-smelling, but it's not rank either. Like burning wood." I paused and looked at my feet. "To be honest, I kind of like it."

"Well, you should be grateful," he said. "For some people it's the smell of rotten meat, their phantosmia. Or sewage. So you could say you got off lucky."

Thus began a battery of procedures intrusive enough to rival the Navy SEAL screening tests. First was an MRI. The earliest booking they could make for me happened to be at three in the morning, and except that I have a mild case of claustrophobia, I might otherwise have dozed off in the scanner.

A few months later I found myself sitting in a dark room with my head wired into an EEG machine by a network of electrodes that made me feel vaguely like one of Dr. Frankenstein's failed experiments. The technician plugging me in was a young woman, and even though the lighting was dimmed, she had to lean in close to me, so I couldn't help but notice that her mascara was smudged.

"Everything alright?" I asked.

She paused and then feinted with a weak smile. "All's fine," she said. "Just got some bad news this morning."

"Sorry to hear that." I'd meant it in that generic way we usually say such things, but the tone of my voice caught me off guard, and I realized suddenly that I really was sorry for her.

It must have caught her off guard, too, because she lifted a fleeting hand to glimmering eyes, smudged her mascara worse than it was before, and sighed. "It's my mother," she said. "She's been sick for a long time and today they moved her into palliative. She signed a DNR a ways back, and, well, I'm just not ready for that." She seemed suddenly to realize where she was and feigned another smile.

"I'm sorry," she said. "You didn't come here to listen to this."

"No," I offered, speaking as kindly as I could. "My father passed of cancer this year. I get it."

She began explaining the EEG to me, that I needed to wait a good twenty minutes because it would only pick up seizure activity if it happened to occur while I was being scanned.

"Do you have any symptoms now?" she asked.

I sniffed deeply and there it was, fainty, the scent of something smoldering, very softly but unmistakably at the back of my nose. I hadn't noticed it before but couldn't escape it now that I did. It persisted through the entire test.

I had slipped out of work over lunch to take the EEG, and because the clinic was only a few blocks from our building, I'd walked. My phantosmia had been only very faint at the clinic, but it was growing gradually as I walked back, and for the first time I even dared to savor the scent.

Not that it smelled good. It was the kind of smell you'd want to wash out of your clothes after a weekend of camping. But it was so mysterious and earthy that it made me feel deeply connected to everything happening all around me, for all it being the smell of something that was not there.

I was passing the S.I.S. with these empty efforts to name my phantosmia swirling around in my thoughts, and the scent was, by this time, almost overwhelming.

I noticed a man slumped against the wall near the door. Recognizing the soiled parka, I spoke out his name almost before I realized what I was doing.

"Hi, Adrian."

He was obviously not used to being called by name, and he looked up with glassy eyes.

"Do I know you?"

"We met a few months ago, over there." I nodded my chin in the direction of our building across the street. "I haven't seen you around since then, though. Where have you been?"

"I spent some time in Kingston," he said vaguely. "But the scene there was pretty rough, so I'm back here."

"You keeping well?" I asked. Immediately I felt how stupid a thing it was to ask, but Adrian seemed not to notice. He shrugged.

"As well as I can. Hey, you wouldn't happen to have…" he trailed off.

I reached into my jacket. All I had was a twenty—I'd shoved it in my pocket that morning to cover lunch for the day. But it was already past one, and anyway my heart was feeling so light at that moment that I felt as if I'd never need to eat again. I held it out to him, my head roaring with a fragrant cloud of billowing smoke.

He said nothing as he took it, but for the flash of a moment I thought I saw a smile glimmer behind the guarded eyes.

About two months after this interaction, I found myself sitting in another examination room, awaiting the arrival of the otorhinolaryngologist my doctor had referred me to. My episodes of phantosmia had come and gone with no predictability; weeks would go by with nothing, and then I would have two or three in a row. One lasted a day and a half, so long that I began to worry in a way I hadn't since the days when it first started.

In that time, I'd begun to notice some subtle changes in me. I seldom laughed at Ed's edged comments about the rest of the staff anymore. I found a genuine curiosity growing in me, to understand what made Alice so aggressive in her approach with our clients. And my own demeanor with them, though it had never really been hard, had become so gentle as to be almost compassionate.

All the while, my interest in the S.I.S. across the street grew to the point of being an obsession. At times I would catch myself standing in the window at the far end of the office, watching the lineup across the street like a watchman in a lookout tower. I started keeping change in my pocket specifically for Adrian, and watching for him intently when I came in to work. He was as unpredictable as my ghost smells, though, and sometimes days, even weeks would go by with no visitation.

And then I'd see him standing in line, huddled in his soiled parka, or I'd come across him sleeping something horrid off on the steps of our building, and I'd call him by name and offer him what I'd been carrying around in my pocket for him. He never remembered me, but he always took the gift.

I couldn't connect the dots very clearly, yet, but a hunch was forming in me that somehow or other these things—Adrian, and the S.I.S., Alice, and Ed—that they were all connected in some mysterious way to my phantosmia. Certainly, it had only started after the site had opened, though not immediately after, so that hardly seemed like concrete evidence. Sitting in the examination room, I was just wondering if I ought to tell the otorhinolaryngologist about these coincidences, when the door swung open and she stepped in.

She was a stocky woman with the look of someone perpetually waiting for the punchline of a joke that would never come. She held my chart in her hand, and I couldn't be sure, but there seemed to be a grin on her face as she scanned it.

"It says here that you've been experiencing phantom smells?" She looked at me with crinkles forming at the corners of her eyes. "Good ones, I hope?"

"Kinda," I said. "Smoke."

"Well, Mr. Sheppard, let's see if we can't figure out what's going on in that honker of yours."

She began a series of rather unpleasant investigations which involved pushing a scope uncomfortably far up each nostril in turn.

"No tumors or inflammation," she offered, scribbling some indecipherable notes on my chart. "Let's call that a relief, shall we? Now, Mr. Sheppard, I'd like to try another test." She pulled a small wooden box out of a cupboard, which she opened to reveal a good dozen glass vials, each one plugged with a plastic stopper.

"I'd like to see how your sense of smell is generally," she said. "Each one of these is scented with an everyday odor. I'll have you close your eyes and smell them, one after the other. Can you tell me what you smell with each one?"

I did as she said and held the first vial under my nose. "Fish," I said. "No question."

"Good. Here's the next."

It was onion. The next was rose—or possibly lavender—after that came tar, then garlic.

"Nothing wrong with the sniffer so far," she said, but when she handed me the next vial I stopped. Not that the smell was difficult to identify; it was just so immediately and painfully recognizable.

I swallowed. "Cigarettes?" I asked after a long time. I opened my eyes.

"Most people find that one easy," she said.

"I did too. But my father died of lung cancer—he was a smoker all his life—and even to this day the smell takes me back to his bedside."

"Well, Mr. Sheppard, the olfactory system *is* psychosomatically connected to the limbic system, making odors an evocative mnemonic." She started chuckling. "Smells can trigger powerful memories, I mean."

I nodded. "It's just: I didn't see him much the last few months—before he went, I mean. I don't know, but maybe I blamed him for what happened. Isn't that awful?"

Unexpectedly, the doctor placed a hand lightly on my shoulder. "It's already hard enough," she said, "for sons to lose their fathers. I don't suppose there's any need to make it harder."

I nodded solemnly and closed my eyes again, taking the last few vials in turn. The scent of vanilla was unmistakable, and the scent of licorice after that, then mint, then apple. I opened my eyes after the last vial. It was hard to tell after wading through so many smells, but it seemed as if another episode of phantosmia was beginning.

I looked across the room at my otorhinolaryngologist. "So, what's up doc?" I said at last.

"Well, Mr. Sheppard: your MRI looks perfectly normal, and your EEG showed nothing. Your blood work is all fine, as are the x-rays of your sinuses. I can't find anything wrong with your sniffer to look at it, and you passed the olfactory test with flying colors."

She closed my file and looked at me squarely. "I think you're perfectly normal."

"Normal? Doc, I smell smoke that isn't there. How can you call that normal?"

"In the majority of cases, phantosmia is entirely harmless. Most instances resolve themselves in a matter of weeks, though for some reason yours doesn't seem to be going away. Tell me: is there a history of migraines in your family?"

I thought for a moment. "My dad got migraines, yes."

"Well, I think your particular phantosmia is a rare form of the migraine aura."

"I'm smelling the sparkly lights that people with migraines get?"

She laughed. "Sort of. The same neurological phenomenon that triggers the sparkly lights in some can trigger different responses in others, including olfactory hallucinations. It's rare, but not impossible."

I sighed. Something inside me fiercely resisted so simple an explanation. I'm not sure what I was hoping for, but it wasn't this. "But I don't get any headaches," I said feebly.

"Occasionally people get the aura without getting the migraines. You should consider yourself blessed."

I rose to go. "So, there's nothing I can do about it?"

"You told me the smell was not unpleasant," she said, the creases around her eyes crinkling playfully. "Perhaps you could learn to enjoy it?"

I was due back at work that afternoon, but I took a meandering route to my building. I got off the bus a good ten blocks early and walked the remainder. The very faint odor that had started in the doctor's examination room had persisted, and it seemed to grow stronger with every step I took toward the office. I was scheduled to meet with Frank at two o'clock. He had kept up with his meagre payback plan throughout that year, and had even found steady work, so that afternoon we were going to renegotiate his payments.

The memory of my first call to him sprang starkly to mind, and I wondered how different his story would have been if Alice had stayed with his file. I thought of Alice herself, and then of Ed, and the deep sadness that seemed to saturate everything they did at ACC Financial. More vivid memories came to me, of their rigid resistance to the S.I.S., and of the derelict souls that used the clinic daily.

It was hard to know for sure if the smell was prompting these memories, or the memories the smell, but the fragrance continued to grow, becoming almost heady as I rounded the block and the Safe Injection Site came into view.

The usuals were milling about by the doors, and a scrubs-clad woman with latex gloves was talking to two of them. As I neared, I could hear laughter passing between them, softly but unmistakably. Not cruel laughter like Ed might have laughed but real, human laughter, like warm friends might share with each other.

I had no clue what the joke might have been, but as I approached, I recognized a soiled parka standing among them, unmistakably. I inhaled deeply, more deeply than I had in a long time, and cleared my throat.

"Hi Adrian," I said. And as he turned, I felt myself delirious at last with the heady fragrance of something beautiful burning.

19.

Jonathan

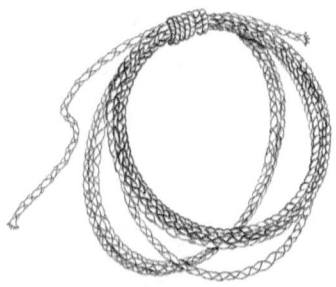

Before that day, I had never really understood that my cousin Jonathan was different. It's true that sometimes when we fought I called him "brown bread," but that was only because he always called me "white bread" first. And even though I said it in reference to his skin color, as a child of nine it was no more xenophobic than if I had pointed out his brown eyes or black hair. We both loved Lego and Atari games, and on these things, the things that mattered, we were more alike than any bond of blood could have made us.

Jonathan was not his original name, of course, though I did not learn this until after I was an adult. It was at his funeral, and my aunt Jenny explained to me how he'd come to them with the name Dakota. My uncle Jon had always wanted a boy named after him, however, and their daughter Jess had been their only biological child, so they'd renamed him Jonathan. As a result, I grew up calling him Jonny and knew no better. I didn't even appreciate what it really meant that he'd been adopted until we were young men and had gone our separate ways.

There were enough signs of the difference between us on that road trip, however, that I might have picked up on it if I were older. My mother and I were vacationing with Uncle Jon and his family for the summer, touring southern Alberta in the refurbished school bus he used as a camper. The bus was more than big enough for the six of us, but it wasn't air-conditioned, and hours on the road beneath the baking prairie sun made it unbearable at times.

Jonny never really complained, though. Unlike his sister, he tended to face hardship with an almost stoic determination. She, on the other hand, complained enough for us all. When it got really bad, Jonny would try to distract her with some playful insult or mischievous prank, but this would only make things worse, and she'd start bickering with him or taking it out on me.

This resulted more than once in a squabble fierce enough that Uncle Jon pulled over and made him get out and walk. He never made Jess walk, only Jonny. And though he'd never dare to pitch me out of the vehicle with my mother there, I looked up to Jonny immensely, so I'd usually get out to walk in solidarity with him.

Uncle Jon would then drive a hundred yards or more down the road and wait for us to catch up, the idea being that between the exercise and the fear of being abandoned, we'd have learned our lesson by the time we caught up to them. Jonny never seemed to learn his lesson though, and within the hour he was finding new ways to get Jess going.

On one of these roadside disciplinings, after an especially fierce melee between Jonny and Jess, Uncle Jon actually drove far enough down the road that he crested a little hill, and we couldn't be sure if he'd actually stopped for us this time.

Though I was mustering everything I had inside me to keep from crying, Jonny looked unperturbed, almost serene.

"Don't worry, Tom," he said, nodding his chin toward the disappearing taillights of the bus. "He won't go far. And anyway, I could use a good walk." Then, abruptly turning his attention to the grass growing along the ditch, he said, "Look! Spear grass."

He stooped and pulled up a few stalks.

"You know why they call it spear grass, don't you?" He started peeling back the leaves and pulling out one or two of the seeds with their long, thin tails. He held one up to me, a wiry strand with a sharp barb on the end.

"Come have a look at this," he said with a grin. And as I was stepping up close to see, he flung it at me suddenly, with a practiced flick of his fingers. It hit me on the upper arm, where the sleeve of my tee shirt covered the skin, but even so it stung sharply, and the barb clung to the cloth, so that it kept stinging as I moved my arm to pull it free.

"Geez, Jonny, that really hurts," I said, nursing the spot sulkily.

He gave me a push. "Don't be a baby, Tom. If you want, I can show you how to do it." He stooped to pull up some more spear grass, but as he rose, he gestured toward a road sign up ahead.

"Look at that," he said.

Uncle Jon had put us out of the bus near to one of those brown-colored signs the province uses to mark sites of interest on the prairie landscape. It read: "Head-Smashed-In Buffalo Jump, 16 km."

I was still somewhat sullen from the sting of the spear grass, and my fear of being abandoned was turning into bitterness.

"Maybe that's what we should do to them," I said, nodding in the direction of the vanished bus.

"What do you mean?"

"Smash their heads in." It hadn't occurred to me how horrid a thing I was saying; I was only trying to impress Jonny. But he gave me a stern look and shoved me, not unkindly, but so hard I nearly fell over.

"Don't talk like that," he said.

"Why not?" I asked, regaining my balance. "'Cause he's your dad?"

"He's not my dad, Tom. He's my elder. And you have to respect the elders." He started walking down the road, bringing his shoulder against mine with another firm shove as he passed me.

"And anyway," he said, "Head-Smashed-In is a special place. You shouldn't joke about it."

Later that day, after we'd caught up with the school bus and were miles down the road from Head-Smashed-In, we saw a sign announcing that we were passing the Siksika Nation Indian Reserve.

Jess said something about how maybe we should drop Jonny off there, how he'd be right at home.

Jonny didn't say anything, but he fixed his eyes on the sign as it passed, even turning over his shoulder to watch it disappear behind us.

"But I'm not Siksika." He said it quietly, but Uncle Jon must have been listening to us closer than we realized, because he spoke up from the driver's seat. "No, you're not, Jonny. You're an O'Connor like the rest of us. And don't let no one tell you different."

Jonny was very quiet after that, and for the rest of the day's drive there was no bickering between us kids.

We pulled into our campsite late that day. An orange sun was hovering just above the lip of the horizon, swollen and enflamed in the settling prairie dust. The campground was in a wide shallow valley, surrounded on all sides by the faces of dusty brown hills. Though the prairies all around were as bare as the day God made them, there were all sorts of cottonwood and poplars growing in the wind shelter of the valley. From somewhere far away I thought I could smell something sweet floating on the evening air.

Jonny was off and running as soon as the bus doors folded open.

"Don't wander too far," Uncle Jon called after him. "It's gonna be dark soon, and we still haven't eaten."

Jonny didn't look back, or even slow his pace, but he did wave his hand in the air twice, to show he'd heard. I watched him for a second and then gave my mother a questioning look.

"Go ahead then," she said. "Heaven knows you could do with the exercise after sitting in that oven for the last six hours."

I called out for Jonny to wait up and set off after him. "Just don't go too far," I heard my mother calling from behind me. "And stick close to Jonny."

By the time I'd caught up with him, we'd already reached the far end of the campsite and come to a worn-out playground. The climbing apparatuses were made of old tractor tires, huge pieces of black rubber half buried in the ground, with smaller ones bolted together to make forts and climbing walls. I hoisted myself awkwardly to the top of one of these, calling out for Jonny to join me. But he was already on the other side of the playground, where there was an open field, and beyond that a fenced area surrounded by bleachers.

"Jonny!" I called from the top of my tractor tire fort. "Your dad said don't go too far!"

"I told you. He's not my dad," Jonny called back. "He's my elder!"

I clambered down and raced to catch up.

"Why do you keep saying that?" I asked as I pulled up next to him.

"Because he is," he said. "'Cause I'm not an O'Connor, Tom. I'm Ojibwe."

"What's that mean?"

"It means," he said, throwing himself toward me and catching me in a playful headlock. "I'm not a piece of white bread like you!"

We scuffled for a minute, and though we were both laughing as we did, it was never clear with Jonny whether any fight was ever just for fun. I tried to pull his leg out from under him, but he shifted his weight so that we both went down in the dusty grass, my head still locked under his arm. We rolled around for a minute more, each trying to top the other, but Jonny was two years older, and eventually he won out.

"Say it!" he said, sitting on my chest and pinning my arms to the ground by the wrists. "You're a piece of white bread! Say it!"

We had played this game often enough that I knew what was coming and braced myself for it. He leaned forward, so that his face was close to mine. Then pursing his lips, he let a trailing blob of spit slowly slip down, lowering it until it hung barely an inch above my face. I grimaced and tried to shrink into the ground, but just before it dropped free, he sucked it back in, still laughing.

"Say it," he said in an exaggerated tone of warning, "or next time I'll let it drop!" He let another blob down from his mouth, hanging it over my face as long as he could before it dropped, and then sucking it up.

"No!" I shouted, writhing under his weight. "If I'm white bread then you're brown bread! You say that!"

Jonny misjudged the timing on his next spit bomb and before he could suck it back, it came free and fell into my eye, wet and blinding.

"Augh!" I cried, and the disgust of it gave me the momentum I needed to finally break loose. "Jonny, that's so gross!"

He rolled away laughing and lay there, staring up at the purpling sky, while I sat up, sweaty and itchy, wiping spit out of my eye.

When I could see clearly again, we both got up and took our bearings.

"What's that?" I asked in the direction of the fenced off area at the far end of the field. "It sorta looks like a hockey rink."

Jonny started moving toward it. The sun had disappeared behind the edge of the valley, and a dusky light had fallen over everything. I wondered briefly if my mother would have thought that the far end of the field was too far, but she had also told me to stick with Jonny, so I followed him.

"It's for the rodeo," said Jonny.

It was a wide arena, fenced in with heavy-duty wire fencing, not barbed, but sturdy, with thick wooden fenceposts. On either side were sets of bleachers, four or five risers high, and at the far end was a complicated-looking contraption of steel fencing and metal siding that I learned later was the cattle chute. Jonny stepped up onto the lowest wire of the fence, leaning his weight on the top wire and rocking back and forth. I climbed up next to him.

"The rodeo?"

"Yeah. Dad brought us here last year. Year before that, too. Every year there's a huge rodeo. Cow roping and bull wrestling. Guys walking around in cowboy hats and spurs."

"You mean real cowboys?" I said innocently, admiring his experience of the world. "Like in the movies?"

He looked at me a second, then punched me in the arm. "Yeah, Tom. Like in the movies."

"You think we'll see some?" I asked, rubbing my arm.

"I think we're too early this year. The rodeo doesn't happen till later in the summer."

We heard someone calling at the end of the field we'd come from. I turned toward the sound, though Jonny ignored it and kept swaying back and forth, leaning over the top wire of the arena's fencing.

"It's your dad," I said, but Jonny still didn't turn. "It's time to head back."

Finally, he spat over the fence and heaved himself down. He bumped me hard as he passed me, though when Uncle Jon came into view, waving at us from the far side of the field, Jonny lifted his arm and waved back. Then he picked up his pace and began jogging lightly toward the campsite.

The next morning, I was up and out of the school bus long before Jonny. I downed two individual sized boxes of Frosted Flakes as quickly as I could, drinking the last of the residual milk from the wax paper lining and wiping my face on my sleeve. Then I turned in the direction of the tire park.

Jess said that she was going to stay at the campsite and play solitaire, but we could go climbing on a bunch of filthy old tires if we wanted to. I took it as a favor that she didn't want to join us but asked her to tell Jonny where I was when he got up.

When I got to the park, I saw three boys standing near the rodeo fencing. They were huddled together and looking intently at something, but I couldn't make out what it was. All three were dressed in straight-leg wranglers and plaid shirts, and two of them wore what I assumed were real-life cowboy hats. One had on a pair of genuine leather cowboy boots, and frequently kicked them so that little clouds of dust coughed up and drifted away while they talked.

When I got closer, I saw that he was holding a long length of rope, which is what the three of them were examining so closely.

"You tie it like this," he was saying. "So when you pull it back, the loop goes tight." The boy put his wrist into the loop at the end of the rope and pulled it tight to demonstrate.

"Where'd you learn how to do that?" asked one of the others.

"My dad taught me. He's been rodeoing for ages."

I was standing close enough to them that they noticed me.

"Hey kid," said one of them. "You wanna play with us?"

"What you playing?"

"Cowboys," said the boy with the boots on. He kicked up a little cloud of dust and swung the loop of his rope back and forth a few times.

"That a real lasso?" I asked.

"Sure is," he said. "Watch this."

He swung the rope in a big circle over his head and then tossed it in the direction of a fence post. It landed easily over it, and the boy yanked fiercely, pulling it tight.

"So, you in?"

"Sure," I said. "How do you play?"

The boy grinned and gestured to the far side of the rodeo arena with a tilt of his head. "Come on."

He climbed the fence and started across. The boots must have been new, because he seemed to walk somewhat gingerly, the straight-leg wranglers making his gait look more bowlegged than it probably was. Every now and then he gave a swinging kick with his toe and tossed up another cloud of dust. We all followed him up to the shiny metal cattle chute at the far end. He climbed up onto the fencing till he could see into it.

"So," he explained. "You can work the gate there, Chet, and I'll sit up here with the lasso. You get in the chute, kid; you too, Andy. You guys can be the calves. I'll be the cowboy."

"Why do you get to be the cowboy?" asked Andy sourly.

"'Cause it's my lasso," he snorted. "And anyways, I got real cowboy boots."

This logic didn't seem to placate Andy, but he accepted it, and with a grim look he clambered over the fence and into the chute. I might have looked grim, too, if I'd known what was coming.

"Okay," said the boy with the rope. "When I say go, Chet'll open the gate. Then Andy, you come running out fast as you can. Like a calf. Ready?"

Andy didn't answer, but he set his stance and poised his weight, ready to bolt as soon as the gate was opened.

I was standing behind him, watching closely so I'd know what to do when my turn came. A great creak sounded, and the gate swung open. As soon as he could make it through, Andy burst forward, pelting as hard as he could.

It was not nearly hard enough. The boy with the rope swung his lasso with what must have been a practiced hand, giving it a great heave at just the right moment. Andy grunted and fell, the lasso tight around his shoulders.

"Yeah!" cried Chet. "Got 'im, Jason!"

The whole thing seemed a bit unfair to me. Jason was perched on the crossbar right above the gate, and all he really had to do was drop the loop over our shoulders as we ran past. I was about to say so when the gate creaked closed again.

"Okay kid," Chet said. "Your turn."

I dug my heel in and watched Jason closely. The gate swung open, but I didn't run out immediately.

"C'mon kid," said Jason. "You're supposed to run out like a calf."

I said nothing but steeled myself to sprint. Chet hammered on the side of the chute. "C'mon!" he shouted. Andy had dusted himself off and found a seat on the fence. "Come boss!" he hollered. "Hey boss! Come boss!"

I swallowed a gulp of air, and with a look of flint on my face I made my break for it. I tried running zigzag out the chute, hoping to dodge the rope, but this was hardly Jason's first game of cowboy. He reached and tossed the lasso over me as I passed, letting me run far enough to build up a bit of momentum before yanking it taut.

It hurt, but not badly, and the last thing I would have done was to start crying in front of three older boys.

"Got 'im!" shouted Chet. Jason yee-hawed

I scrambled to my feet as quickly as I could and shrugged my way out of the lasso.

"No fair!" I hollered, banging the dirt off my pants. "You're sitting right there!"

"That's how the game's played," said Jason placidly, using his palm and elbow to coil the rope slowly.

"Let me have a turn," said Andy, jumping down from the fence.

"No. You be the calf again."

Andy opened his mouth in protest, but Jason shut him down. "It's my rope. And besides, Chet's turn comes before yours. You be the calf again. You too, kid."

Andy and I played the calf three more times. Each time, I watched closely as Andy got yanked to the dirt; I was trying madly to figure out some way to avoid the same fate. But each time my turn came, I felt the rope slip around my shoulders, pull taut, and throw me to the ground.

Chet had a turn with the lasso, and Jason again. Andy argued vehemently for his turn, and even got Jason to agree that after a few more times he could give it a try, but no one even suggested I might get a turn myself.

I had just stepped into the chute a fourth time, determined this time to escape the lasso, when I heard a tentative voice speak my name.

"What you doing, Tom?"

I looked through the bars of the cattle chute, and saw Jonny standing by the fence, outside the arena.

"We're playing cowboys," I said, smacking dirt off my legs with a kind of pride. For all it being unfair and painful, I had started to own the game.

"Who's that?" said Chet.

"That's my cousin," I said. "His name is Jonny."

"You wanna play, Jonny?" I asked him. But Jonny said nothing. He looked up at Jason, still sitting on the crossbar over the cattle chute. Jason looked away and struck his rope against the side of his leg two or three times.

"No," said Chet suddenly. "He can't play."

"What d'you mean?" I asked. It was a sincere question, but I felt a strange heat rising in my throat as I asked it.

Jason jumped down from the crossbar. "Chet's right. He can't."

"Why not?"

No one spoke, and my perplexity seemed to shorten my breath for a moment. "Why not?" I asked again.

"He can't play with us," said Jason. "'Cause he's an Indian."

His eyes were fixed firmly on Jonny as he said this, but to my surprise, Jonny didn't return his stare. He cast me a sad look and then looked at the ground hard, as if he would bore a hole into it if he could.

"Yeah," said Andy. "We don't play with Indians."

Jason started climbing back to his perch, as though that was all that needed saying. "C'mon Chet," he muttered. "Let's go again."

The cattle gate swung open, widely, but I stood stock still for a long moment. Jonny had turned and was walking back toward our campsite. I had never seen his shoulders so stooped as they were in that moment. Something somewhere between fury and shame was swirling inside me, and I gave a great guttural groan.

I bolted from the chute with all my might, though I wasn't playing cowboy this time. I was running after Jonny, wishing with everything inside me that I was standing next to him on the other side of the arena.

I knew the boy with the lasso had roped me even before I felt the line go taut and I lost my balance. I fell hard in the dirt, a great cloud of dust reeling up as I landed.

I wanted to scream. I wanted to swear.

I rolled over on my back and grabbed the rope, heaving on it as hard as I could, hoping to pull Jason down with me. But he was older and heavier, and anyway I was hurting pretty badly from playing cowboy all morning, so I couldn't move him. He heaved back, and the rope bit deeply into my shoulders.

I punched my hand against the ground and shouted out in pain and rage. If the cowboys were at all startled by my outburst, it passed quickly. Jason gave the rope a final yank with a savage laugh, and all three started waving their hats in the air, whooping wildly.

20.

A Feast of Epiphanies

Casper never would have called Natalie that afternoon except that he really needed the bread tins. They hadn't spoken in months, not since he'd moved out at her request and set himself up in his new apartment. But the pastor of his new church had come up with an idea for the new year, that each family in the congregation should take a turn making homemade bread for the communion service. They celebrated communion at the start of each month, and Pastor Milo said it would make the whole experience more meaningful if the bread they served had been personally made—with tender loving care is how he put it—by one of the many lovely households that made up their little family of faith.

Maybe he'd done it to spite her, to show her how well he was moving on without her. Or maybe it was simply to prove to himself that he really did fit in with all those lovely households at church, however dingy his private life seemed by comparison. Whatever the reason, he'd signed up for the "Our Monthly Bread" project, as Pastor Milo playfully called it, determined to make a loaf of bread with as much tender loving care as he could manage.

It hadn't occurred to him till he was watching some breadmaking tutorials on YouTube that Friday evening that he'd need some bread tins. He owned a set—they'd been included in a big box of old kitchenware that his grandmother had given him when he'd left for college—but he'd never used them. They'd been stuffed into the back of a kitchen cupboard when he and Natalie were setting up house after the wedding, and they hadn't been touched since.

When he had moved out, however, he'd left everything behind except his clothes and a few irreplaceable personal items. He wanted the break to be as clean as possible, and the thought of sitting down to divide up all the random accretions of their life together seemed excruciatingly sad to him, so he simply told her to keep what she wanted and give what she didn't to Goodwill.

It was the kind of thing you say in the blur of a messy separation, never guessing you'll find yourself some months later, wanting to make a homemade loaf of bread for your church's communion service and needing a set of tins.

"Do we—I mean—do you still have that old set of bread tins?" he'd asked at her lukewarm hello.

"You're calling me about bread tins, Caz?"

"Yeah. They were my grandmother's, and I need them."

"What for? You've never made a loaf of bread in your life."

"Look: do you have them or not? I think we used to keep them in the back of that—what do you call it?—the lazy Susan thing?"

"I didn't get rid of them, if that's what you mean. So unless you did, I guess they're still there."

"Well, I need them. Do you—" He squeezed his eyes shut, grimacing against the great surge of regret and humiliation welling up inside him. "Do you mind if I swing by tonight to pick them up?"

"Sorry Caz, I'm out tonight. But I'm working tomorrow. If you want, I could bring them by on my way home."

"You're working tomorrow? It's a Saturday."

"Don't get started, okay? One of the things about us being separated is that you don't get to comment on my hours anymore, remember? Just tell me if you want your tins or not. I could bring them by around four."

"Well—" Casper grimaced again. "I guess if that's the best you can do, it'll have to be fine. I'm having Mom and Mel over tomorrow afternoon for Ukrainian Christmas Eve. You can just text me when you get to the apartment and I'll come down to get the tins, if you don't want to risk bumping into them."

Casper's mother had been quite hard on Natalie when they'd separated, and more than one vaguely insulting phone call had been exchanged between them before she and Casper finally parted ways.

There was a long pause on Natalie's end. "Nothing's simple anymore, is it?" she said at last with a sigh.

It was Casper's turn to pause. After another long silence, he said, "No, Natalie. It's really not."

"Well: I'm sure it'll be fine, Caz. Who knows? It might even be nice to see you all again."

Casper wasn't sure there'd be anything nice about Natalie dropping by during one of his family's awkward celebrations of Ukrainian Christmas, but his resolve to get his grandmother's bread tins had become an almost overwhelming force inside him, so he agreed.

He was bitterly frustrated after the call, so he tried to distract himself by packing away the meagre Christmas decorations he'd put up in his apartment.

He knew this would disappoint his mother. She always insisted that the tree and its trimmings should stay up till after the seventh of January, Ukrainian Christmas Day. But Casper had found the whole rigmarole of putting up a tree to be almost unbearably depressing this year. He'd left all his Christmas ornaments behind with Natalie, and somehow his pathetically decorated tree seemed only to remind him, every time he saw it, of how alone he really was. The sooner it was packed away, he figured, the quicker he could put the whole gloomy situation behind him.

It was not much of a distraction. The radio was still playing Christmas music, and at one point he found himself lost in thought over a syrupy rendition of the "Twelve Days of Christmas." He did the math absent-mindedly and realized that this Friday afternoon, as he tore down his pitiful tree on the fifth of January, it was technically the twelfth day of Christmas. It crossed his mind, ridiculously but painfully, that there was no hope he'd get twelve drummers drumming this year, since he had no true love to give them.

He went to bed miserable and intensely alone.

The next morning was January sixth, Christmas Eve Day by the Ukrainian reckoning, though his new church had celebrated on the twenty-fifth like everyone else. He was grateful he had the golubsty to prepare for the family gathering that afternoon, as well as the communion bread to bake. Normally Natalie would have made the golubsty for their Ukrainian Christmas dinner. They were very finicky, as cabbage rolls go, and he knew it would take him a while just to watch the playlist of YouTube videos he'd compiled to learn how to do it himself. Add to this his first ever attempt at baking bread and it was enough to keep his mind off Natalie all day.

By four o'clock that afternoon, a huge dish of golubsty was warming in the oven and he was working away at the bread dough, dusted with flour and somewhat disheveled, when the intercom to the apartment's foyer buzzed. He braced himself as he reached for the receiver. He couldn't decide if he was hoping it would be Natalie—so he could be sure she'd be gone by the time his family got there—or if he was hoping it would be Mom and Mel—so he'd at least have some small amount of moral support when Natalie did arrive.

Whatever his preference, it turned out to be neither.

"Merry Christmas!" came a gregarious voice, bellowing through the crackling receiver down in the lobby. "It's your Uncle Buzz."

Casper was genuinely startled. His dad's brother had kept in touch with them after the funeral, off and on while he was growing up, but he hadn't heard from him in over a year. "Buzz? What on earth are you doing here?"

"Your mother got in touch with me to say that you were all getting together for Sviatyi Vechir, and she thought you could use some extra company this year."

Casper passed the back of his hand across his forehead and squeezed his eyes shut. He'd always found Buzz to be a bit much, and he wasn't sure he had the capacity for him this evening, of all evenings. But he had no choice now, so he took a deep breath and pressed the button to release the door. "Well, come on up then. It'll be good to see you."

Moments later Buzz was standing in the doorway, poorly shaven and tousle-haired, his overcoat crumpled and his scarf shabby-looking.

"How's the friendly ghost?" he brayed, flinging his arms wide in greeting.

"Merry Christmas, Uncle Buzz," Casper mumbled as the man yanked him into a smothering embrace. Buzz squeezed him tightly then released him abruptly, giving him a staggering smack on the shoulder.

He pushed a brown paper bag into Casper's chest. "I come bearing gifts," he said, as he pulled off the crumpled overcoat and shoved it into the closet next to the boxed-up Christmas tree. Casper reached into the bag and pulled out a large clear bottle.

"You know, Uncle Buzz, most people bring wine."

Buzz waved his hand dismissively. "There's a bottle of wine in there too. But it's your first Ukrainian Christmas as a bachelor, right? So tonight, we celebrate!"

Casper looked closely at the bottle of vodka. "I think you might want to take this back to the liquor store. There's some kind of crud floating in it."

"Read the label, wise guy. That's Smirnoff Gold there. We're talking some premium vodka. And it's got little flakes of real gold in it, for an extra touch of class. That bottle almost bankrupted me, Casper."

Casper stepped from the foyer and set the bottles on his makeshift dining room table. His apartment wasn't large enough to have a dedicated dining room, but he'd set two plastic folding tables together in the living room to serve for the evening's festivities.

"Why on earth would they put gold in it?" he wondered out loud.

Buzz opened his mouth to explain, but just then the foyer intercom buzzed again. This time it was his mother, with his sister Melania.

"Glad you made it," said Casper. Leaning over the receiver and hiding his words behind his hand, he added softly: "Uncle Buzz is already here, and I could use the help."

His mother's voice fluttered at the receiver down in the lobby. "Well, I'm sorry Casper, but I just didn't want you to be—"

Casper pressed the button to release the door, cutting her off with its metallic buzz. When he turned from the receiver, he saw that his uncle had already found his way to the table and was pouring a swallow of vodka into a tumbler.

He lifted the drink in Casper's direction, as if to offer him a touch of class. Casper shook his head and looked away while Buzz downed it with a shrug and a gasp.

"You're not wasting any time, are you Uncle Buzz?" he mumbled sadly.

"I'm telling you Casper: this is premium stuff."

A hundred rejoinders ran through Casper's mind—was it the same premium stuff as what had killed his dad that night?—was it premium enough that Buzz wouldn't have to worry about dying in a DUI himself?—was there enough gold in the bottle that if they saved it they could use it to pay for the funeral, just in case?—but he bit his lip and looked away, breathing a sigh of relief when the sound of a knock finally rattled on the door.

Mel was first across the threshold. For all it being the start of January in Toronto, she was radiantly tanned.

"How was India?" he asked, smiling his first genuine smile in days.

Mel beamed, throwing her arms open and inviting him into a hug. "Amazing!" she said. "But I missed you."

Casper hesitated. She was dressed stunningly, as always, in an expensive-looking cashmere coat and a paisley silk scarf. It made him suddenly aware that he was still wearing a baking apron and was covered in flour from the bread.

"Well?" she said, still extending her arms.

"Look at me, Mel. I'll get flour all over you."

"Shut up, Caz, and give your sister a hug. I haven't seen you in months!"

Casper acquiesced, and as he stepped into her embrace, a heady smell overpowered him, like the billowing clouds of incense in the churches of their childhood. From a distance, the fragrance would have been charming, but pressed up so close to it as he was, it simply made his nose sting. He tried to stifle a cough and ended up spluttering weakly.

"Do you like it?" Mel asked, releasing him from the hug. "I got it in the duty-free shop at the airport in Calcutta. It's called Encens Mythique, by Guerlain." She pronounced the French with an exaggerated accent. "Would have cost me a fortune to get it here at home."

Casper rubbed the tip of his nose with the back of his hand. "What can I say? It's classic Melania. You never do anything by halves."

"I was wheezing the whole cab ride over," said his mother. She leaned forward and gave Casper a perfunctory peck on the cheek. "Here," she said. "I brought varenyky." She held up a large ceramic pan, wrapped in a towel to keep warm.

"I don't know how you could even make out my perfume, Mom," said Mel playfully, "the way the cab was filled with the smell of your cooking."

"Don't knock Mom's varenyky," said Casper, giving his second genuine smile of the evening. "As far as I'm concerned, it's the best thing about Ukrainian Christmas Eve."

His mother ignored their banter and pushed past him into the living room. "No tree?" she said, more as a commentary than a question.

Casper's smile faded. "No. I already put away the tree. We're nearly two weeks past Christmas and I thought—"

"You know how I feel about the tree at Ukrainian Christmas."

"Yes, Mom, I know. I just thought that maybe this year it wouldn't hurt to pack it up early."

His mother nodded, but clearly not in agreement. "And why are you covered in flour? You said you'd make the golubsty. You don't need flour for that." She looked at him sharply. "You did make the golubsty?"

"Yes, Mom, I made the golubsty. At least, I did my best. But I'm also making bread. My church is doing communion tomorrow and I'm making the bread for it."

His mother arched an eyebrow. "Communion? In the Ukrainian Orthodox Church it's called the Eucharist. And—" An unkind scoff escaped her here, which she tried to pass off as though she were clearing her throat. "We'd hardly get some divorced layman to bake the bread for it."

Casper took a steadying breath and held it for a moment. "I'm not divorced, Mom. I'm separated. It's different. And so is my church from the Ukrainian Church."

His mother had already stopped listening. She reached into her purse. "Here," she said after a moment's rummaging, and for the first time since she'd arrived, her tone took on a tender note. "I brought you this."

She produced a small vial of some yellowish liquid. "It's oil," she explained when Casper hesitated to take it. "Just olive oil, but it's infused with essence of myrrh. I thought you could use it. Anoint yourself with it maybe, or, I don't know, put it on your salads or something. To be honest I'm not sure how you're supposed to use it, but they say it has medicinal properties."

"Why would I need that, Mom? I'm fine."

"Sure, you're fine now. But you weren't. And I just—" The note of tenderness now was unmistakable. "I just don't want you to have a relapse."

Caper flinched visibly. "I'm not going to have a relapse. I'm seeing my therapist regularly, and I'm keeping up with my meds. The doctor says I'm fine."

"Maybe so, but what does it hurt to do all we can to be sure? They say this myrrh is direct from the Holy Land."

"For the love of God, Caz," said Mel. "Just humor her and take it. It was all she could talk about on the cab ride over."

But something in Casper's gut dug in its heels. "No. I'm not a basket case. What I have is a manageable mental illness. And that's what I'm doing: I'm managing it. I really don't need your voodoo remedies."

Sometimes their mother acted more hurt than she really was, but it was always hard to tell. She looked from Mel to Casper and chewed her lip a moment, then in a very thin voice she said, "Fine. My daughter thinks I'm a broken record and my son thinks I'm a witch doctor."

"Mom, I don't think you're a witch doctor. It's just—"

"No, Casper, you've made your point clear enough." She returned the vial to her purse and kept her eyes averted. "If you'll excuse me then, I'll put the varenyky in the oven to stay warm. You don't mind me using your oven, do you?"

She left before Casper could reply. An awkward silence followed.

"Veseloho Rizdva, Melania!" said Buzz suddenly from his spot at the table.

"Merry Christmas, Buzz. I didn't even see you there."

"Can I pour you some refreshments?" he asked.

A strange look crossed Mel's face. "No, Buzz, I think you're drinking for two tonight." Removing her coat, she handed it to Casper and nodded in the direction of his apron. "You're baking bread now?"

"Just this once," he said. "Like I told Mom, it's for my church. But speaking of bread reminds me, Mel." He hesitated. "Nat's stopping by tonight."

Mel looked at him with a lifted eyebrow, an expression that reminded Casper annoyingly of the look his mother had given him moments ago.

"Well, I needed bread tins, and…" He trailed off. The whole thing was starting to feel ridiculous to him. He was spared the trouble of explaining, however, because at just that minute the intercom buzzed for a third time.

It was her.

"Do you want me to come down?" he asked into the receiver.

The voice on the other end sounded strained and sad. "I don't mind coming up," it said.

He hesitated briefly and then squeezed his eyes shut and pressed the door button. "Come on up then," he said.

It had been so long since he'd last seen her that he found himself fumbling for words when she was finally standing there in the doorway, with three battered bread tins in her hands and a guarded look on her face. She had clearly just come from her work at the law office. Her hair was painstakingly arranged, her clothing crisp, her makeup impeccable.

"Here are the tins, Caz," she said cautiously.

He took them, but still hadn't found his words. Maybe they'd all tumbled down into the great chasm that had opened in his gut at the sight of her.

"Well," she said awkwardly, perhaps misunderstanding his silence. "I guess I should get going then."

Casper opened his mouth, and a thousand things flashed through his mind to say. Before he could choose from among them, though, an unsteady voice bawled at them from the living room.

"Natalie! Fancy meeting you here!" it said. "Veseloho Rizdva! Merry Christmas!"

Natalie looked past Casper toward the voice. "Is that you, Uncle Buzz? I didn't know you'd be here tonight."

"Neither did I," laughed Buzz. "It was his mother's idea."

"Well, Merry Christmas to you."

"You're staying tonight?" It wasn't clear if Buzz was asking her or telling her. She clamped her mouth shut at the question and inhaled deeply. "No," she said after a slight but weighty pause. "I don't think that's such a good idea."

"You can stay if you want."

Of the thousand things Casper might have said, this was the last thing either of them expected to hear coming from his mouth. A startled look flashed across her face, but he had already plunged forward and didn't feel he could turn back.

"Mom's made varenyky," he said. "I mean, I'd understand if you didn't want to... but it is Ukrainian Christmas Eve..." He sputtered out feebly, but not before repeating the offer. "You can if you want."

Natalie closed her eyes against some hidden hurt, but after another long inhale she sighed and said very softly, "Okay Caz. I'll stay."

Casper could not tell if the ache in his gut now was relief or regret, but he nodded. She was removing her coat and looking around the place, and he realized she hadn't yet seen his apartment. "It's not much," he said, taking her coat. "But its cozy enough."

"No," she said. "It's nice. You look like you landed on your feet."

"Come and share a drink with an old man!" bellowed Buzz from the living room.

"Go ahead, Natalie," said Casper. "I need to check on my bread dough."

When Casper entered the kitchen, he found his mother standing over the large mixing bowl he had prepared the dough in, furtively screwing the cap back onto the vial of oil she'd shown him earlier. The air was strong with a sickly-sweet smell.

"Mom? What on earth—?" Casper began, but his mother started with a blustery explanation.

"I just don't want it to happen again, Casper," she said quickly. "We almost lost you."

"Did you put it in the dough?"

"Well, you wouldn't take it. And they say it has medicinal properties. So when I saw what you were making there, I just thought, what can it hurt?"

Casper crossed quickly to the counter and seized the bowl, holding it to himself as though guarding a newborn. "That bread's for church tomorrow. I don't need you ruining it."

"Nonsense! A few drops of olive oil aren't going to ruin a loaf of bread."

"Well, I'm not even going to be eating it." He set the bowl on the counter and stood with his back to her. He inspected the dough gently, like an anxious father trying to soothe a baby back to sleep. He couldn't see any traces of the oil, though the room still smelled strongly of myrrh.

He patted it down and covered it with a clean dishcloth, like the YouTube video had explained to do. Then he set the bowl on the floor, to the side of the counter near the heat register, so the heat from the vent would help it rise.

When he turned back, his mother was leaning against the counter, watching him with folded arms.

"I see you're using your grandmother's bread tins."

"You recognized them? Natalie dropped by with them. She's—" He swallowed grimly, dreading what was to come. "She's staying for dinner tonight."

"Over my cooling corpse she is." Although it is true his mother often acted more hurt than she really was, he knew this time she meant it sincerely.

"Don't get dramatic, Mom. She just stopped by... and it's Christmas Eve."

"That's exactly my point," she said. "I don't want her to spoil our Christmas together. No one told me—"

"I didn't know I needed your permission to invite a guest to my apartment," said Casper. He was keeping his voice low only with great effort. "And if it comes to that, no one told me that Uncle Buzz was coming for dinner, either."

"I didn't want you to be alone for Sviatyi Vechir, Casper!" She was making much less effort to keep her voice down. "And anyway, I have something I want to talk to you all about, and I thought it might help to have him here."

He gave her a sharp look at this, but she pressed past it. "But don't try to tell me that's the same thing as having her over, after what she did to you."

"What did she do to me, Mom?"

"You know as well as I do that she abandoned you when you needed her most!"

"Abandoned me? Do you even hear yourself? She didn't abandon me! She just took a job that any up-and-coming lawyer would have killed to get—"

"And you just recovering from—" It was still hard for his mother to say the words openly. "From your episode. That's a fine time to launch a career, just when your husband needs you the most. I never would have done something like that to your father."

"Well, you never had the chance, did you?" He stopped abruptly, startled to see Mel standing in the kitchen doorway.

"You guys wanna join us in the living room?" she asked with an affected playfulness. She flashed her brother an imploring look. "It's a really small apartment, Caz."

When they were all seated at his improvised dining room table, he could tell from the look on Natalie's face that he had not been nearly as successful at keeping his voice low as he'd thought. Only Buzz seemed untouched by the smothering tension in the room.

"Veseloho Rizdva!" he said with a stagger in his voice, raising his glass so unevenly that much of the drink slopped onto the table. "They say the gold in the glass helps you feel the effects of the drink more deeply." He drained what was left in his cup at a toss.

"I think you're feeling the effects deeply enough already," said Mel.

Uncle Buzz waved his hand dismissively. "Nonsense," he said. "It's Sviatyi Vechir. Casper's got a new apartment. We've got the whole family together again." He gestured toward Natalie as he said this. "Tonight, we celebrate!"

However awkward the situation was, Natalie had always liked Uncle Buzz. "I never used to celebrate Ukrainian Christmas," she said, "until I met Caz. I even learned how to make golubsty for the occasion."

"His name is Casper," said his mother icily, still refusing to look toward her. "I've never liked Caz as a nickname."

"Maybe I shouldn't have stayed," began Natalie, but Buzz roared her down.

"Nonsense!" he bellowed unsteadily. "If we can't put the past behind us on Christmas Eve, then we never will." He was unexpectedly lucid as he said this last part and it caught them all off guard.

"And anyway, Mom," said Mel tentatively. "I call him Caz, too."

"That's who I got it from," said Natalie warmly. When she and Casper had been dating, in the early days, she and Mel had been very close. It was sad for her to be sitting there and acting as though they were perfect strangers.

"His name is Casper," their mother said softly but unshakably.

Either Natalie missed the note of finality in her voice or chose to ignore it. "I know, but somehow Caz seems to fit him better. Casper always made me think of... you know..."

"The friendly ghost?" said Mel, and for the first time that night real laughter was heard at the table.

"You know I hate that," said Casper, though he was smiling too.

"The friendly ghost," said Uncle Buzz, punctuating it with a blow of his palm on the tabletop. "That's what I told your dad they'd call you!"

The mention of Casper's father abruptly cooled any warmth this discussion of Casper's name had kindled among them, but Buzz carried on unawares.

"'Don't call him that,' I said. 'They'll tease him worse than if you call him Hercules.' But he insisted. 'It's a family name,' he said. And it *is* a family name. Like mine."

"Buzz is a family name?" This from Natalie.

"Balthasar," said Uncle Buzz with a skewed grin. "It was our gido's name."

"Buzz is short for Balthasar?" said Natalie, looking toward Casper. "You never told me that."

Casper shrugged. "What did you think it was for?"

"I don't know," said Natalie. "I just thought it was a nickname. Like the astronaut."

Uncle Buzz poured himself a wobbly shot of vodka. "Gido was Balthasar. And his dad before him... was Casper. But I told Dimitri not to name his kid that... that the other kids'd pick on him." He set down the bottle and lifted the glass in an indistinct toast to no one in particular. "And did they?" he asked in Casper's direction.

Casper wished intensely that Buzz would stop referring to his father. He kept his eyes fixed on the table, but Buzz's glass hovered uncomfortably in front of him, waiting for an answer, so finally he mumbled, "Sometimes they did."

Buzz nodded triumphantly and took a gulp of his drink.

"Well," said their mother at last. "Since we're all sharing, I have something I wanted to talk to you all about. Something I've been wanting to say for a while."

Casper noticed his mother's voice was trembling, but this barely had time to register, because Mel cut in suddenly.

"Before you do, I have a revelation of my own." Her mother lifted a hand to stop her, but Mel took a deep breath and plunged forward.

"I'm pregnant," she said.

A stunned silence followed this announcement.

"Oh God," their mother said finally.

"Congratulations, Mel," said Natalie.

"Mazel Tov!" said Uncle Buzz. He lifted the remains of his tumbler and swallowed it off.

Their mother scowled in Buzz's direction, then asked, "How can you be pregnant?"

"I hardly think you need me to teach you the birds and the bees, Mother."

"That's not what I meant, and you know it. Who? And you unmarried?"

"That's your biggest concern? That I'm not married?"

"Children need a father, Melania." The unintended irony of her comment clattered clumsily down around them.

"I can't imagine," muttered Mel.

Her mother tried to salvage what she'd said, doing more damage as she did. "Well then, of all people, you ought to know how true it is. Children need fathers."

"Mom," said Casper imploringly. He placed his hand on her forearm, but something seemed to have risen up within his mother and it was intent on being heard.

"No," she said, waving off his hand. "It's true. You know how hard it was not having him, Melania. Is that what you want for... for your..." She trailed off, as if by not saying it aloud she could somehow prevent it being true.

"Well," she said at last. "No matter. I'll simply pray. It's what I did when Casper got sick—I prayed that he would find his way back to the Faith—and—well—even though he hasn't found his way back completely, still, he's better off in that church of his than he would be without it. So my prayers were answered."

"Oh, Mom," Casper began. "For the love of—"

"No," said their mother, still determined to have her say. "I did pray. I even buried a shrine of St. Joseph in your yard. They say it's supposed to help you sell your house, but I thought: what could it hurt? And that's what I'll do, Melania. I'll just pray that you and whoever he is, the father of your... of your... that he marries you."

"You can save your prayers," said Mel, staring bitterly at the tabletop.

"Well, I won't save them. Children need—"

Mel brought her palm down violently on the table, causing Buzz to start in alarm. "Mom!" she yelled. "You can save your prayers! I won't be marrying him, I can assure you." The rims of her eyes were red with pending tears, but she kept them fixed on the table and none fell.

"He's already married," she said at last.

Her mother lifted her hand to her mouth.

"I met him in India," said Mel softly. "He was there for a three month stint, and, well, I didn't know until I found out that we were... that *I* was pregnant... that he had a wife and kids back home." She lapsed into silence.

Natalie really had been close to Mel, back when she and Casper were dating, so almost instinctively, she reached over and gripped her wrist, giving it a squeeze that she hoped would be reassuring. Whether it was so or not, Mel did not shrug it off.

Casper looked at his mother. There were tears streaming down her face, and she still held her hand to her mouth.

"Mom," said Casper gently. It was the first time he'd spoken to her with sincere gentleness that night. "Mom, it's okay. It's not the end of the world. Lots of kids these days grow up in single-parent families. It's not—"

His mother shook her head silently and closed her eyes. "No, Casper. No: this is my fault."

Casper blinked. "How could this be your fault?"

Her silence was almost surreal at that moment. She kept her eyes shut and it wasn't clear if she was breathing, though she was not holding a breath.

"This is what I wanted to tell you tonight," she began, but then trailed off into another silence. Casper was alarmed to see how violently she was trembling.

And then suddenly it came out of her: "So was her father—a—a married man."

She had phrased it in such an unusual way that it took a moment for it to sink in, what she was saying. Mel looked up sharply and fixed her eyes searingly on the woman sitting across from her.

"What do you mean?" Casper whispered.

"Dimitri was drinking so much in those days. He was never home. And even when he was, he wasn't really there."

"What are you saying, Mom?" asked Casper, more urgently this time.

"It was a man at the church who—oh—" There was a great sob pressing at the back of his mother's words."

"Did Dad know?"

The sob seemed to be strangling her words now, but she was able to force them out. "Not at first. He was drinking so much in those days, it was easy enough to convince him that—" and she looked at last at her daughter's face as she said it—"that you were his. And he loved you—Oh, Melania—he loved you as though you were. But he always suspected."

"But did he know?" asked Casper firmly.

She nodded indistinctly and clenched her eyes against her tears. "He pieced it together when Melania was older. You were kids then, but he confronted me about it. I denied it, of course, but he knew. And then he died in that horrific way, and we never—"

The sob surfaced at last, and she broke off once more. All this time, Mel was staring at her with a burning intensity. It looked to Casper as though something was shriveling up visibly in his sister's face.

"And you thought," he said to his mother slowly, "that now—tonight—on Christmas Eve—you thought *now* would be a good time to tell us all this?"

"I didn't think there would *ever* be a good time to tell you. But during your last episode, I started to wonder if your—illness—wasn't—I don't know—punishment for my secret. So I promised that if you got better, I'd tell the truth. And now—" She lifted hollow eyes in her daughter's direction. "Now my sins are coming back to haunt me."

"Dolores…" It was said so unevenly that no one noticed it.

"How could you possibly make this about *yourself*, Mom?"

"Dolores," said the voice again, more steadily than before.

"What else could it be? He visits the sins of the parents on the fourth and fifth generation, doesn't he? Or doesn't the Bible they read in that church of yours have that verse in it?"

"Dolores!" It was Uncle Buzz. He was a good three drinks past sober and was following the conversation only with great effort, but he knew that an awful revelation of great betrayal had been made, and that it touched on his brother Dimitri's memory. He had lurched to his feet, leaning over the table on both fists.

"You swore," he said haltingly, "that you wouldn't sully Dimitri's memory… for his kids…" She tried to speak, but he pulled himself up till he was standing straight, swaying slightly, but erect. "No! You swore that his kids would grow up… to know they were his kids."

"Uncle Buzz knew?" was all Mel could find to say. "You kept it secret from us, but Uncle Buzz knew?"

No reply came. Their mother had sunken into a sob from which there was no reaching her. Buzz swept up the bottle of vodka with a trembling hand and staggered crookedly from the room.

Natalie's hand still rested on Melania's wrist. "Oh Mel," she said, and there was a gentleness in her voice that Casper hadn't heard in a long time. "I'm so sorry."

She looked at Casper. "I really shouldn't have stayed," she said awkwardly.

She made as if she was going to rise, but Casper got up from his chair before she could. "No," he said. "Please don't leave now." He was surprised to see that his hands were shaking. "Please stay." He closed his eyes against the anger that was burning in them. "I think Mel could use you. And I... I made golubsty."

He looked toward the kitchen. "In fact, I should check on it now. And maybe look after Buzz."

He gave her a pleading look, and she nodded faintly then looked away. He stepped from the table and found his way into the kitchen.

Buzz had been sick in the sink. He was still leaning over it on both hands when Casper came into the kitchen. The man groaned deeply, and it wasn't clear to Casper if he was sobbing or retching again.

He stepped up to the sink. "Here you go, Buzz," he said, putting a steadying arm around his shoulder. He'd had some small amount of practice at this with his father. He was quite young back then, of course, but the lessons we learn about these things as children we never forget.

"Come on old man," he said softly as Buzz leaned against him. With his free arm he reached and turned on the tap, trying to wash the mess down the drain. Luckily, Buzz had eaten very little that day.

"She swore," said Buzz indistinctly.

"I know she did, Buzz."

"No." He pushed against Casper's arm. "You don't know! It was after the funeral and she'd told me what happened... and I swore her to... she swore me to..."

Each word was lobbed so haphazardly that it seemed to strike Casper in a different place, in a different way. He flinched against every blow.

"It's okay, Buzz," was all he could manage, though he knew deeply within that it was not okay, and he doubted it would ever be so again. He tried to move Buzz toward the kitchen door. "Let's get you to a bed where you can sleep this off."

"No!" shouted Buzz. He pushed forcefully against his nephew. "She swore!"

It was hard to make out exactly what happened next.

Casper pushed back on Buzz, but only to keep himself from falling. Perhaps he pushed harder than he'd meant to because Buzz staggered against the kitchen counter. He'd placed the bottle of Smirnoff on the edge of the counter when he'd come into the kitchen, and he fell so unevenly that his weight came fully against it, knocking it over so that it rolled back and began spilling out its gold-infused contents.

"Buzz!" cried Casper, rushing over to right the upended bottle. Not that he cared much about the vodka itself, but it was a large spill and had started pooling, trickling over the side of the counter. It was right over the bowl of dough he'd placed on the floor earlier that afternoon. A cascade of spilled vodka was splashing down onto the bowl, soaking through the towel that covered it and into the risen dough.

"For the love of—!" he began, restraining himself with only a great effort. He moved to retrieve the bowl, pushing past Buzz in his haste. The man tottered and then slipped to the floor, striking his head loudly but not painfully against the cupboards as he fell.

Casper set the bowl on the counter and removed the sodden towel. The dough did not look as though its baptism in vodka had done it any lasting damage, though he was sure there was a sour smell of alcohol hanging about it.

"You've ruined it," he muttered, more to himself than to his uncle. He clutched the towel fiercely and began a frustrated effort to mop up the spill, though it was so large that all he managed to do was push it around the countertop.

He looked in Uncle Buzz's direction. The man was still on the kitchen floor, though he'd grabbed hold of the countertop and was trying uncertainly to drag himself to his feet. A painful memory of seeing his father once like this, when he was far too young to lift him, flashed across Casper's mind. He flung the towel onto the counter and reached for Buzz with a heavy groan.

"Come on, Buzz. We'll find you a place to lie down."

He bore the man's weight as best he could and helped him steady his steps as they made their way to Casper's bedroom. He was grateful it was on the side of the kitchen opposite the living room, so he wouldn't have to pass the morose scene of Mel and Natalie sitting awkwardly with his mother.

He returned to the kitchen after settling Buzz on his bed in a crumpled heap. He could hear Mom and Mel exchanging whispered words in the living room, though he still couldn't bear the thought of rejoining them. He leaned over the bread dough and stared at it intensely. As far as he could tell, it was fully risen; at least, the bowl was now filled to overflowing. He was sure there was an awful smell of vodka coming off it—though the spill had been so large that the whole kitchen smelled faintly of alcohol—and he wondered angrily what Pastor Milo would think.

The YouTube tutorials had told him he was supposed to punch down the dough before shaping it into loaves. "To release the built-up pressure of the gas produced by the yeast," is how one video had explained it, "press your fist firmly into the dough once or twice."

Casper squeezed his hand into a fist, much tighter than he had intended to, and pressed it into the dough. It collapsed like a weary exhale. He brought his fist up and back down again, with more force than he realized. He closed his eyes furiously, his head echoing with the words of his mother's awful confession.

He punched the dough a third time, fierce with frustration.

He thought of Buzz, sleeping off a half bottle of vodka in his bedroom. He fought down the questions welling up within him: had it been Smirnoff Gold the night his dad died? The thought unleashed a great rage in him, and he scattered it with another blow down onto the bread dough.

He and Mel had been very close after the car crash. His mother had descended into a dark chasm without her husband—though after tonight's revelation he wondered if it was more guilt than grief that had pulled her down—and though she eventually did emerge from the darkness, she was never the same again.

At least, he did not remember her being so clinging and controlling before that night as she became after.

He punched the dough almost violently this time.

The look that had been on Mel's face as their mother made her terrible confession rose up in his mind's eye. Had she somehow known, he wondered, in some unilluminated place within, that the man she'd always called her father wasn't really hers? Was that why she drew men so magnetically into her sphere, now, so easily and so urgently?

He struck the dough furiously.

And for Natalie to be here tonight—to hear the awful truth—to know—

He brought his fist down a seventh time and lifted it wildly for an eighth.

A soft touch on his arm stayed him. He became aware of a sweet smell, like clouds of incense enveloping him, and as he did, he realized that he had been sobbing, softly but audibly.

The touch became a closed hand, covering his fist and bringing it gently down to rest.

"It's okay, Casper."

Casper shook his head. He couldn't bring himself to look at her, and he slumped his shoulders wearily.

"Mel," he said at last. "I'm so sorry. She shouldn't have—not tonight—not like that—"

"No," she said again. "It's okay, Casper. It had to come out eventually."

"I'm still your brother," he said, chewing his lip bitterly. "You know that don't you? You're still my sister."

Melania didn't speak for a long time. The smell of her Encens Mythique was strong in the air, mingling vaguely with the lingering odor of spilled Smirnoff.

"I'm not sure that's as comforting as you mean it to be," she said finally. The teasing note in her voice was very faint, but even so Casper could sense the untold layers of sadness and frustration it was trying to hide.

"Well, I don't think I could bear to lose a sister," he said with a weak laugh. "So you'll have to keep the job for my sake, if nothing else. And Mel: I'm here for you and your baby. Whatever you need; I'll be the best uncle I can be."

Mel nodded, and brushed away a single tear before it could take shape. "How's the bread coming?" she asked.

Casper looked down at the dough, blinking as though he were seeing it for the first time. It was quite pulverized.

"The YouTube tutorial said you're supposed to punch it down before you form it into loaves," he said sheepishly.

"Well, it looks like you've mastered that step."

Another feeble laugh escaped him. "Maybe," he said. "After everything this dough's been through, though, I can't imagine how the bread's going to turn out."

Mel touched it with her perfume-scented hand. "Maybe I can help you make the loaves?" she offered.

Casper nodded. He was about to speak when he suddenly became aware of someone standing in the doorway of the kitchen.

It was Natalie.

"Your mom's left," she said haltingly, gesturing back toward the living room. "She told me to say sorry to you. For her."

There was no longer any guardedness in her voice, and in some strange way her vulnerability in that moment seemed to hurt him more than all the hardness that had been there before. "So—I guess—" Her words came falteringly. "I guess I'll say it for her. I'm sorry, Caz."

Casper couldn't meet her eyes, but he nodded. "I'm sorry too," he whispered faintly.

She inhaled deeply and held the breath for a weighted moment. "I guess I should get going," she said at last, exhaling sadly.

She turned to leave.

"Wait."

She stopped, but she didn't turn back.

"Do you want to stay?" he asked. "You could help me and Mel make this dough into loaves. They were your tins, after all. And anyways, my mom left her varenyky in the oven. It wouldn't be Ukrainian Christmas without it."

She sucked in her upper lip pensively. "No," she said after a glance toward the front door. "I don't suppose it would. But they're not my tins Casper," she added with a tentative smile.

For all Casper's bread dough had seen that night, they were still able to form it into three small but passable loaves. The kitchen smelled strangely warmed as it was baking, a messy but not unpleasant odor of yeast and myrrh mingled inextricably together.

They ate Dolores's varenyky at the makeshift table while they waited. They sampled Casper's golubsty, too, though they all agreed that they had turned out poorly, and that maybe it was for the best his mother was not there to comment on it.

The loaves of bread were oddly shaped when he finally pulled them out of the oven. So oddly that even Natalie gave a genuine laugh when they emerged into the world, and all three of them watched in a kind of rapt wonder while they cooled on the counter.

"You're sure this was your first try?" Mel asked sarcastically. "They look divine."

"Considering the circumstances," offered Casper in return, "I'm just glad they look like bread at all."

He reached for one of the loaves. An inexplicable urge to say something came over him, and he broke the bread in two, the way he had seen Pastor Milo do, and held it out to his sister. "This is my body, broken for you," he repeated reverently, then added apologetically: "At least, that's how they say it in church."

If Mel sensed the same weight settling over them in that moment, she didn't acknowledge it. She broke off a piece and chewed it as though she were critiquing a rare wine.

"It's really not bad," she said at last. "I mean, I'm sure I can taste the Smirnoff, but it's none the worse for it." She nodded toward Natalie. "You should try some."

Nat hesitated, but Casper held out the bread to her.

"Peace?" he offered.

She said nothing, but unfolded her arms and broke off a piece. Chewing it thoughtfully, she nodded, seeming to agree with Mel's assessment; then suddenly she said, to no one in particular, "Do you know that I was also praying?"

"Praying?" Under the weight of the moment, Casper couldn't raise his voice above a whisper.

"During your—" The word was too painful for her. "During your episode. Your mom said she was praying for you—what did she say?—to come back to your faith? Well, I'd been praying too. Did you know that?" The question sounded partly a confession and partly an accusation.

"Nat, you never pray. You always said—"

"I know what I said. But I did pray. When they admitted you the last time, and we knew what it was—at least I knew what it was— I started praying that it would—that you'd be healed."

"You prayed for me to be healed?" Even at a whisper he couldn't hide the incredulity in his voice.

"Well, I wasn't raised like you, so I didn't know how to do it. But I did. 'If there's a god,' I said, 'then heal him of this.' O god, how I prayed for you in those days."

"You prayed for me." It was more a statement than a question this time.

"I thought maybe you should know. Because after you were better—after they'd released you, I mean—and things were under control again, you said we weren't on the same page spiritually anymore. Do you remember saying that? So I thought you should know how I prayed for you in those days. And who knows, but maybe my prayers were answered."

Casper opened his mouth to speak, but he couldn't find the words to say. He'd always believed it was a miracle, in the biblical sense, that he'd made it through his last episode, though she had never told him before today how she'd been praying for one. And it was true, too, that the space between them had widened into something uncrossable after the dust of his last episode had settled. Before he was released, his therapist had told him he might do well to reconnect with his faith, that many people recovering from mental illness find a community of faith to be a great help. Natalie had never felt comfortable in the little community church he'd landed at, however, and the more he flung himself into it, the more she withdrew.

Of course, her career was gaining an inexorable momentum by then, and she hardly would have had time for religion, even if she'd wanted to join him.

"Maybe your prayers were answered," he said at last. "But I was praying too, Natalie."

"You were?"

"For you. When I was sick. You reach this point where you don't think you're going to get through, and you're pretty sure you don't want to. I didn't think I did, anyways, and I was worried for you, if you'd be okay when I was gone."

"Oh, Caz."

"And I knew how much you'd given up to marry me, so I started praying that—" The confession caught in his throat. It seemed like such a pitiful thing to say, now that he was hearing it out loud. "I started praying that you'd get established in your career, after I was gone, that you'd get back what you'd given up to be with me."

Natalie was looking at him intently as he said this, with an inscrutable look on her face. "You prayed?" she said, softly. "You were in the middle of a full-on psychotic break, and you were praying that my career would take off?"

Casper nodded. He couldn't tell if the look on her face was one of compassion or woundedness. The last fight they'd had, before they finally separated, was over the hours her work was stealing away from them.

"Well," she said with pursed lips. "I guess your prayers were answered, too. Though maybe it would have been better if they hadn't been."

Casper opened his mouth. A thousand things to say rushed through his mind at once. He wanted to tell her how sorry he was, how wrong he'd been, how much his prayers had changed since then. But it all seemed so foolish at that moment that he clapped his mouth shut and said nothing.

"It's like that stupid story," said Mel suddenly. Both Casper and Natalie had forgotten she was listening, and her words almost startled them. She reached and broke another large piece of bread. "You know, Caz," she said with her mouth full, "this really isn't that bad."

"Story?"

"You know. What's it called? The girl sells her hair to buy a Christmas present for her husband?"

Casper didn't get the reference, but Natalie nodded. "That would make my career his gift of tortoise shell combs to me."

Mel shrugged. "I mean, it's only a little bit like that story, but still."

Casper still didn't understand, but he looked timidly at Natalie. "I really am sorry," he said. "Not just for tonight, and for Mom and Buzz and—me—but for everything. I am so sorry, Nat."

"And so am I. But it's late, Caz. Not too late, but very late. And I need to go."

Casper nodded. Carrying one of the two remaining loaves with him, he walked her to the door. "If I take one loaf to church tomorrow," he said hesitantly, "I'll still have one left over. Would you take it? It's not much in the way of gifts, but it's what I have."

She stood silently in the doorway, surveying the apartment and seeing it, maybe, for the very first time. After what seemed a long while, she nodded.

"Thanks, Caz," she said, cradling the loaf of bread under her arm. "And if you're around after church tomorrow, maybe I could stop by. To pick up our bread tins, I mean. And who knows but maybe we could talk some more?"

"Sure Nat," he said. "I'd like that."

After she'd left, he leaned his back against the door and slid slowly to the floor. He cradled his face in trembling palms, and as he did, a faint smell of fresh baked bread washed over him, filling his senses with a deep and probing peace.

About the Author

Dale Harris is a poet, novelist, songwriter and ordained minister living in Oshawa, Ontario. His first novel, *Though I Walk* (Word Alive Press), won the Braun Book Award for fiction in 2020, and his short story, "The New Parson of Petit-Wasmes," was longlisted for the 2020 CBC Short Story Prize. He blogs regularly about God, life, words and spirituality at his blog *terra incognita*. In his writing he loves to explore the spiritual dimensions of everyday things and the mysterious presence of God in both the bright and dark seasons of life. He can be contacted through his website, at www.daleharris.ca.

www.ingramcontent.com/pod-product-compliance
Lightning Source LLC
Chambersburg PA
CBHW020400030726
47496CB00007B/2223